SPELL(

RAJAT CHAUDHURI

NIYOGI
BOOKS

Published by
NIYOGI BOOKS
Block D, Building No. 77,
Okhla Industrial Area, Phase-I,
New Delhi-110 020, INDIA
Tel: 91-11-26816301, 26818960
Email: niyogibooks@gmail.com
Website: www.niyogibooksindia.com

Text © Rajat Chaudhuri

Editor: Vibha Chakravarty Kumar
Design: Shashi Bhushan Prasad
Cover design: Misha Oberoi

ISBN: 978-93-91125-88-2
Publication: 2023

Price: ₹495

Printed at: Niyogi Offset Pvt. Ltd., New Delhi, India

To Anuradha Sengupta

Do the gods light this fire in our hearts or does each man's mad desire become his god?

—Virgil, Aeneid

The ALL is MIND; The Universe is Mental

—Three Initiates, The Kybalion

CONTENTS

Praise for Rajat Chaudhuri's previous novels

THE BUTTERFLY EFFECT

'An imaginative, madcap rollercoaster ride' **LIZ JENSEN, BESTSELLING AUTHOR OF *THE RAPTURE***

'A magic box...brings Allan Poe to mind' **SCROLL**

'Genre-bending' **HOUSTON CHRONICLE, USA**

'Propels the accumulated anxieties of a city into a shape-shifting future vortex' **OUTLOOK**

'Explores a Ballardian near-future' **WORDS WITHOUT BORDERS**

'Projects the tropes of a new politics of imagination' **INDIAN LITERATURE**

The Butterfly Effect was listed in
'FIFTY MUST-READ NOVELS ABOUT ECO-DISASTER'
by Book Riot, USA.

HOTEL CALCUTTA

'Sheer power of storytelling' **THE TELEGRAPH**

'Invites a hungry, urgent reading' **ASIAN REVIEW OF BOOKS**

'An astounding work' **INDIAN LITERATURE**

'A dazzling "wall of stories"' **THE SUNDAY GUARDIAN**

'His themes reveal a deep fascination with human response to the extraordinary' **HELTER SKELTER**

INCANTATIONS

THE HOROLOGIST OF ANANTANAGAR

I'd have never stepped out without a Plan B. Not in a manic city like Aukatabad.

But who is listening? We had stopped listening to each other long before it came to this. Long before there were angry slugs buzzing above our heads.

Still, bullets flying in smog are better than bullets flying in clear light. That way, we get chance on our side. So do you. That's the way we try to get rid of one another. This last time.

Won't be easy though. Not for you. Not for us. Me, him and the one-legged man. The smog has blinded us all. The smog has blinded the city...as it has blinded the world—driving us on to nowhere land.

The bodyguard, the buck-toothed butcher, appears just when we think we have luck on our side. Comrade LJ on his crutch, swift like a cheetah, lunging for the attack but then... the spray of bullets. In the oily haze, only sprays count. Nothing to shoot at. Fiery metal nipping sunflowers waking up to the day. Whizzing projectiles from ten directions and death gasps. Pensioners with their walkers kissing silty loam as hot lead packs their gizzards.

More shots. Crackers exploding on Diwali. That's the day Lord Rama returns to reclaim his kingdom after the forest exile—after fighting the ten-headed demon. This bodyguard's a maniac. He should be in Tihar. He should be in San Quentin. We won't give up so easily!

Kid's pram torn to shreds, flying into lily pond. Big splash. More cries, followed by an abrupt silence. Silence of quiet death. *La petite mort*, hushed orgasmic ends.

'Down, down!' screams a voice.

'Machine pistol…*behenchod*!'

Answering shot from our side, or what seems to be our side anyway. It sounds different, the whistle of the Makarov bullet. I think I catch a glimpse of the one-legged LJ, the muzzle flash of a gun briefly lighting him up. The petroleum darkness of the smog closes in again, exposing no one. Particulates, nitrogen oxides, benzene vapours, smoke from farm fires, swirling. No mercy. No taking sides. Only a bleak, filtering dawn light.

Muezzin's sonorous call to prayer. Volley of shots as I duck for cover behind the public urinal. Is LJ dead? How much longer can I survive this? Sirens in the distance coming closer. Screeching tyres.

A cat snarls near my feet.

Blood fountains dance.

Who can save you? No one can. I cannot be saved from you.

Men rushing in this direction.

But first things first.

My name is Chanchal Mitra.

I am from Anantanagar. The city of the East. Anyone from these parts would know that we, the Mitras, are from a respectable tribe. In fact, there are whole streets and neighbourhoods of this city named after us, our kin. Sweet shops, bakeries, twin-chair saloons.

Yes, we are honourable folk; you can even call us the old aristocrats. Old and mighty, we used to be. But never the upstart rich. Not a whit of a link with you who sleep now. Never! We are not parvenus tearing it all up. Keep this in mind, and we can be friends.

Now that I am feeling a little better, we can talk.

See the sun rising.

The sun rising, the maids arriving in every house on Four Horse Street in their synthetic saris; the mongrels on the street fighting as people troop out for work. My office begins late, perks of the profession. I watch through the window and wait for the onionskin papers to arrive. Later, I walk down the street to the bus stop to catch the 12:45 to the newspaper office and every step is slippery here. Every face, that of a demon or an angel, and they're all laying traps just as a wind picks up. The wind blows hard through those streets.

Slashing open the glass roof of the bus stop, it cuts through the window slats of crumbling houses that stand like rotting corpses of soldiers refusing to lie down. The wind roars through the dark alleys—smelling of fish curry—and howls along the avenues, reeking of diesel death, screaming through every broken door it can find. Buffeting people with its heavy hands, it commands them in its thundering voice to cower in fear or sing its praise. That voice calling for sacrifice. That's how a storm speaks. The wind will blow hard again very soon.

Evenings empty like gutted animals. Shadows creeping out of pools of darkness, congealed around the sodium lights of Anantanagar. The world caving in and consuming us.

The wind piercing my eardrums. The maw of mother Earth wide open. Gaia's hungry flames flickering with animal heat. Shipwrecks galore. Plunging into a dominion under the thrall of an endless night.

In this darkness, there's only the tick-tocking of time.

The clocks.

They're all still here, one-eyed monsters with the ashen face of grave-diggers, bored looks of body-snatchers, bleary-eyed like morgue attendants—ticking away the wretched moments.

They're everywhere in the house. 'Get to know them as you grow up,' father had said gravely one day. Ancient grandfathers, stately and self-important, hoary timepieces with rotten teeth in their ivory casings—ticking for a century or more, and watches from a more familiar past. Our house, a museum of time. A museum of living time, hungry time with a scratchy, rasping breath, time frothing with bile juices and bubbling with sulphuric acid. Time dripping *aqua regia.*

But museums house the dead. The clocks knew. So they were preparing. Deep in their murky mechanical bowels, coded in the chatter of their well-greased gear trains, they were planning it out.

How could I know what was on their minds? From the days of the water clocks in Egypt on to the metronomic rhythm of atomic time, somewhere in between, the keepers of the hours had developed sense organs. A taste for rust-salt, red-brown, IV lines. Metallic black in the dark, metal taste, metal flash.

The Goth.

The Goth. Tallest of the seven grandfathers towering over us in the rooms and passages of our old house. I never asked father why it was named after a Germanic tribe. After mom left, back in my school days, the clocks crept in and filled up all corners of Mitra House, where the sunbeams didn't dare. Father, my military engineer dad, collected them from the British auction-houses with intimidating names—meant to throw off scum like us—loaned some from friends, and scoured the old bazaar with its warren of alleys at the end of which sat dreadful beings twisting time in their gnarled hands, so pale they looked like dead maidens. Near the police headquarters it still stands, the biggest clock market in our world where he bargained assiduously with dead shop-owners, still sprawled over the cobwebs of four dimensions; often, they took him along...and he remained unseen for days in his horological quests.

When the municipal corporation of this city came up with the gamble to set up an old steam clock, mostly to divert attention from a kidney harvesting racket, he was excited to no end. But the engineer in him would be chuffed when clocks didn't work, for in restoring the heartbeat into their mechanical madness, he perhaps discovered connections with some bigger contraption that invisibly bred chaos in our lives.

The Goth's been running slow by several hours. It's his new game. Imposing in its giant oakwood frame of ten-and-half feet, burnished black on the inside, its pendulum chamber double the volume of a striptease booth on the street of pleasure.

Father fighting a losing battle with the old master of the hours—rude, curmudgeonly, vicious-faced—tolling at its own sweet will. Sometimes when we sit down for lunch, it announces with authority that it's the hour of breakfast; or when, in the middle of the night, I turn from side to side in my bed, dreaming of my dead mom—who resembled that famous queen of Bhaskarnagar—The Goth tolls the hour for vespers. But the idiosyncrasies of the machine only strengthens his resolve to twist it back into shape, and in fact when all the timekeepers and gadgets in the house—the dusty theodolites of Alderworth, the Kodak Brownies, the Wurlitzers, the noisy valve radio sets—are performing flawlessly, I see a shade of black on his sunburnt face. As if he's always expecting them to break down, and awaiting the serotonin bath of accomplishment in putting them right.

Ruthless summer day. April, I suppose.

Father poring over The Goth's metal innards for the last forty-eight hours; the tomb of power behind the dial with the moon wheel and the engraved map of the known world, 1654. Hidden by the etched bronze dial, the mammoth gears with their sharp three-inch teeth and witch-like grimaces, the wheels, the barrels, the anchor escapement swaying to the beat of seconds and the two tightly coiled steel springs—each big as a cartwheel—delivering torque in Newton metres to the heavy lyre pendulum, the brass bell and the Scythian dagger hands pointing out time.

It's dark inside The Goth and he is wearing a coal miner's helmet with a headlamp. There, he sits on the edge of the metal frame of the clock movement.

Sometime in the afternoon.

I step out for a walk to the riverside. A lowering sky and the evening sun lost in a mile-high cumulonimbus. Crowds on the strand this day, watching dead fish in the water from a toxic spill. An east-Asian vessel still disgorging its poison into the river. A beggar on the bank, with polio-deformed feet. Akbar…I know him well. Every month, I get him some provisions from a shop nearby. He *salaams* seeing me, and I ask him how he is.

'*Mast*,' he replies.

I return at the stroke of five. The house consumed by silence. Back in my room reading the papers and hearing Dad mutter as he speaks with The Goth, and there is this sound of the lyre pendulum: tick-tock…then silence; tick-tock again, and more words and interjections. I cannot discern whether they issue from a human mouth. A regular conversation he is having with The Goth, God knows for how long. The light is quickly falling outside.

I had dozed off. A metal wrench clatters to the floor, waking me up. I can still hear him as I fold the newspaper and put it away. More sounds from that room. Then the click of a lever, and the purr of the gear, louder like a growl this time. Now one long throaty growl—teeth-gnashing, snarling, wild.

Really loud!

An ear-splitting cry of steel, a scream beyond any sounds on this side of the forest—cold, blood-curdling scream of metal lashing against woodwork, the wood splintering like a burst casket releasing the spirit, torque unleashing an iron horse, lash of metal on curd-soft human flesh, knife-like teeth, the teeth that is the blade and the knife digging deep, piercing soft muscle tissue, slicing open a ventricle, disconnecting arteries and snapping bone like safety matches.

No sounds from that room anymore.

The storm howling overhead, lashing Anantanagar with fury, spraying chilling rain through the windows of Mitra House, whipping Four Horse Street mercilessly and drowning the city in a dungeon of darkness, as the electricity department switches off supply for fear of short circuits.

In this darkest of evenings, between booming thunder like the muffled howl from a torturer's pit, between streaks of lightning blinding a city homebound—though home doesn't remain a home anymore when everyone you knew to be your own has conspired against you or left—there are three sharp taps at the front door.

My heart's racing. Fast, run fast. But why should I run? Run away? The rain is heavier outside. But I am at the front door. Curtains billowing. The rain gushing in through twenty windows and flooding this dead soldier's house.

The shape of a stranger through the curtains of rain. Muscles stiffening, nerves taut—I dither.

'Who is it in this deluge?' I call out at the storm.

'I come from another world, let me in,' thunders the voice. I unlatch the door and step aside, holding the flickering candle high. He walks in, the rain glistening on his battle-hardened face, gleaming in a wreath of crystal fires on his shoulder-length hair. Raincoat flapping like a cape, wellingtons squelching on the wet floor now reddening with a trickle of blood. On a leash held in his hand, a giant king crab walking in now, making circles in the water flooding the veranda.

'Major Gupta,' the tall stranger proffered a strong hand, 'you don't know me. Rabi was my friend. We fought many battles together. He had saved my life.'

I flinch from his piercing stare. We shake hands as a chill goes down my spine. How does he know about the dead? Perhaps he doesn't? I try to get a better look at the face, speckled with shadows of the dark house dimly lit by the shortening candle, and the breath of the freshly departed on my back.

Who is this stranger whose forehead furrows with a hundred lines that writhed like water-snakes while he spoke? A powerful jaw shaded by grey stubble, a weather-worn face with the unmistakable marks of aristocracy intact and an inward gaze.

'I see it in your eyes but how did it happen?' he asks.

How do I even explain it to a stranger. So I tell him; and listening to me, he falls silent. He drifts away but still watches me from the corner of his eyes. 'Shouldn't we close those windows first?' he says at last. The windows are closed, and he says he is a doctor of some sort.

He takes charge, he takes care of everything.

So smooth that we are back in the house after midnight. Whatever had to be done for the dead, we are done.

The house after midnight.

Mitra House with the great clocks. The rain pummeling the city again. Rivers of rainwater everywhere, and the lights still out.

All through the night, we are talking.

Watched by the great clocks, we whisper into the night. The clocks watch us, and they see him leave when the sky begins to turn red in patches.

Like wounds freshly opened.

BLUE HALOS

She seemed to make that remark very casually. 'Are we sending the assistant away tomorrow, Vincent?'

If she could manage on her own, Vincent had answered, knowing pretty well that Zeeta, his lab coordinator, preferred caution. There had been issues with the assistants earlier, and the company had framed new protocols for secrecy which they had to follow.

Vincent peered at the white hot road blazing for miles ahead of him in the Aukatabad summer. Thoughts crept into his mind, lingered and dissipated, leaving the earthy scent of reefer smoke. The TUV was cruising at a comfortable seventy-five. There was no hurry. What will this day bring back, a day which had dawned as ordinarily as any other? He could only guess. After a decade in this business, he still couldn't be sure. The deeper he had delved, the more surprised he had been. Surprised and wiser.

'The Dark Side of the Moon' pulsated through the car speakers, as the first of the flyovers zipped by. Glassy shopping malls, the steel and chrome geometries of mega corporations flashed past, shimmering in the heat. The burning air echoed the howls of farm labourers whose bones were turning into buttery dust under the newly-sprung city of glass. *In hoc signio vinces*!

He had risen early and, after a brisk morning walk, made coffee and a cheesy chicken omelette for himself. Then he had called Zeeta and left some instructions before setting out. It was a good ninety-minute drive to the lab from his apartment, which was closer to the centre of town. He had been living here in this studio accommodation right from the time he had moved to this city with a teaching assignment after completing his organic chemistry degree in England. Rents were going through the roof and he did not find any reason to move to a bigger house. He was single and content. His work at the research institute provided enough challenges to keep him occupied.

The sun was already burning through the windows. Vincent adjusted his powered shades as the car swung into an unfinished road that went up to the research institute, about a kilometre into barren emptiness.

Zeeta would have arrived by now and set things up. Lucky to have such an efficient colleague, who could be trusted. Her background was impeccable, and she had come with a good recommendation. Her slicked short hair, black shell academic glasses and full lips—which she coloured in blood moon shades—hadn't distracted him when she joined his team, but he had noticed the younger assistants look at her with worshipping eyes.

It remained like that till the time the roots and mushrooms had begun to arrive in his lab. He never discovered how these were sourced, what efficient supply chain obtained for him whatever he required. Some of these substances were banned across the globe. He knew his brief, that he should not be asking questions.

Their parent company was a giant pharmaceuticals operation spread across continents; but they did take up independent projects, and he was not supposed to ask too many questions. All he knew was that the current work involved unusual levels of secrecy and confidentiality. The small research team was carefully vetted and special procedures were followed, involving multiple levels of checks.

He had begun the new set of experiments with Santa Maria. This was the name he used for three different varieties of marijuana. He preferred using this name for his lab notes. This made it difficult for them when it was found.

Now, as he swiped through the plate glass door, he remembered those early experiments with Santa Maria. The receptionist, a light-eyed girl from the hills, gave him her practised smile and he waved back. As soon as he was gone, she pulled out her mobile and noted down a number on a notepaper. Leaving the desk phone off the hook, she hurried towards the fire exit.

Vincent swiped again, entering the lobby area where a lift was waiting to take him three floors down. A few minutes later, he walked out of the lift and into the changing room to put on his purple lab coat.

Santa Maria had not been much of a revelation, though it made him hold Zeeta's hand for the first time. 'We can stop here and allow the world to freeze,' he had said, 'and then we need not sweat over these chemicals, these foods of the gods.'

'Let me make you some tea,' she had said, looking strangely into his eyes, letting him hold her hand. He remembered how it seemed, sipping for ages that Darjeeling as the world began to turn into stone. A black obsidian. He had asked her out for dinner sometime around those early days of this project. A few weeks had passed.

She took good care of the lab. Everything would be in order when he arrived. Once a substance was checked out, he would write down the experience. The assistants would help them mix reagents, measure temperatures and prepare new formulations for testing. They would collect inputs on other experiments done in the past and collate the findings for Vincent to study. When everyone left, he would transfer some of the observations to a secure computer. Sometimes she would help.

Zeeta had begun staying back late; she would not leave until he was done. This bothered him. The protocols of confidentiality were strict, and he worried that he may be hauled up by his invisible masters. But nothing like that happened. Only…one evening, after an eventful day spent on a medium dose of Blue Halos mushrooms, they had forgotten they were supposed to return home.

'This is the maestro among shrooms,' he told her as he scribbled some notes. They had drunk the magic mushrooms steeped in warm drinking chocolate. The Blue Halos tasted odd, so he had suggested this method of masking the flavour. The synesthesia triggered by the fungi had almost faded by then; the door knobs did not look like jelly any more, nor did they turn into bioluminescent bobtail squids with the light of another world. Still, he was drained with the experience, left with a lingering happiness akin to the afterglow of a hay roll.

'Thanks for asking me to be part of it today. In any case, we will be short of assistants with security-clearance for a few more weeks as everyone is coming down with respiratory illness from this smog,' she said.

'I guess we should be careful…none of us wear masks,' Vincent said, 'we cannot afford to lose a single day now,' he added.

'I'll ask them for a circular,' Zeeta said, rising up to get some water.

'I'm starving, can we find something to eat?' he suggested.

Sending off the driver, they drove out to one of the chic dhabas with amber light ribbons twisted around rosewoods and an LED-lit mobile tower, pretending to be a palm tree, looming over a dusty courtyard. Stuffing themselves with butter chicken, they went on to a motel, beyond the last flyover of the city of glass, where all through the night their work-soiled dresses pirouetted in the ceiling-fan breeze under the pink-blue fairy lights of the cheap deluxe room, heavy with the aroma of *chameli* room-freshener, while a blood moon drifted across the heavens.

THE MAN WITH
THE MISSING EAR

'Most people crashing to their end down two-thousand feet-deep ravines have their skulls smashed, their clothes in tatters and their faces painted by Fauvist masters with the brightest of red corpuscles,' I'm saying to a man with half his ear lobe missing, who is occupying a couch in my *chilekotha*—the attic—completely sloshed and almost choking on his hiccups. He makes a gurgling noise, opens one eye and takes a swig from the tumbler. But he doesn't pass out, and is careful enough to check the shotgun in his belt from time to time.

I continue without bothering to note his reactions, 'Nothing like that happens to the Chief Minister despite the fact that he must have accelerated down that steepest of rock faces with the wind splitting his clothes apart, till close to the ground he would have experienced the moksha of weightlessness. Wind drag would have countered his acceleration; and if you remember classroom physics, as my dad would say, drag here depends on the square of velocity, the density of air in that gorge and the reference area of the object hurtling earthwards—in our case, the Chief Minister was six feet, and the drag co-efficient, always written as Cd.' The man raises an eyebrow and seems to contemplate upon the difficulty of extracting an ice cube from the plastic tray.

'An elegant equation,' I continue, 'that brings together the above would have ultimately helped him achieve weightlessness at some point…and then it would be classic free fall. Free fall till he heard the brook rise up to sing him a lullaby.' I was getting in the mood. The man with the missing ear had brought a good whisky but it looked like he will crash in my *chilekotha* tonight.

I was remembering the night we received the news.

Late summer. Humid like hell. Wet bulb temperature hovering near death's door.

Trying to concentrate on my job at *The Trumpet*. I'm in charge of the business page. For a few weeks a colleague's been on leave, so I do the night shift. Boss slips out early this evening, scratching his dirty beard. He seems to be in a hurry. I'm told he is seeing a bar crooner who does sleazy dances for a tip. He leaves some instructions for me to finish my work and wait for a correspondent to phone in the report of the Chief Minister's interview.

The CM's touring Thunder Mountain, where an insurgency has been brewing. I chew through my tiffin—oily fried rice with leathery poultry chicken and shrimp. The cook has forgotten to put in the salt, and I don't have the time to make the journey to the pantry to heat up the grub. Phone rings. My colleague at the other end is breathless and incoherent.

'Calm down', I tell her while trying to dislodge bits of chicken stuck between my molars with my Chinese toothpicks.

She tries to say something but loses her words.

'Where are you? Are you okay?' I ask. When she finally breaks the news, it takes a few moments to sink in.

'The CM has been attacked,' she blurts out.

'My god!' I quickly send an urgent note out to my colleagues while listening carefully to what she has to say. The news begins to seep in. Agencies are flashing first reports. Soon, it will be a torrent. In less than an hour my boss is back, as are all the seniors. The office is buzzing again— phones ringing off the hook, comments from the leader of the Opposition, a quick few lines from the police chief, a press conference has been called, cancelled, called again. Someone's already heading that way.

It's late when I finish. I am returning home long after midnight. There is a huge procession of the ruling party along the Avenue of Egos. The crowds are restless, belligerent.

It is around this time of the attack on the CM that it begins. We grow feet, more and more feet, like centipedes. Jet engines thunder above us in droves, desire kisses the stratosphere, dirt's swept away, miasma vacuumed. They even demolish the hovel where Akbar lived near the river bank, but I manage to get him a place in an abandoned warehouse belonging to the rail company.

Frenzy, feverish frenzy overtakes us all. We move at a dizzying pace. Steel, concrete, cement, stock market pulse beats, exotic vacations, infotech gurus and aerodrome-sized establishments to lose freedom, win it back again. And *you* are in all of this. So am I.

Moneybags making a beeline. Someone's busy signing agreements. An acquaintance from university days, now a door-to-door pyramid scheme salesman, pops up on my way to office, 'Have you heard, the biggest fashion house on this planet is setting up shop right here in Anantanagar?'

'Is it?' I ask.

His face crumples into a pitiful smile, blanched of colour for a moment. 'We are blessed!' he whispers.

Is he stoned, like he always used to be? I study his face. The colour comes back. I bid him good fucking luck with his sales pyramid.

But I notice that day that the brass nameplate on the gates of our house had tarnished. It could do with a good polish. Earlier, dad took care of such things. Now I get a tin of Brasso but Mastan, my pet Doberman, chews up the applicator. A shoe brush can do as well, I tell myself. A frayed one is lying in the store. Pouring some brass polish over the plate I use a good twenty times till 'MITRA' shines and shines brighter than the greedy eyes of the *dalal*s who prowl Four Horse Street.

We are scared shit of these characters. But there's a glint in our eyes that won't fade. Four Horse Street is a historical neighbourhood…there are many beautiful houses here, grand mansions built by eccentric ancestors with eclectic tastes; and heritage buildings too, all pretty and crying for repair. These *dalal*s and their bosses, the promoters, consider these ripe for the taking. These appointed tormentors stalk Four Horse Street with the attitude of butchers in a slaughterhouse—eyeing for the fattest pig, dreaming of pulled pork, a large juicy animal turning on the spit, dripping lard, drip by juicy drip. Licking their lips, setting their wolfish gaze on their dinners of frozen music as Goethe had it.

These *dalal*s, they use coded signs to mark out properties. Peeing dogs leave their scent so that they don't end up fighting each other over territory. But fights do break out, *peto*s are hurled that take away arms and legs, and nights echo with the romantic whistles of stray bullets.

These old buildings: the Brit-built ones like great grandfathers, those of the *babu*s like profligate maternal uncles with many secrets…and the more recent ones like ours, in a mix of styles, are their common enemies. Driven on by their promoter bosses, the *dalal*s go about targeting these grand mansions, these haunted houses, these greying three-storeys with plans of high-rises, multi-storeys, shopping malls and hypermarkets. Each time they succeed in coercing the original owners, usually with words, square feet and smoking Mungeri *katta*s in their belts, the promoters descend with their sledge hammers and labour platoons. The grandfathers are snuffed out. The street and the city wakes up with new face paint.

I play the trumpet.

The Communist-run government struggles in a democracy opening its doors wide to the world, not knowing what will get in through that hole. A soup of dialectics pours forth from the mouths of apparatchiks, ores of protest melt in the blast furnaces of consumer heat.

It keeps us busy.

We make headlines that slither like snakes. Venomous, hard-hitting, eyeball-uprooting sexy copy. We top circulation figures for the last five years in the East. Trumpets blow louder. Blowing, fingering, blowing and fingering; and yes, I made that up about the circulation but we do have a humongous readership.

The Trumpet stands at the southern end of the Avenue of Egos where, after putting the day's edition to bed, we pack the bug-ridden couches of the old bar where tiger moths on the hand-blown tulip lamps throw indecipherable signs on the marble tabletops. Nobody really knows why the moths have such a liking for the lamps in this bar. 'Maybe they are commie snitches keeping an eye on this bourgeois fish wrap of a daily and its reactionary employees,' a colleague comments, but no one pays too much attention to the moths anyway.

The Avenue of Egos with all its secret places, bars and casual acquaintances is a strange attractor. After a day packed with newsroom chatter and meetings with sources planted deep inside red brick buildings—wherefrom the city and the state is run in a fashion which is a mix of a football club and a film society—the avenue with its flame trees and cosy restaurants is like holiday memories from younger days. When everyone was still alive...mom and dad, and the uncle who jumped before a running train.

Stepping out of office late in the evening, my usual order at the bar is a cooler this summer, after the attack on the CM. Then vodka man arrives, always ordering five large ones with coke, and blabbers endlessly about Ramsay Brothers' movies until one day I discover he is a doctor at the morgue. Good company, I like him. More people come—the late night disco girls with black nail polish, the promoters smelling piss-money and more shadowy figures, but by then the moths cut off all the light and I shift to whisky.

I must have met Comrade LJ around this time.

For three-and-a-half days, after the CM is pushed into that ravine in a grievous attack while touring Thunder Mountain, the city prays silently. But before weightlessness could take over, he gets snared by a strong branch of a tree a few hundred feet down the way. The impact puts him out, and he suffers a stroke and passes into a coma.

Football matches are cancelled, and townsfolk take French leave and go off to the hills. The temples organise the death-defying *mritunjay yagna*s, and in the clandestine betting-circles, the odds that he would return to consciousness remain high. Yet he chooses to become a part of our memories.

Starting out for office one of those days, I spy a blue chalk marked sign on the neighbour's wall. I am about to stop by and ask him about it, but don't. The coded sign, which looks like a hooked fish, remains on the perimeter wall till the day the demolition team appears. I remember the singing bullets of my sleepless nights and the greedy-eyed *dalal*s. I miscalculate thinking they wouldn't bother a journalist. Yet, I soon realise they are coming when the hooked fish appears on my front door.

That's how I meet Idris Alam, the man with a missing ear lobe. Idris is the most depraved specimen of humanity I will ever come across. Which is what drew me to him, like a paroled prisoner to a striptease joint.

Idris is a promoter's agent and he arrives with a proposal. He is slit-eyed and rat-faced, and whoever took half his ear had made a clean cut of it. They want ten houses in a row to be pulled down in order to make way for a multi-storied diamond souk.

'Where will I go?' I ask Idris with exasperation.

He screws his eyeballs and glowers, 'You'll be getting two flats in a housing complex,' he says coldly. I see his missing ear on fire, blood dripping from his eyes.

'Complex it is,' I mumble, but suggest if we could work out a deal so that our house can be spared. A meeting with his promoter boss is arranged.

Meanwhile, my colleagues at *The Trumpet* are busy pushing conspiracy theories about the assassination. The first fingers are pointed at the Red Dawn ultra-leftist groups that have been pricking a thorn here and there in the distressed backside of the administration. Not to be left behind, our competitor, *The Incendiary*, suggests that the hill insurgents must be behind it. Trumpeters and Incendiarists try to outdo each other in this game, roping in the flimsiest clues and sources of support for their pet theories. This takes a nasty turn when the opposition leader's underworld links are splashed by *The Incendiary*, both in print and on their TV channel. Not ready with anything sensational, we go on to defend the man in question by getting poets and footballers together in his praise, and pressing the police chief to write an eulogy of the famous collection of moths that Chakladar, the man in question, has at his villa just outside the city. How could a person with such a love for winged insects ever plot such a dastardly act? The gossip fluffs and froths, and the moths of Chakladar become famous across the land.

In the meantime, Idris arranges my meeting. The promoter, a colourless man with a feet-long tongue, is adamant. 'Why are you being sentimental about this tired pile of bricks,' he keeps repeating while chewing scented tobacco. But my profession helps. I bargain and lose, give some more line and get revived. Mitra House, our handsome two-storey home from grandfather's time, will survive. But I will have to cooperate. My profession provides access to the secret lives of people—which ones in the heritage buildings committee can be easily blackmailed or bought over, who can be coerced because we have a file full of evidence about his whore habit, which municipal officer has the best-dressed skeletons in his cupboard—and I will help them with these details. They will do the rest.

Things begin to work and the hooked fish sign disappears from my front door. In a year Idris graduates to a sedan from his Japanese motorbike. Idris and his bosses succeed in targeting distressed owners of houses which have been quietly removed from heritage lists, offering them thousand square feet of salvation. Idris and his gang begin visiting me often. I hate them, and I love them too. What use are these shit piles of ancestral homes anyway?

My inputs have proved valuable. They send me packets of biryani and scotch of uncertain origins, which I secretly pour into Mastan's bowl till he bites the priest one day. They drop wads of cash in my empty fish bowls.

I'm getting kind of friendly with this guy Idris. We chat about the CM's death, he tells me he hates the idle rich. 'After days of back-breaking work, sometimes I slip out at night and hide in the shadows of the stables at the racing ground and throw bent nails before big cars. It's lovely to watch the tyres burst and the drivers lose control.'

'You are a genius,' I tell him, and go with him one night, then another. If the driver is dead, he pulls out his teeth with odd-looking pliers, wrapping them up carefully in a blood-soaked handkerchief.

'What do you do with these?' I ask, shivering with excitement.

'Why, I have a toothed pussy on my bedroom wall.' And he proudly shows it to me one day, lit up with concealed art gallery lamps. A fine and oversized specimen of plasticine art, the molars and incisors gleaming on the ridges of the labia majora.

Soon, Idris begins getting potted cacti for my garden. I discover that he is a green finger, running a nursery on the outskirts, and then one day a woman appears with him to help in the house. Her eyes are dark like murder, and the train of her hair reaches out through the sitting room window.

Champakali does the dishes, manages the kitchen and provisions, and enters monthly accounts on the computer. She says she's been to high school but I often find her to be better informed than the average undergrad. In fact, her interest in books strikes me as slightly odd. I am intrigued by this but never try to uncover her antecedents. There is a lot on my plate already. *The Trumpet* is sprouting more business pages and the pressure at work has grown tenfold. I have to read and watch TV. Idris' potted cactus plants are filling up the house. We sometimes go out at night to throw bent nails before speeding luxury automobiles and drown ourselves in Moscow Mules for the rest of the night. Woodpeckers drill the trees all day, and I read and work, and read and go to play the trumpet, watch TV and scour the internet for business news. I read stone drunk; I watch, download, re-watch the videos and the live programmes and commit everything to memory till I'm senseless. And Champakali is hovering there somewhere in the penumbras of late night lights of Mitra House, for she never seems to sleep. And I'm memorising every word escaping *your* mouth.

1,000 MILLIGRAMS

'We're almost there, I can hear it knocking at the door,' Vincent whispered in a sleep-soaked voice. It was early morning and the spring bed at the motel had given him a backache.

'What, who?' Zeeta responded, her eyes still shut tight.

'I have a feeling we're very close to what we have been looking for.' He stepped off the bed and hit an empty whiskey bottle left by a previous occupant. It rolled along the frayed carpet and hit a wall.

'Mushrooms? Pscilocybin?' she responded faintly.

'Not there but somewhere close. Closer each day,' he said.

'And how would you know when we get there?' she asked, her voice still on the edges of sleep.

'We are looking for perfection, perfect harmony—you know I can't tell you more,' he said, raising an eyebrow.

'Harmonies within or tuning ourselves to harmonies in chemicals?' She was suddenly inquisitive in a playful way.

'Someday everyone will know. What they missed in the Good Friday experiment ...' his voice trailed off as he went into the shower stall. The double-blind Good Friday experiment which established the conditions when psilocybin influences mystical experience was one of the entry points to his work. But here he was, going way deeper.

The refreshing burst of warm water cleared his thoughts, and he closed his eyes and stood under the shower dreaming of isomorphs and neurotransmitter receptors, and slowly the puzzle seemed to unravel. He was almost there. Meanwhile, their motel nights had become frequent.

This morning, as they exchanged glances, all these memories flooded back, like the contemplative carnival of a marijuana high. It had taken much longer than he had anticipated but they had made great progress. Zeeta waved. He waved back and pushed the door of his cabin. The blinds were lowered and the room was dark. He switched on a light and made some phone calls. As he spoke in a low voice, it was difficult for someone passing by to overhear what he was saying.

He stepped out of his cabin, put on the coat and entered the lab. Bhimsen Joshi's rendering of *Raag Asavari* was playing on the speakers. He asked her to turn it down. Though music was very much part of the experiments, he didn't want to hear Joshi's stentorian voice right now.

'Can you change the music, please?'

'Oh, surely,' she said, crossing her legs. A soft instrumental began to play.

'Hope no one is around on this floor today?' he asked.

'Nobody will be here unless they are required,' she said in a dutiful voice.

He smiled. 'Got everything ready?'

'Everything ready, sir,' she said confidently.

'Okay, then, ibogaineBZ2, 1,000 milligrams,' he said calmly, and went behind the racks to undress.

'Sure, sir,' she said

Vincent lay on the couch at one end of the long lab room. At this end, a small door led to the emergency exit stairs. From here, he could see rows upon rows of experiment tables, the racks with solutions and reagents, ceramic bowls, jars with solvents of many colours, a distilling setup with a swan-nosed flask and more tables with more glass objects, a spectrometer, more instruments, a refrigerator and shelves of books at the far end. Near his feet, a screensaver silently zoomed images from the Mandelbrot fractal on the computer at his work table.

Zeeta helped him take off his boxer shorts, smiling slyly as her hands rubbed him.

'Now, make it fast, we might need the best part of two days for this,' he said, breathing heavily.

'Okay, Okay,' she said as she played a bit more with him, the blood rushing in at the beckoning of her smooth grip. He turned to his left and curled up a bit, exposing his buttocks. She took up the bulb-syringe from the tray and delicately inserted the cream-white nozzle inside him. He moved a bit to make himself comfortable. She went deeper. Four inches of nozzle was inside him now. 'Go!' he whispered.

Zeeta began to squeeze the red bulb attached to the nozzle and the root extract of the *Tabernanthe iboga,* mixed with an infusion of substances he had prepared earlier, flooded his large intestine. She watched him closely, stopping if he looked uncomfortable, till all of it had been administered.

He had a smile on his face. She went for another smaller syringe-bulb, this time laying him on his back and going slowly and more cautiously. His eyes were wide with a rising euphoria.

For some time, he lay on the table. He didn't move but kept staring at the ceiling. Zeeta looked a little nervous, she could feel the sweat breaking out on the back of her palms.

He rose and went to the washroom. She sat on the couch, watching him carefully. He returned and walked clumsily to the table. His pupils were dilated and he seemed to be focusing at an invisible distance. He hovered around the table then went in the direction of the racks.

Now, he was mumbling and his feet moved awkwardly. It seemed that his feet had suddenly forgotten the rhythm of walking together. Now, one was more heavy than the other as he struggled to lift it from the ground; now, they seemed to be pulling in different directions. He smiled, he kept smiling, the smile grew wider then, 'Kingdoms of light!' he exclaimed. He was fumbling, his hands shook, he steadied himself on the leather chair in front of the computer.

'Should I get the tea?' she asked, holding him in a steady unwavering gaze.

'Now I know where to look. Now I know...' he went repeating. He opened the desk drawers looking for something. She stood back, studying him closely. She knew the classic effects of ibogaine; they had discussed it hundreds of times. But what else had gone into infusion BZ2 that he had prepared for this enema? His lab notes will have the details, and this computer. Besides, there was the unused sample. She swept her gaze across the racks. Light from the corridor was filtering in through the glass door at the far end.

He was rubbing his chest as he kept rummaging through the drawers and finally fished out a pen. He started writing while he went on mumbling, 'No tea, no tea... chocolate it has to be...thick solid slabs of the darkest dark...'

'You want hot chocolate? I'll get it. We have some from the mushroom experiments,' she said.

'Shrooms...yes lovely shrooms...eternity in their gills...' there was a slur in his voice now. 'But I have to write this down.

It's all here, in here, he touched his heart, his fingers moving across his hairy chest. All of it, I have to write about the fairies,' he began scribbling madly.

'Maybe you could get dressed first,' she said tentatively, 'I will help…' but he waved her off.

Early next day, the security team entered the lab through the emergency exit when their phone calls went unanswered. Taken aback by the loud music, they listened for a few moments. It was Lou Reed singing 'This Magic Moment'.

Then they saw him. Vincent Dutta hadn't dressed and seemed to be sleeping with his head on the table. They covered their noses at an odd smell of vapours, checked him for breathing and dialled an ambulance. Lou Reed sang heartily through the concealed speakers, the laboratory was cool under fluorescent showers and the lab coordinator, Zeeta, was unreachable on her number.

DAULAT-E-DUNIYA

I lived a quiet life right up to the point Idris, the man with the missing ear, appeared. Dad was wedded to science, a fanatical believer in functionality, and this belief bred in him an austerity where embellishments and the extraneous had very little place. I followed in his footsteps. His collection of clocks was an exception.

The rooms of our house still lie neglected, dust motes floating, heirloom chairs sagging slowly with the weight of phantoms, female spiders busy pheromone-coating their draglines. Cobwebs on the ceilings, cobwebs on the windows, webs on the ebony table with a secret compartment I hid stolen cigarettes in while in high school, rusty iron boxes of vinyl— Gauhar Jaan, Stan Rogers singing 'Northwest Passage', beaten trunks stacked with the secrets of three generations that hadn't been opened since the Great War.

The rooms we use are sparsely furnished—bed, my table facing the garden, framed photographs on the wall, bookcases, a couch and an easel from my college days. Using it as a clotheshorse now. Same for the other rooms. Then, there are my father's workbenches lined with rotting valve radio sets, Phillips amplifiers and overflowing toolboxes with greasy pliers and swan-neck spanners in the storeroom adjoining the kitchen. He used to spend hours working on gadgets that friends gave him for repair. I haven't touched anything there since that day.

This green secretariat in my room, I had bought it from an auction, as well as the two nightstands that I am using to display some of the cactus plants that Idris brings. The television next to the window has developed boils on its skin, but it is an old Sony and I don't let it go. The Goth and his parliament of timekeepers still remain posted all around the house.

When my dad, mauled by the brutal clock, speared by metal sharp, zooms off to the other side, I am pushed into a gutter. Sewer rats drag me there in my sleep. Perhaps I sleepwalk into it. Pitch-black tunnel stinking of vomit, at one end of which the menacing clock grins wickedly through its seventeenth-century dial. The other end invisible, cul-de-sac.

In this stifling hole, lights blink on sometime. Blinding reds, chilling blues, dirty greens and toxic yellows. Animal eyes. Radiation leaking from escaped lab rats. Sometimes these are *The Trumpet*'s neon flashes, burning like the eyes of an egomaniac in his own private Tihar. If I had been sleeping, then why do I feel so tired always? Think I already mentioned it's a bus ride from Mitra House to *The Trumpet* office. Half an hour, that's it. But you can also take the Metro, which is a little further off. I take the bus mostly, and find the same faces whatever time of day this is, travelling, making the same gestures, clenching and unclenching their fists when they see me, tch tch-ing, gnashing their teeth or giving pitiful looks while making signs of the hooked cross in the air with their umbrellas. A band of circus men from another town.

And then, I'm waiting for a source at the shopping mall, sipping a bitter coffee when there's a roar of exultation from above. A sound reverberating through the food court. Camera girl rappelling down from the crowded upper balcony. Buyers gathering already, enjoying the *tamasha*, smelling Issey Miyake and term plans. Dimwit, lazyfucks. *You* here too. Who can escape your shark eyes and your swagger, like smoke coiling on cubes of frozen carbon dioxide. Camera girl now dangling by orange ribbons, another with burgundy hair on a terracotta swing, grabbing a feet-long dildo-mic. Firing questions at me, and ten stage hands from ten directions rushing in with thousand watt studio halogens fixing five in front, two lighting up my cranium, one behind and three, jammed under the chair. Asslights.

'How're you today?' she trills.

'Fine.'

'Who are you waiting for?' the burgundy head charges ahead.

'You.'

'Watching girls?' she challenges playfully, adding, 'What did you buy?' Before I can respond, she commands, 'Show us.'

I begin to unzip my jeans.

No, I'm not here. Somewhere else this gotta be. 'Coffee,' I say timidly. Shoppers forming a noose around me, police constables, some of those bus passengers, the teeth-flashing circus men. And there *you* are, watching from a distance.

'Only coffee, when there are so many promotions! Haven't you heard of Buy Everything Day?'

'Aaaaaw!' Collective despair steams from the crowd. The noose tightens.

'Err...no,' I mumble.

'Today, you must buy everything you notice,' she smiles provocatively, her pearly white teeth glittering.

Don't you know, girls with all their teeth extracted can give the best blowjobs? Get those pulled next time. I know someone who can make better use of teeth anyway.

'We are from Splurge TV and have an exciting gift for you,' she says.

'With or without teeth?' I begin to say, but she butts in, 'Tell us the name of the salon that opened here today, and we will give you a coin from the era of Samudra Gupta.'

'Does it offer teeth extraction?' I blurt out.

'I err…' she looks at the camera girl…

'Then get all of those pulled and it will be a super prize.'

She smiles, pretending I had joked, 'Won't you like to own a Samudra Gupta coin?'

'Samudra Gupta? The emperor?' Samudra Gupta turns out to be a jeweller who has newly set up shop at the mall. My head throbs, the noose chokes my breath, I wish the lights burn out and I can flee, but luckily the person I had been waiting for appears. Like an angel, he extricates me with some effort. Shaking fists at the thousand watt lamps, we walk fast, double fast, run, out and away to an old-fashioned tea shop on the Avenue of Egos.

I'm still playing the trumpet.

As we speak, yacht companies from Hellas, tech conglomerates from the Middle Kingdom, buccaneers from Malacca, and fashion moguls from Milano arrive in hordes, setting up shop on stolen land; and to their honour, the black ditches of the city get dredged with World Bank dollars, the homeless are packed away into hiding and snaking overpasses are built. And then after the Chief Minister's final tryst with weightlessness followed by a split in the ruling party, the centrists come to power. Things move faster, here and all across the land.

The yacht maker diversifies into helicopter rentals, a food giant sweeps in a blue-chip cosmetics brand, the tech magnates unleash sly algorithms, the pirates build smart cities pouring tonnes of cement that further heats up the planet while a local moneylender begins oil explorations in the bay.

The poor of Anantanagar, who had set up small shops everywhere—and those from the villages whose lands had been snatched by the smart cities and tech academies—creep and crawl all over, overflowing into the shopping malls, fighting with the uniforms, snatching careless cappuccino cups of dreamy-eyed duos sitting in sidewalk cafés on the boulevard that heads towards the river.

This is the route I take while walking to the *ghats* from home. Teeming with employees of finance companies, bleary-eyed call-centre crowds, venomous managers with salt and pepper hair fishing for weekend fun and the lone *phuchka* stall where sultry eyed receptionists of multinational companies congregate. Sometimes, on my way back from the river I stop for *phuchkas* or grab a coffee at the shop next door—a square room of blue glass and moody Turkish lamps. Sitting with my espresso in that kaleidoscopic heaven of colour, redolent with coffee aromas, I eavesdrop on the confident chatter. It's rejuvenating, and I wonder whether I'm getting screwed the wrong way.

Men and women in corporate gear locked in bluetoothed soliloquies—celeb promos, performance bonuses, windfall dividends, American Express, Far East cruises, 3BHKs, vacation homes, cock worship. Climbers all. Climbing, climbing fast to reach the critical mass of accumulating so much joy that the world would never be saved. Let the world go to hell, different story…doesn't bother me a whit.

By the end of the workday, these crowds are flocking at the Chinese joints at the city end. Out there, cow piss imported lagers and dense fogs of weed smoke drive discussions about being passionate in conception and detached in execution, or some new cock doing the rounds that season. Old timers sit at the back with their hard drinks and wary eyes. On my off days I step into one of these joints, the red-walled one with *Kuan Yin*, the Avalokitesvara bodhisattva on a pedestal. A snifter or two with a quick meal and replenishing my stock of bamboo toothpicks, I hurry out; but if they spot me, I'm drawn into the excitement of their lives.

'Mitra!' they holler across the tables, 'join us bro!' I sink into that fug of smoke and slurry speech, and those spirit-fuelled *adda*s become reckless. On good days, there are fights. Which is why the shaved head sitting next to me tonight has a stone eye.

Probably he was there with us last evening when we steered through the strategic vision of the oil-exploring moneylender, detouring through words the Father of the Nation may have spoken on to the Malacca pirates, all of it still buzzing in my head after midnight, me struggling to remember where I had picked up this gunk. Whenever this happens I check for the toothpicks in my bag to be sure that I had been to the Chinese bar, but these often disappear.

Didn't I just mention that I struck up these casual friendships along the boulevard? Mostly young professionals, managers and finance guys. One evening they invite me for a boat ride. Men and women—a mixed group. Charged up by Malana cream and the stench of rotting fish from the chemical spill, we have long, animated conversations and *you* effortlessly make your way into it. I ask them if they believe in God. They slur and stutter so I tell them where to look. I have the authorised biography with me and I read a few lines.

A wind rises. The water becomes choppy.

I narrate anecdotes like the one about your days in the Swiss college where a small accident led you to start an online pet sales start-up. 'How imaginative', they roar, from Malana heaven, and the boat lists over the dark waters.

This is cyclone season. Cyclones are growing stronger. We should go home.

More stories.

They want to hear more. I feel flushed, bathed in adrenaline. Like a priest at a temple mediating between the deity and the devout. Finally, the *majhi* rows us back. But I miss Idris on these trips.

Once the row of houses is gone from Four Horse Street, the diamond souk is completed at a dizzying pace. As if the glass structure was buried long back, beneath the alluvial plains; and this day at the push of a button and the snip of a ribbon by the Minister of Commerce, it reared its head and claimed territory.

The Diamante is a pyramid of clear glass rising ten floors, and from its peak protrudes a seventy-foot chrome needle, which erupts into a freeze frame fountain of crystal blocks gushing and falling all around. At night, when the souk is lit up and the laser beams embedded in the crystal drops switched on, the lights befuddle merchant ships bringing in Nipponese automobiles and coal from the southern hemisphere. I often find myself gaping at the sparkling pyramid, and the fire of its heart warms me up on cold winter nights.

The laser beams whisper *your* name and I am at the Chinese watering hole again, looking for those spunky manager friends from that night on the river. On my work table at home, the stacks of onion-coloured *Daulat Times* and *The Business Bee* grow. Cartons of pink newspapers and magazines all over. On my phone, on the internet, the interviews run nonstop.

I'm breathless when I read the news and watch *you* on TV. Like I've just run a marathon or a relay. Relay's the word. I wish when you are here next time you'll grant me an audience. I have made a request for an interview.

Late into the night, Champakali makes me endless cups of tea. She mixes my drinks, and I read and I watch, I read and I drink. I watch and I replay. All through the night, the Diamante twinkles like a wishing star.

But then it happens. Late one night I tear up the business papers. The buggers were telling only one side of the story. I hate my job. I hate everyone who pens these lies. On my way back I had seen a wasted consumptive girl being pimped by a beggar in an alley behind the diamond pyramid. They appeared in my sleep. In there, the beggar was screwing the girl in the Burning Man position while fire consumed them both. A shanty has been burnt to cinders tonight.

A condo will come up soon.

They have set the planet on fire.

I dream of Idris and the toothed pussy.

Past midnight, too late to call him now.

I jump out of bed yelling *your* name. I aim for the nearest carton full of business papers and give it a square kick. It tumbles down the stairs to the main door, choking in the alphabet streams of its rose-tinted desires. Letters, and then whole sentences stream out of the papers and slither away through the dining room, towards the sitting room and then out of the house, ready to pounce on the next innocent.

We are innocent.

I grab a meat cleaver.

We lick the blue skies with our forked tongues.

I will chop off the balls of those managers.

Champakali comes rushing, Mastan by her side. Her eyes go wide when she sees the knife.

'Who subscribes to this pile of rubbish?' I bark.

Mastan growls angrily at me. She takes a look at the snaky lines of business news slithering away, and then in a calm voice, says, 'You must have. I don't follow business news'.

I fling a pile of *Daulat Times* at her. She ducks. With a crash the bunch hits a sideboard, shattering some plates. I hurry into the kitchen, grab a bottle and take a swig. I look at the meat cleaver still in my hand and think of the managers on the boat that day. Tender meat. Idris has impressed me with his dental art.

My head aches the next morning. But it's not a hangover ache. It's an abomination. I skip office.

The journo's job doesn't appeal to me anymore.

'Gifting of flowers will never go out of fashion and the margins are good,' Idris tells me one day while downing shots of a smoky malt in my *chilekotha*. Over the months, he has morphed into a drinking buddy. Indeed, he has opened doors which I would have never tried. He prefers the *chilekotha* because he is scared of Mastan; he is scared of all dogs. No connection with his missing ear, I suppose. But he insists we sit upstairs knowing Mastan isn't allowed here.

Idris keeps hammering on about the profit to be had from the flower trade while getting fearfully drunk on whiskey. All through that week. I know he is trying to hide some of his money from the property broking, and then he has this nursery. Neat plans.

I think about it over days.

'Let's begin small,' I tell him at last, 'flowers and chocolate. Don't burn money over a fancy shop, just a small boutique will do. Most orders will be online.'

'Why chocolate?' he asks.

'Huh! Bloody brain food! Didn't you ever go out on a date in your college days?' I snap.

'College?' he narrows his slit eyes and knocks back a double.

'Oh, I should have known. Sorry but chocolate is a must. Flowers and chocolate cannot be separated.'

'And Black Forest', he slurs, but in a few weeks he puts down quite a sum for our venture, a little flower boutique on the northern bank of Teardrop Lake where the bone-tired go to cleanse their lungs at end of the day. So that was that.

As I was saying, Idris has been a big influence.

MANDELBROT'S FIGURES

The backlit dial of her watch showed that it was still early hours. Here, all seemed to be quiet. She glanced back once at the table—the Mandelbrot set was still churning out its infinitum of images on the computer screen. Her heart was still thumping in her head. Everything, she has to remember everything that had transpired from the time she administered the enema the previous day. How could she forget. But no, she has to move fast. She checked her bag again, everything she needed was there. She took out the duplicate key, silently thanking the receptionist, unlocked the door and tiptoed into the emergency exit. Orange LED strips guided her as she stealthily climbed the steps to the ground level, where a door opened to the parking lot.

As Zeeta crept across the silent parking lot, negotiating icy shadows, she feared that one of them would burst into life: she noticed her hands shiver.

A cobbled path cut through the lawn, meeting a service road beyond the perimeter wall. With luck, there would be no guards there. The *mali* was up early tending the plants, but she could avoid him by looking the other way. Will he find it odd? Perhaps not, because she had worked night shifts before. She knew the elderly man. He had given her primrose cuttings at the beginning of summer. The wildflowers were still blooming in her window case.

She slipped out through the gate and, in half an hour, reached the highway. The *mali* hadn't seen her. In a few hours, she would be relieved of a great burden. She clutched her bag close to herself as she tried to hail a taxicab.

The taxi sped through the city of glass on its way to Aukatabad which was shimmering in the horizon like a dubious promise. The summer sun was burning away the morning smog, and was already harsh by the time she reached the outskirts. It scorched souls. Like dried petals, they lay scattered on the kerbside. A scent of nothingness rose from them that left the whole city weary. She had asked the driver to take the outer ring road. Staring at the dusty miles stretching ahead and the traffic slithering into Aukatabad, she unmindfully opened her bag. She dug her hand inside, and ran her fingers over something and smiled. Now only if she could arrive in time.

But the taxi was slowing down. She looked ahead, and then at the rear view mirror. Were they being pulled over? No. Nothing of that sort. The trucks, tourist buses and cars ahead of them were crawling. Slowing down further till everything came to a standstill. Minutes passed, the heat became unbearable, ten minutes went by. Nothing. Half an hour. The passengers got down from the buses. They were marching ahead to see what was the matter.

She didn't want to get down even though the taxi was turning into a frying pan. '*Kya hua bhaiya*?' she asked the cabbie, but the driver didn't seem interested in investigating the reason for the halt. He took out a pocket mirror and began to comb his hair.

She slid her hand inside the bag again, and now found something soft and pulled it out. A half-eaten bar of Atman dark chocolate gone soft in the heat. Zeeta tore a piece and took a bite. It melted fast, spreading its luscious richness. She was wondering if she should switch on her mobile. No, that would be tricky. Vincent Dutta's master would not take very long to figure things out. And she was trapped in this sweltering heat, hemmed in by dead automobiles.

The chocolate was a gift from Vincent. She felt better as she took another bite. Perhaps a breeze had begun to blow. Was it getting a bit chilly? What! In the middle of summer? A wind. Did she catch the whisper of a cool wind? Or was it someone trying to reach in through the window? An ice-cold hand.

MEET YOUR MASTER

The click of your shoes on the pavement sounds like whip cracks in my ears. Louder with every step. Coming up Four Horse Street, which shoots west to east across the city before losing its way in the jungle of concrete that overran the wetlands like gene-spliced fungus of an apocalyptic imagination.

The immense heat of the afternoon is an attack on civilisation. This year, it is worse than the last. The avenues of Anantanagar shimmer in the fiery blaze, tar melts like liquid nightmares, the art-deco mansions hiss and crack while hulking SUVs climb mirror-clad avenues swooping up into *jannat*s of petroleum dreams. Unnoticed in the mountains, the glaciers melt away, drop by drop—like the terminally ill shuffling along till the end, glioblastomas growing, the teardrops of a future waiting in the wings. Sorcerers crouch at every corner, casting spells, selling hope and tricks. Illusions aplenty. Blackwater refuse of the grey sprawling city—the emptiness of bloated bellies, aborted foetuses, the wasted wants of a megapolis swim below its foundations through choking sewer pipes.

The flowers are selling well. I've been devoting more time to our new enterprise. If you have ever been in this business, you know how creative and fulfilling this can be. Working on the arrangements, the right shade combinations for various occasions, and then, of course, the suppliers, nurseries, stocks, inventories. Meanwhile, Idris adds to his collection on the bedroom wall. I haven't met the managers since I quit office but I will have to, very soon.

I spend the first half of the day at the boutique with the shop assistant. We discuss how we could get to know the regular customers better, and speedily address complaints. Then, after a quick lunch at the Tibetan joint close by and picking up quite a bit of cash to clear some dues, I arrive home.

The TV is chirping away. Tuberoses spreading their cloying sweetness in the thick of a summer afternoon. I've been watching that TV for the whole week. Glued to the screen, unable to pull myself away. I never switch it off, even when I go out; I leave it talking to itself. This way, I miss little. From the moment I enter the house I can hear its confident chatter.

A heap of used teabags on the table. With me away at the flower shop, Champakali has become careless. I rarely see her these days. Tea stains spot the sheets and whisky bottles clatter under my bed when the spirits have a party.

You are everywhere now. An explosion, on every screen. A hankering to know you, in your fairy-tale. An endless desire to excavate even a few shards of a broken mirror that speaks the truth.

I watch nonstop, I play the social videos, each one as soon as they appear, like blessing and respite. Soon it turns out I can predict what you're going to say next and I am right, always. So much so that Idris and others are betting on my words. Some smart asses have even made money from the company shares. I can smell the sweat on your brow, the warm air you exhale.

Other than books and newspapers, my green secretariat table is overflowing with clippings. Carefully sorted—onionskin papers, dailies, prints from websites and, besides these, stuffed thumb drives and hard disks.

The pictures of Prana the cat always follow you. Prana and Atman, Atman and Prana. Prana the life force, Atman, immutable soul. Prana, your darling pet, the nation's sweetheart—your only competition in the wide world but for that German thorn, which will be dealt with soon.

I think the grandfathers are now never wound on time. They are tolling different hours; and so, morning and evening, day and night muddle up. Champakali is becoming more and more careless. Why is she not winding the clocks in time? What is she up to these days? And my room always smells of spoilt food and unwashed sheets, drowned in the babble of television voices where the endless footage shows a palatial home in Aukatabad, meetings and press conferences or shots of the villa in Bournville, the town the Cadburys founded.

Your footsteps ring louder in the stillness of the afternoon. The street outside suddenly empty, the crowds around the Diamante wiped clean. Not a single cabbie or food delivery guy in sight. Through the window of my room, I see you coming— through the gate, across the tuberose beds with cautious steps, your eyes cold like an evening funeral.

Something flashes in your hand—a cane, an umbrella? But you are in the passage already. The main door bangs shut. So you have the keys? Where is Champakali?

A flock of pigeons take flight, punctuating the emptiness of the afternoon with their wing beats. And through the hall I can hear your heavy steps. Coming closer, stopping for a moment.

Now, you're right outside my room. Panic! No time to lose. The connecting door to the store room is open. I creep into the darkness of my father's dead radio sets.

Dismembered audio amplifiers, thermionic valves, picture tubes, naked wires pushed into plugs, alligator clips attached to jumper cables—there's a lot of electricity here. Potentially. Enough to power a revolution, or at least to power me up. Wires going out from every socket to the dismantled equipment. I softly step up to the switchboard and flick on all the power switches.

Through the crack of the door I can see you as you stride into my room with slow purposeful steps. Chin lifted, stiff with determination. You walk right up to the table and stare straight in my direction.

Irresistible. This attraction of electricity. Billions of electrons rushing through copper. Through naked circuits. Through the teeth of the alligators. I step closer. A radio begins to crackle.

You know I am here. I am transfixed. I can smell the sweat on your brow.

Through the crack in the storeroom door I can count the creases on your grey Armani jacket. So familiar.

I grab the naked alligator clips with my bare hands.

It's perhaps the warmth of your breath that heats up the air. Perhaps it's the air that catches fire.

The moths fly off from the tavern that night. In their hundreds, they flap out of homes and offices, from railway terminuses and cemeteries, and begin circling over the city. 'Is it climate change?' some ask. A few hundred escape from the deputy CM's collection and join the free. They fly and dive and spin and flutter in the hot air, and out over the poisoned river. For some days they take siege of the city, darkening its skies, brushing against faces, hanging like a spell from the clouds of Anantanagar's sweltering summer nights.

HYPNOSIS

The taxi was hemmed in from all sides. Cars, buses, motorcycles, minivans. People were waiting despondently in their vehicles while many, mostly long-distance bus passengers, had stepped out on the pavements, investigating the traffic jam. That cold brush on her cheeks. But there was no one outside the door. Was an invisible being warning her about danger? Despite the heat, she was shivering. She got out of the cab and walked up to the pavement. She felt better immediately. She could ditch her handbag with its contents and walk away…vanish among the faceless millions.

She was gliding over plate glass. As she walked ahead along the footpath, the people on the pavement parted to make way but her body didn't brush against theirs. They seemed to drift past. As if she was all of water and they were sailing by. The automobiles shone with an animal intensity. The Jaguars, the Camrys, the Dzires were glowing and alive, these were no more metal and plastic. The vehicles looked like living beings bristling with chromosomes and that sight made her burst into laughter. She went on laughing, hardly able to control herself.

She was far ahead now, almost at the head of the long line of vehicles. And now she noticed the drivers of the cars in the front were not in their seats, nor was there any policeman. The automatic signals were blinking amber as the empty cars eyed each other, and the occupants milled in their hundreds around a roadside temple. She walked into that crowd. Nobody paid her any attention as people jostled and fought to enter the sanctorum. She glided through the press of bodies.

Some of these people were trying to form a queue but the crowd was in no mood to wait. Many in the crowd had bottles, cans and small tins of milk in their hands, and they held these carefully so that the milk didn't spill. What was happening? Where was all this milk coming from? Where was it going?

Then she noticed the milkman; there was another queue before him. During Shivaratri, some Hindus offered milk to Lord Shiva but this was not the time; and now she saw the deity. The centre of all this attention was the elephant-headed Ganesh, and not Shiva, the Destroyer.

A miracle was afoot and this had drawn the crowds. She got excited and fought to reach the front. And it was easy for her as she could slip in like the wind, flow like water. Nothing could obstruct her. And right at the front she saw the priest, guiding the devout. Shiva was also there, but Ganesh was stealing all attention.

The faithful bent down with their cans and PET bottles, bone china mugs and bell metal glasses, and lovingly held these at Ganesh's lips; and calmly, the deity sipped the milk and soon the containers emptied. The next one in line would stoop low before the God hoping his offering would be similarly accepted, and so it was. 'Sixty degrees, sixty degrees!' the priest raised his voice, guiding them about the angle the glass needs to be tilted so the God can drink. And she watched, everyone watched, as the idol went on imbibing gallons upon gallons. And not only here in this small temple but all over Aukatabad and beyond, in big and small towns and villages, on pavements and huge marble temples, throughout the day the God of prosperity didn't disappoint his followers.

Zeeta watched for many minutes till she remembered where she was and whatever had happened the night before. Fear crowded back as she turned around and began to retrace her steps. She slithered through the growing mass of people and TV crew. The taxi driver was still at the wheel, though most of the others had disappeared. She got in.

She hadn't noticed a TV crew follow her when she came out of the temple. They walked up to her side, sticking the mike through the window. She refused to talk, shielding her face from the camera. But they went on insisting. They told her that the city had come to a standstill and offices had closed.

'Did he drink from your hand?' the man with the microphone asked her repeatedly.

'Oh, no! But yes, he is drinking. I saw,' she said, lowering her dark glasses.

'Is he drinking with his mouth or drawing it in through his trunk?' the man asked energetically.

'Mouth, mouth,' she said testily, how else do you expect him to drink?'

'Don't you think he will soon lose his appetite?'

'I don't know, ask the priest,' she said, exasperated. The camera crew was already drawing attention and people began to mill around the taxi. This was really getting risky, she tried to roll up the windows but the microphone was in the way.

'What will happen if he suddenly decides he had had enough for the day, do you think there will be a law and order problem?'

'I don't know!' she screamed, 'why are you asking me, ask the police, ask the military, why me!' she yelled, and tried to roll up the window again. This time she succeeded because the interviewer had retreated, and was beginning a piece to the camera.

'That's it,' he was saying, 'as we have been telling you from the very beginning, Milk is vanishing by the gallon.

Lord Ganesh has been drinking it up, thousands of buckets disappearing before our eyes. The military is on standby, the police is on the streets, in case a law and order situation develops when he refuses to drink any more. We were the first to show you these pictures, you have heard it from the devout and we will show you more pictures throughout the day. But before we take a break we leave you with some questions to ponder: do we have adequate supply of milk in the country to satisfy the god's thirst? What will we do if Ganesh is not satiated in the days to come? Should we ask friendly nations to send us milk aid?'

By the time the traffic eased there were already rumours of milk being sold in the black market and stories of milkmen being waylaid. Milk riots had broken out in the northern regions.

Amidst these odd distractions, she had almost forgotten Vincent. Now as she remembered everything, she looked into the rear-view mirror and noticed a grey Scorpio a little behind them. Something about that car looked familiar. The man at the wheel had a vicious look on his face. Zeeta felt a tingle on the nape of her neck. She sunk lower in her seat and politely asked the driver to step on the accelerator. But it was not easy to speed up. Everywhere, the devout spilled onto the streets, disrupting traffic.

Half an hour, and the Scorpio was still visible in the rear-view mirror. They were crossing the campus of a technology institute when she abruptly asked the driver to take a turn. Their taxi swung into an empty street and gained speed. There was a screech of brakes behind her, and then angry blaring of horns. She switched on her cell phone. Thirty missed calls! She quickly dialled a number and whispered into the receiver.

'We will meet you at the sandwich bar,' the person on the other side said.

'That's way too far and I am being tailed,' she objected.

'Shake them off and do as you are told.'

'But I am close to the first rendezvous,' she countered.

'Change in plans. You'll come to the sandwich bar,' said the voice.

The sandwich bar was the code for an old Ashokan pillar near the Mutiny Memorial where people came to feed pigeons. 'That's way off my route and…' she exclaimed.

'We don't encourage insubordination,' the voice cut in. There was a click. The line went dead.

She popped the sim out of her phone and threw it into a ditch through the window. They were on a single lane and the taxi was cruising fast. A little way ahead she took out her phone and flung it into a high drain flanking the road. The driver twisted his eyebrows, *'Memsaab*?'

'I will go further north. Just keep going, I will tell you where to stop,' she instructed him calmly.

'No problem, *memsaab*,' the man nodded and looked at her in the rear-view mirror, and in his momentary distraction a thin naked boy ran into the street, directly in the path of the speeding car. There was an ear-piercing screech of brakes, followed by a tremendous collision.

He died instantly as his taxi swerved and hit a tree at eighty kilometres per hour. The force of the impact hurled Zeeta against the windshield, and shards of glass punctured her lungs in three places. Another bar of Atman dark chocolate wrapped in gold foil flew out from her bag and landed on the street, which the scrawny boy snatched up and ran away with. The wreck burst into flames. Zeeta lay huddled in a swamp of blood while the dead driver's exposed ribs jammed against the wheel, pressing against the horn. It blew incessantly, shredding the silence of that empty stretch, dragging the visible and the invisible worlds closer to each other.

THRALL

ESCAPE

The train was splitting apart a sea-blue afternoon with windrows of wheat on one side. On the other, they had put animal hide up to dry. His eyes popped open, the smell waking him up. On this side of the track are rows of tanneries, using methods of curing leather that ran as far back as the early Mughals, if not further. The stench permeated these desolate miles where kettles of vultures circled overhead, thriving on rotten carcasses. The air-conditioning had failed and the coach was slowly turning into a steam bath.

Yesterday he had been jolted up from sleep and found that murderous dog licking his ears. A Dobermann—evil incarnate. Always a cat person, he hated these saliva-dripping abominations. '*Hut, hut!*' he tried to shoo him away. The dog obeyed. He must have dozed off on that couch and rolled on to the floor. Hopefully no bones broken.

He stood up slowly. Backed against the wall, a green secretariat table was groaning with the weight of piled newspapers and magazines. Chairs, an easel, personal effects.

A dingy little room. Putrid vapours rose from a plate of stale biryani, and a fetching news anchor was screaming the headlines from a battered TV. A shaded reading lamp on the table hid more than it revealed. But he could read his name. *Jayant Roy Kapoor.* It was everywhere on those stacked dailies and magazines, *Daulat Times, Business Bee, The Trumpet*... But the face in those pictures was someone else's. And who the bloody hell was that?

He grimaced, his head throbbed with pain. Did he hurt himself? A window was open. Through it he saw a pretty shopping mall bathed in a cascade of diamond-shaped stones. He had seen pictures of this before—the Diamante. But that's in Anantanagar. Friggin' heavens! How did he end up in Anantanagar?

He stepped out cautiously. No one was around. The rooms in use were sparsely furnished but for the enormous grandfather clocks standing at every corner, displaying different hours. Did he end up in a bloody museum? The tick-tock, tick-tock of the pendulums hurt his ears.

He needed a leak. The door to the loo was jammed so he went out through the back door into the garden. Tuberose beds, pomegranate trees, a lot of potted cacti. Moths hovering about purposelessly, hanging like curtains. He began to unzip but then heard footsteps behind him. Swinging around, he saw a man coming through the gate.

'Wait,' he ordered and finished his business. The stranger stuck his hands in his pockets and watched him with a half-amused look on his stupid mug.

'Watering the garden?' this man asked him in a thick accent.

'Who are you?' he asked.

'Idris Alam. I am the caretaker of this place,' the man said, cracking his knuckles.

Ignoring him, he fished for his cigarette pack. It was empty. 'Hey, can I get this around here?' he waved the pack at him.

'Yes, sir,' the man replied, his broken teeth flashing in a grin. But he found him a pack of twenties and hailed a cab for him.

Jerky ride through heavy evening traffic. He was pissed to find the stranger next to him, in the taxi, watching the road. When did this joker climb in? All along, this guy was giving him sideways glances, so he had asked the driver to pull over and ordered the fellow to shift to the front seat.

'What's your problem?' he said, giving him a cold look before shifting to the front seat.

'Listen here, in case you don't watch TV and live under a rock, my name is Jayant Roy Kapoor, and everyone in this country knows me by that name. So address me respectfully when you speak unless you want me to drop you back into the gutter from where you emerged.' His co-passenger kept quiet. From the back seat, Kapoor watched his jaw bones moving.

'We're going to the Imperial, which is not your street-corner dhaba, so behave,' he added, offering him a cigarette. The man snatched it shamelessly and lit up.

They didn't speak the rest of the way. Just as the taxi swung in through the hotel gates, this fellow took out a handkerchief and patted the sweat off his face.

Kapoor noted that the guards at the entrance failed to recognise him.

Unpardonable! His Swiss hospitality training couldn't condone such a slip. But he won't bother about this right now. The Imperial's standards have hit rock bottom since they sold to Samtani's chain. He harboured a lot of respect for Raj Samtani; like him, Samtani had built it from scratch but he didn't have class. Warmth was definitely missing at his hotels.

He headed straight for the dimly-lit bar on the first floor.

He needed a drink to clear up his mind. Things were getting a little foggy, first with that house of old clocks which was definitely in Anantanagar, though he had never left his city Aukatabad, and now this character latching onto him for a drink.

The fellow was poring over the liquor list, which he had grabbed as soon as it appeared, and soon enough hailed a waiter.

'Black Dog double, load it up with ice,' he ordered, 'and you, sir?'

Kapoor liked that. Finally this guy was acknowledging the boss, 'Stoli for me with crushed ice, please,' Kapoor said.

The icy air-conditioning of the hotel was freezing his balls off by then. He downed the shot quickly while the other man, who had said he was the caretaker of that house of clocks, nursed his scotch.

Kapoor scooped up a handful of peanuts and chewed slowly. What had happened in that room with the dog and the piles of business papers? He had felt dizzy and possibly sat down on that couch to catch his breath. But there was pain too, pain that could be real, or somewhere in his mind like shadows of birds circling above.

Dumbfucking pain, this slow head throb that might never leave him...he drained another glass. Those pictures on the magazine covers in that house. The headlines, 'Atman Group's Flagship Chocolate Company Locked in Turf War With German Competitor', 'Business Conglomerate Atman Group Helmed by Jayant Roy Kapoor Bids for Telecom in Africa', 'Indian Chocolate Emperor Planning Major Marketing Blitz'... But the man whose face was plastered across the newspapers? That's a bloody impostor!

The lights of the bar hurt his eyes. Showcases of leather-bound books lined the walls but he doubted they were real. He dug into the ice pail and popped an ice cube straight into his mouth. Freezing heat. The man sitting with him raised an eyebrow. Ignoring him, he took out his handkerchief, patted his sweating forehead and marched off to the loo.

The looking glass was spotless clean. He stared at his reflection for a minute. A drawn and tired face. He splashed on some water and patted the wet handkerchief against his cheeks. 'Nazi bastards! That German company Ritz, they must be propping up that impostor, or else…'

A roar of water followed by a gurgling sound. A toilet flushed. 'Bloody Schutzstaffel,' Kapoor raised his voice. 'Nazi wankers,' he screamed at the mirror. Another toilet flushed in the cloak room. And again. Every time he cursed, a toilet flushed but no one came out of the lavatories, and only a little later the caretaker of the house of clocks appeared at the door.

They returned to the bar. This fellow was looking a bit soft, having downed a few in his absence. 'What were you doing in there for so long?' he asked.

'You don't ask me questions,' he thundered.

The other man was definitely shocked when he heard him say that. Maybe it was how his voice had changed in anger… 'You were in the loo over an hour,' this man said quietly while trying to call the waiter.

This joker was getting too far! It was stupid for him to get him here just because he had got him that pack of cigarettes. 'No more drinks for you,' he barked. The other man eyed him silently but didn't react.

As he waited for another vodka, Kapoor felt a creeping uneasiness in his chest. Fatigue was slowly overpowering him—like he was being weighed down by stones and a part of him struggled desperately to surface. Knackered, he felt spent and down to the last drop. A new waiter arrived. He suspected him to be working for Ritz, the German competitor. Hitler's chocolate makers!

The waiter had brought his drink and a carafe of water. A voice said that the water was poison. They looked at each other and left the bar, leaving the vodka untouched.

A vegetarian dinner at the lobby-level restaurant was served, and that was when this guy tried to talk with him. About his work, about something he was engaged in.

Was he seeking help? The man's words couldn't filter through the walls of his exhaustion. He was too drained to follow what he was getting at and kept nodding. It was getting late. His eyelids were heavy.

'If you need anything contact my office, they will help you,' he told him finally and, wiping his hands clean, stood up to go. Dinner was over.

The other man offered to pay with a card and he thanked him for it while bidding him goodnight.

Kapoor checked into a room at the Imperial.

Thoughts began whizzing in his head as soon as he closed his eyes. Forthcoming shareholder meetings, volatile stocks, frictions with that insufferable Ghaswala on the board of directors of the pharma business, the impact of fluctuations of crude prices, new oil exploration blocks in the Bay and the nagging climate warriors always after them, but mostly about the flagship chocolate operations. That was his baby, his first-born. Atman chocolate's factories spread across continents, global value chains, prices of shares, local issues like the complaints about child labour on cacao farms, advertisement campaigns, new launches, thousands of employees dependent on his insights, his strategic thinking, his skills in running this juggernaut of a business empire.

They didn't collide but kept him awake. Like buzzing bees, the network of connections between thoughts and the material world. Kapoor's heart was beating faster now. He could hear it pounding away, he could feel his chest billow with the air of secret excitement.

But what if someone was planning to unseat him, some bugger in league with the Nazi chocolate-maker, planning to throw a bloody spanner in the works. His skin crawled, his hair stood on end, literally, as if he was in a bloody pool of static electricity.

He was sick again, and went to the washroom where he retched badly.

Assailed by nightmares! A storm-ridden sea infested by dangerous creatures—giant cat heads sucking in whatever swam past them, excreting green slimy poo; crocodiles dark as cocoa beans and big as cargo containers; sharks with human heads.

Between waves of slumber and wakefulness, he could hear a voice…a slow droning loop. Was it the voice of that schmuck who took a ride with him in the taxi and joined him at the bar—where did he go? He got up sweating heavily and checked around the room to make sure that fellow was not hiding behind the curtains.

An English breakfast appeared on the table next morning. He was feeling famished and attacked the sausage first. They tasted good but were a little oily. He speared a grilled tomato to balance the flavour when the phone began to shrill. Someone was waiting for him at the lobby. Must be that fellow from last night. What did he want now? No, he won't meet him again. He will check out and slip away. He won't spend another moment in this city where he hadn't arrived but was here nevertheless. That's something he will have to sort out later, but for now he will have to return where he came from. He dialled the front desk and sent for the bill.

Stepping out stealthily, he took the elevator to lobby level but just as he was slipping out through the banquet exit, he heard him call out, 'Hey!'

What fresh hell is this? Kapoor rushed out hoping he could jump into a taxi at the gate. But the man was right there, coming after him. He should have asked the hotel for a drop off.

There was only one way to get rid of him: he ran. But his feet dragged. Still he ran. But the man was faster than him. He was closing in. 'Stop! Stop him!' the guy yelled, which got a group of street kids amused and they began to run after them—he dashing ahead, his pursuer a few feet behind him giving chase, and this clutch of boys coming right next. And their cries drew more onlookers; auto-rickshaws screeched to a halt, buses blared their horns angrily and a hawker of cheap knickers upped the price of his merchandise.

Luckily a bus came along and he scrambled in.

The signal changed. The bus lurched forward and his pursuer missed it by a whisker. It took him straight towards the river and across it to the central train station. He jumped off and rushed to the ticketing counter.

Kapoor kept looking back as he stood in the queue. A sea of faces but Idris Alam wasn't among them. Maybe he was there, but he couldn't spot him. There was definitely someone watching him, someone watching him from close, he could feel their presence but this was not the time to bother. He went through his pockets and found a card but the ticket clerk wouldn't accept it. So he paid with cash and bought a ticket for Aukatabad.

The train was scheduled to leave late in the evening.

He managed to get a bed in the retiring room and stretched himself out to rest a bit. While floating off to sleep, he remembered those photos on the magazine covers again. That face! That impostor. He has to expose that bugger, he could be working for the Nazis. He has to reach out to the legal team once he arrives.

He had a sandwich at the railway canteen with the swing door and old-fashioned chairs. He sat there for a long while. It was evening already but still a few hours before the train left.

Afterwards he took a stroll along the riverbank with the ferry ghat and old warehouses. There were more moths hovering here today. The air was thick with these winged insects. Somehow this area looked familiar, though he had never taken a train from this city. Just that everything was different this day. Even the moths and the way they were dancing on the water was different. Besides, how could you leave a place where you hadn't arrived? He will have to figure that out.

Finally, when the train rolled in, he couldn't find his compartment for they hadn't put up the passenger manifest. He entered through a door and, a little later, was sitting on an upper bunk of a three-tiered coach with blue seats. Passengers were jostling in and he kept a watch from his perch just in case that caretaker of the house of clocks appeared again.

CLARA HAS
AN AUDIENCE

Though it was an adult human head, it looked no bigger than a coconut shell as it dangled by a thread from an iron hook on the polished teak cabinet. The room was dark, except for a focus lamp directing an antiseptic glare on the leathery skin which had once been white but was now blackened by charcoal fires. The bulging lips were sewn together with orange thread hanging in tassels below the chin and the eyes were tightly shut. Her ear lobes had been slit open and pierced through with pieces of yellowing bone needles. The skin near the right ear is furry and damaged perhaps from the fire; otherwise, she has a calmness of aspect and she seems to be at peace. Her wavy honey blonde hair hangs loose, forming a golden halo which envelops the bull-necked man sitting on a chair, his back towards the shuttered windows. He has close cropped hair and his skin is pale like people from the north-western part of the country. He is watching her intently.

A woollen carpet with embroidered cat heads covers the room from wall to wall. The man is in his pyjamas and a slightly frayed grey top, but the Patek Philippe Sky Moon Tourbillon on his wrist is a giveaway that he is no ordinary guy. It's close to midnight and the palatial mansion where he is sitting in grim vigil with the blonde is dead-quiet. Outside on the grounds and beyond the high-security, electric-fenced perimeter wall, the guards look nervous. They have hurriedly finished their roti-tadka dinners, feeding part of it to the mongrels that roam the road outside, and were now pacing the front of the building with wary sleepless eyes. Some bad news has come in during the evening and they have been put on high alert.

The pale-skinned man looks on grimly. The muscles of his slightly florid face tighten with concentration as he leans towards her. Alcohol wafts from his breath when he speaks. 'It has happened again! First the contamination in our chocolate factory up north, and now this genius dead in the lab with a nozzle stuck in his bloody arse!' His booming voice seems to emerge from the bottom of a well. His shark eyes light up with unearthly rage as he screams, 'Are you listening, Clara?'

Silence.

Jayant Roy Kapoor sighs, his eyes still glued to the shrunken head before him. He smells something in the air and his mind floats back to the events of the day. The chief scientist was found dead in the lab and nobody's got a fucking clue. He was half in the mood to call up Ghaswala and give him a piece of his mind—security across all their operations was hired from one of Ghaswala's firms, which recruited only ex-army guys. But he relented at the last moment. Long experience has taught him to avoid hasty decisions.

But now he needs to speak with this woman. She would know. Only the dead know the answers. He focuses on Clara again.

'It was you! You and that bunch of hippies and ex-KGBs you were hanging out with in that Calangute villa, till I picked you out of that cesspool. They gave you these ideas, their mushrooms and acid did—that screwed up your mind and then you infected me!'

There is a tap on the door. He checks the time on his watch, frowns and walks up to a video phone and hits a button. A face damaged by a scar and with heavy hooded eyelids flashes on the screen.

'Bullet! Why have you come here?' he snaps at the man.

'Sorry sir, I just came to report...' the buck-toothed man begins to say.

'Didn't I tell those assholes not to send anyone in when I am in my speaking chamber? Now, have you got hold of that two-penny slut?'

'Not yet, sir...there was a problem.'

JRK suddenly erupts with anger. He throws an angry glance at Clara and screams into the receiver, 'Get lost and don't come back without her. If you do, I will get you transferred to Congo and you can screw pygmies to the end of your days. I want every pinch of the substance and the formulas she has made off with. As for Vincent Dutta, give him a good burial.' He clicks off the videophone.

JRK returns to his seat and tilts the backrest till his eyes level with hers. There is a crack of thunder outside. He twists his face as he examines Clara's severed head, as if seeking affirmation for his outburst. She doesn't seem to have any opinion on this matter.

TRAIN TO
BHASKARNAGAR

Primordial darkness. Hot and stygian. A sound coming from far. A heavy mechanical throbbing and pounding. Diesel locomotive. We are on a train.

I stretch out my hands and feel around in the darkness to get my bearings. It's pitch black. A terrible stink rising from all around me. And then my hand strikes something and a light comes on. Naked filament bulb pouring straw-coloured piss-light from a low metal ceiling. Train toilet. When will they replace these lights with energy-saving LEDS? My face, in the scratched basin mirror with lipstick marks, is white as bone. I press the push tap. A jet of warm water sluices down the metal basin. Splash on some. The faucet gasps and spurts, wetting my shirt.

There is a thump against the toilet wall and muffled voices outside. I unlatch the door and swing it open.

The glint of steel catches the eye even in dim railcar light. A skinny fellow of average height pinning a woman against the wall, threatening her with a cut-throat razor. His bloodshot eyes are wild and he is trying to snatch her bag but she is holding on to it with all her strength. It's dark outside and the train has stopped in the middle of barren emptiness. All passengers seem to be asleep.

He sees me and signals me to back off with a jerk of his head else he will slash her throat. I retreat a step, then another. Luckily at this time the train whistles and lurches into motion, throwing him off balance on the moving joint of the floor plates. I lunge forward and grab his arm holding the weapon, twisting it all the way back. My heart thumps madly as I grapple with him but he is no pro. He kicks ferociously, hitting me a few times. Perhaps he's just a junkie looking for easy cash.

Released from his hold, the woman steps back and strikes him on the face with her hand bag but he sinks his teeth in my wrist. I howl in pain but don't let him go, twisting his arm even more till the razor clatters to the floor. The noise and screams wake up some passengers, and now two or three of them rush in to help, raining kicks and punches on the poor snatcher.

Someone goes looking for the railway guards. More passengers appear and a doctor among them helps to wash the open wound and applies an ointment. I walk back slowly to my seat and this is when I realise she is in the next berth. 'I am sorry for all this trouble, I hope your hand does not hurt too much,' she says.

She is definitely much younger to me, with dark gleaming eyes and flowing hair that is really long. I twist my wrist and say, 'It's nothing...' I ask her to be careful next time, even as a finger of pain prods my bones.

'I have painkillers, let me know if you need any,' she says before lying down on the lower berth. The other bunks on our side are empty, except for mine at the top.

I tell her I will be okay, before lying down again and switching off the light.

Darkness. We are on Train 1899. It's going to Bhaskarnagar, the historic city of the north. That's what the ticket in my pocket says. Crawling for miles through the remains of a summer night.

I can't sleep, and toss from side to side worrying that the crook might return with an accomplice. Lying on the bunk, I watch for movement in the dim-lit aisle while trying to remember recent events. But memory fails me. Pain licks my injured hand through the night.

The woman from last night is sitting opposite to me. She looks real in the morning light. But one can never be sure. She is reading a book and popping salted cashews from a large packet.

I ask her what she's reading and regret this immediately. Too intrusive. She says it's a crime thriller set in the early nineteenth-century, in a faraway city.

I don't know the author's name. Must be an entertaining book, I tell her, and say I wish I had a magazine to read.

'I'm sure you will find one at the next station,' she says, adding, 'Does your hand hurt?'

I tell her it's bearable but that's a lie. Now I notice the odd burn marks around the bite wounds. Where did I get those from?

'I'm so sorry, this happened because of me. Let me know if you need the painkillers. I also have Dettol,' she smiles.

'I will do that,' I say, and ask her where she was headed.

'Bhaskarnagar. I will get off at first light. And you?'

'I'm going there too,' I respond a bit hesitantly.

She gives a questioning look, perhaps noticing my hesitation.

To change the subject, I ask if she's going home.

'Home? No, call of duty,' she smiles.

'I just hopped onto this train on a whim,' I tell her, and look around unsurely.

'I would love to do that when I am free,' she says.

'No one's stopping you,' I say.

She doesn't react to that, and instead asks, 'That man who attacked me last night, what do you think—petty thief? But how did he get in?'

'Junkie, most probably. Didn't you notice that glazed look in his eyes. The train staff rarely takes the trouble to lock the doors at night,' I tell her.

'You reacted fast!' she laughs. She's attractive I think... pretty too.

'Ha! I'm amused. It's just reflex, 'I say, adding, 'I used to be a wicket-keeper.'

We both laugh and she asks me what I do.

I tell her I used to work for a newspaper till very recently, covering economic news. But one was getting tired of it. What lies at the end of our growth dreams, I wonder aloud, and point at the distance where black smoke was belching out from brick kilns. 'This is a road to the bottom of the pit…we are beginning to breach all planetary boundaries. Our cities are suffocating, and so are our villages,' I say.

'But there is no utopia,' she says.

'There is disease,' I reply, 'and there is slow death of everything precious. We are burning up the future, and the kids we see today will be roasting on the fires of our greed.' I apologise to her for being morbid, and say, 'I quit the hack's job and now am on my own.'

She nods repeatedly, watching me as I speak, as if she is memorising my expressions.

'It's always a good idea to explore, more so if you have hope on your side. Perhaps there is a middle road.'

'I guess,' I tell her, but here my thoughts get broken up with no certainty emerging…so to avoid more conversation, I look out through the window as a dismal town rolls by like a forgotten movie played in error.

This train full of people going north powered by fossil-fuel that was burning up the planet. The aircrafts zipping across the skies, pumping grim futures into the horizon of possibilities. Isn't endless growth another name for mass suicide? When evolution decides to short circuit and fall back into the wells of its own undoing. My newspaper job was a well-burnished lie, but what now?

The blood on my knuckles has dried…whose blood it was, his or mine? Where is that poor junkie who was seeking a few moments of escape from a wretched existence? I wish he would pardon me for what I did to him. Only if he was here now, I would have asked for forgiveness. The sky is ablaze with the fire of summer. The rushing landscape dotted with tired water lotuses breathing the emptiness of loss.

A tea-man comes along. He sings as he serves tea but the song doesn't lift my mood, nor does his tea. It's too sweet. At another station infested with belligerent monkeys, a doe-eyed village girl appears with a basketful of little framed deities. The gods and goddesses look attractive in their dazzling dresses, and she sells quite a few. Following her, a scrawny teenager comes wielding an AK-47, and his plastic guns are also lapped up by the passengers. Then the girl with her gods and the boy with the guns get down together and are talking with each other, and the girl is all smiles.

She's watching the two. 'My name is Sujata,' she tells me after a while, adding, 'Don't hesitate to get in touch if you need any help in Bhaskarnagar.' She offers me some sweets from a box she pulls out from her knapsack, 'These are really tasty, try one.'

'*Ladykeni*s are my favourite,' I tell her. The *ladykeni* tastes delicious.

'Sorry, for I didn't bring anything I can offer.'

'Please have one more,' she says, smiling.

Shamelessly, I take the offered sweet and, finishing it, tell her how tasty they were.

'I'm not carrying my visiting card but my name is Chanchal Mitra,' I say, and giving her my address, invite her to get in touch when she's in Anantanagar.

'Mr Mitra, I should thank you again for last night,' she takes out her book.

'You can call me Chanchal,' I tell her, and climb up to my bunk for a nap.

'Chanchal, Chanchal,' I can hear the faint ring of my name through a fog of sleep and wake up to find her asking if I would like to buy a book or magazine as a vendor had appeared. I get a news magazine but before I can crack it open, Kapoor grabs it and begins to read. I realise he has taken the same train and is travelling with us.

We have just left a junction station and are clattering over a turnout into a branch line. The wheels shriek and squeal as we resume our passage through the deserts of an empty afternoon.

CHOCO RAJA

Sweaty hell! Kapoor grimaces with disgust. Scorching hot winds sandpaper his face with dust whenever he steps out of the air-conditioned space for the loo. Crappy train compartment from before the war. Damn. He remembers boarding last night but he had overslept. Half the day was already gone.

The young female passenger is offering him sweets. He notices she has long and beautiful hair, and marble black eyes that twinkle like stars. Her lustrous hair, like those in a shampoo advertisement, touches the ground as she stands.

'No, no thanks,' he won't have the sweets.

'Please take one, I can't eat all this,' she insists, smiling through dark hypnotic eyes.

'But…' he doesn't know her, yet her face looks familiar.

She is well-proportioned but athletic, and there is a rhythm in the way she moves her hands when she speaks. Her body is supple, trained—she could be a classical dancer or someone well-versed in martial arts. He sizes her up secretly from behind the pages of the magazine but can't decide if she could be working for his secret enemies.

'You cannot refuse these *ladykeni*s,' she insists.

'Do you work for Ritz?' Kapoor asks in his most matter-of-fact voice.

'Sorry, what was that again?' she says, with genuine incomprehension.

'Nothing! I thought you work for that German chocolate-maker.' Perhaps she is not with the Germans, but that impostor in Aukatabad may have employed her. Maybe they are all thick in this plot, the German company and that impostor, and now this woman. Okay, so she wants to bump him off, under orders from that wanker so that his deception is complete. Ha! Not so fast, darling! Jayant Roy Kapoor wouldn't have been where he is today if he could be taken down so easily. Just let me get back to my city.

Despite the risk of eating anything offered by a stranger, he takes a *ladykeni* and bites into it. His teeth sinks in the syrupy softness. Too sweet, nothing special. But her dark gleaming eyes somehow make it tastier, as dusk unrolls like winding-sheet over the skies of the north.

The confounded train crawls for kilometres. It stops at every village, every town, every hint of human habitation on its way. She reads most of the time, her legs stretched out on the opposite berth. Her black leather knapsack below the window on which she has rested an elbow. Two passengers on the aisle seats get off at a small town. They are replaced by a father-son duo.

She gets tired with the book, puts it down and keeps gazing into the approaching evening. Because Kapoor sits facing her, their eyes meet a few times and she consciously averts her gaze. He tries to make conversation so that he can look a little more into those eyes.

'I think it will be dark soon, look at those clouds,' he says.

'The sun has set awhile,' she says, looking out through the window.

She is at least ten years younger to him, he reckons.

After sometime she packs away her book, and says, 'You were telling me something about Germans?'

Kapoor looks her straight in the eye. Her face has been carved with much concentration. Almost classic in its fine outline, accented by those kohl-black eyes and fine lips. Her hair, which she had tied up in a bun, seem to have a life of their own. They untie themselves every now and then, dancing to secret rhythms as she moves. It touches her slim waist and rests there awhile before springing to life again.

'I have serious issues with that German company,' he says.

She nods, 'I hope you don't mind sharing with me.' Her eyes sparkle with curiosity.

She can't recognise me, this is good and bad, Kapoor tells himself. 'I have stakes in the chocolate industry but this

German competitor has been coming in the way. Not only that, they are unscrupulous and they, along with some small players, have been ganging up against me.'

'Chocolate!' she says, looking slightly amused, 'that's wonderful'.

'Chocolates are our flagship business,' Kapoor says, and stretches out his hand, 'Jayant, President of Atman Group,' they shake hands awkwardly. 'Of course you know our business conglomerate. After finishing my studies in Switzerland I started with chocolates. It was a tough fight with the *firang* multinationals having grabbed the market and refusing to budge. But now we are ahead. Why I chose chocolate, that's a different story, but we have diversified over the years—petroleum, telecom, pharmaceuticals and IT are our workhorses,' his face flushes with pride.

'That's extraordinary,' she says.

'We now manufacture chocolate for half the world,' he tells her, with a confident grin.

'Amazing, I would have never thought...' she begins to say something.

He cuts her off, 'Well, people on the street don't recognise my face, though I'm very much in the news. That's for movie stars. It's good in a way. But those who really matter, know. My Davos speeches are analyzed by finance gurus, our expansion plans are dissected on TV talk shows, and we supply chocolates to the US Marines. Perhaps the only one more popular than me on these TV shows is Prana,' he says, adding, 'I'm sure you know who that is?'

'Ah yes, you mean the cat that's on the logo of Atman Group?' she says.

'Yeah. That's him, my favourite pet. Though I do have more exotic creatures in my menagerie in Aukatabad.'

She nods thoughtfully, watching him. 'Are you going all the way?' Kapoor asks her after sometime.

The sun has set and the lights of the train have come on. Everything looks bleak under that light—the cheap PVC seat covers, the narrow bunks and the dirty aisles jammed with lunch trays.

'The incompetent buggers running this country are not keen on full privatisation of railways. That's the only way to turn it around,' Kapoor tells no one in particular, sweeping his gaze up and down the aisle.

The few passengers in the almost-empty compartment have resigned themselves to the journey which seems to have no end. Some are reading magazines, others are deep in conversation. And most of the talk that filters through is about the prospect of politicians in elections, promises of a good career for sons, and good grooms for daughters.

'Yes, I'm going all the way to Bhaskarnagar,' she replies after a while.

'Really, so this train goes to Bhaskarnagar, does it?'

'Definitely. And you, where are you headed?' she asks.

'You can call me Jayant or just Kapoor, though the media prefers JRK. I am going to Aukatabad.'

But before he can complete, she says, 'But this train doesn't go to Aukatabad, that's a slightly different route.'

'What do you mean?' he says, looking exasperated. Which is when the ticket examiner appears in his flapping black jacket and dirty white trousers.

Kapoor fishes out his ticket. The TTE studies it carefully and shakes his head. His ticket is for Aukatabad but he has taken the wrong train. Because the train is quite empty and the distance he is travelling is almost the same as the journey to Aukatabad, he is let off with a fine and a small bribe.

'So it seems I will be stuck in Bhaskarnagar. Is it still the pretty little city like before?' he asks her.

'I guess so, haven't been there recently.'

' I thought you live there.'

'Not really. I'm travelling for work and will be gone soon when it's over,' she says. Will be gone soon...will be gone soon...he focuses on those words as they echo in his mind. Why was he feeling like this? He realises he is watching her shamelessly and averts his gaze. Something is happening to him alright, but he's not sure what this new fuck-up is...

The train speeds on through a thickening darkness while he imagines her in the backdrop of the turrets and parapets of the old forts of Bhaskarnagar—slate grey, earth-brown or a dazzling orange against a mellow dawn light. The polished brass cannons like guardians of old, handsome men in brightly-coloured turbans, slow-walking elephants, their *howdahs* bursting with *goras*, and the camels with their sleepy smiling faces. He wanted to see her against this dream tapestry in a queen's finery, and he will be spying secretly through the crenellations of a tower parapet.

What could he do to possess those eyes? How to drown in that raven-black night, he wondered, as he again tried to steal a look and got engulfed in that quicksand.

'Would you like to be the face of our chocolate brand?' Kapoor blurted out without any preamble.

'Face of the brand?' she looks perplexed but listens attentively to what Kapoor says next.

'Well, as you must have heard, Atman group will soon launch a campaign with the government to popularise chocolates and make them affordable. Operation Choco Raja, we call it; we are aiming for the grassroots because to build a strong nation we have to strengthen the foundation. We are telling people that *chocolate is food suited for kings and queens*, chocolates are nutritious, rich in antioxidants, chocolate lovers live long and happy lives. Chocolates ooze warmth, chocolate bars kindle solidarity, evoke compassion and fellow-feeling, chocolate stimulates affection and inspires romantic feelings; in fact, the whole emotional shebang can be finetuned with chocolate. I believe, chocolates can indeed make our nation stronger. We want everyone to be able to afford it and we need a face for this campaign,' Kapoor goes on breathlessly. When he speaks, everyone listens. He has that sort of confidence.

'Umm, that's interesting,' she tears open a packet of cashew and pops a few into her mouth, adding, 'But I am not into modelling. Not my line.'

He hesitates before speaking again. 'I didn't mean that. Don't mind my over-enthusiasm but I believe you can fit perfectly in our campaign. You could be an ambassador for Choco Raja,' and he goes on to explain that the campaign managers will need to find someone who embodies the message we hope to convey.

'You think I fit the bill?' she says, trying to hide her amusement.

'Absolutely.'

'Thank you, I will have to think about it. Let me know when you are ready to take this risk with a novice. If you are indeed serious, you can drop a message at this office and they will know how to contact me,' she gives him an address and a number and smiles, holding her gaze for a moment. Kapoor dives deep for words but doesn't find any.

As she prepares to turn in for the night, her hair unfurls from the bun, spreading into a fan. What if he doesn't take the connection to Aukatabad straight away, he wonders. Let that fraudster remain in charge for some more days, let him dig a deeper grave, then when the time is right he will get all his men around and get the bugger thrown straight into prison. Let him play the president of Atman group for some more time. Meanwhile, Kapoor has more serious business to deal with, more pressing thoughts. He wants her to be part of everything he does from now on. Yes, everything, and not only the chocolate campaign.

The coach lights had been switched off for the night. There was a moon tacked low in the sky. The stars had been devoured by invisible beings travelling through space-time. Their blue fires simmered in the bellies of those creatures. The moon hovered so low that he feared it might fall from the sky. The train stopped everywhere, picking up passengers. The stench from the bathrooms which hadn't been cleaned for hundreds of kilometres wafted in now and again in great choking gusts. The passengers pinched their noses and shook their heads in despair. 'It's a bad line,' someone sighs. 'We usually avoid this route,' another answers between sounds of someone snoring. 'This whole bloody railway is crying for privatisation,' Kapoor comments over those voices.

Kapoor fights sleep. He struggles. He doesn't want to get lost again and wake up somewhere far from the woman in the next berth. So he focuses on her, keeps talking with her in his mind till an ocean of sleep closes in.

An apparition hovers around him, somewhere between sleep and wakefulness. A dark-eyed woman with a waterfall of hair. She is draped in a red-bordered cotton sari and was forming the powerful swastika mudra with her hands. She is enveloped by darkness but she was catching light, light from another star. Light not of this world. Suddenly, there's the crack of a whip, a cold blade of lightning splitting darkness apart, and followed by cries of agony. Gasps of the dying. Pain enters his body uninvited and soon he is twisting and squirming sick...

'When does the train arrive in Bhaskarnagar?' Kapoor asks, his heart thumping against his chest, forehead wet with perspiration.

'At first light,' she says. So she was awake.

'Do you know a hotel where I can put up for a couple of days? I have to remain incognito, they shouldn't recognise me.' Kapoor asks her.

'There are many. The smaller ones in the new part of town are discreet. But are you sure about this?' she says.

'What?'

'I mean, I can offer you a place too, before you return to Aukatabad. I thought you will take the next train or flight.

My employers have a guest house and there will be spare rooms.' She sounds worried.

'Thanks, let me think ...perhaps it's best for me to put up in a hotel. We can meet in a day or two, after I have had adequate rest and you can give my offer due consideration. Right now, I feel terribly tired and not up to any more travel. Aukatabad can wait. Meanwhile, I need to chalk out my moves for I have a fight ahead,' Kapoor tells her.

She seems to hesitate before she speaks, then making up her mind, says, 'Okay, as you wish. Do get in touch if you need anything. I will be around in Bhaskarnagar for a few days.'

'I will,' Kapoor says, feeling the warmth of an ardour enfold him.

He keeps lying on the bunk, fighting sleep. He fears invisible hands coming closer that will try to strangle him the moment he closes his eyes. He wraps his hands around his throat to protect himself. His heart is thumping so loudly that he fears everyone in the train will wake up. The hands come closer, relentlessly. To stop himself from screaming he bites the soft flesh of his palm once, twice, many times. The Mount of Venus is soft meat. Then up the thumb. Sharp incisors dig deep. Blood colours the low moon red.

Her hair tumbles off the bunk. He secretly caresses a strand. Darkness lights up with crimson. The long curly ribbons dance in the light of the dead moon crucified on the murky horizon.

PEACOCK PALACE

The weasel-faced man driving our autorickshaw doesn't utter a single word along the way. Right from the time he starts the diesel engine with an ear-splitting noise, he seems to know our destination and doesn't ask me or Kapoor for directions.

I'm thinking of this woman on the train, Sujata. It was Kapoor who had been chatting with her mostly but now he was completely silent. Depressed perhaps, because she didn't bid goodbye? There was a rush of passengers boarding another train and in the push and jostle, we lost her. My phone is also missing…did I lose it in the crowd? Or perhaps I didn't bring it with me at all? Dawn is breaking above the rose-hued walls of the city. Camels carry men and loads, padding along; the station road is empty, except for the odd motorcyclist thundering past, wreathed in the vanity of petroleum.

We are rushing into a canvas from another era, picturesque in a dusty, sandy way. Pretty, but greying at the corners, vibrant but harsh in its contrasts. The driver steers the noisy auto with the calm confidence of a Zen monk. I go through my trouser pockets and count the money. Will do for a couple of days. The freshness of morning was cleansing my mind but my body weighed heavy with fatigue. Every muscle ached, my eyelids felt heavy like stone and my injured hand was a scream no one could hear.

The name of the city appeared on shop signs. Long ago, I had holidayed in Bhaskarnagar with friends. There was a palace right in the centre of town and there was the Garden of Time. Next to it was the House of Secret Delights.

But this is hardly anything to help me find my bearings early in the morning, with sleep-weary eyes and the tiredness of a long train ride. I wonder if I should ask the *autowallah* to stop and find out where we are headed. But I don't. I let him decide, and soon, passing through the city gates and empty parks guarded by long-dead leaders, we arrive in a neighbourhood of hotels and a suburban railway station. We stop in front of a small hotel. I pay weasel-face and walk into the two-storey building with a red and white sign that reads 'Peacock Palace'.

The sleep-deprived man at the reception pushes the guest register towards me. He has a thick handlebar moustache and may have very well been the security guard doubling as receptionist for the night shift. A pot of wilting petunias, which look like they had been watered in the last century, is placed at a corner of the counter. I consult the tariff card. I have cash to last a day and some more. Weasel-face had overcharged. But I need to rest now. Then I can go out and try to buy me a ticket to Anantanagar. I check into a first-floor room, which offers an unflattering view of the railway station.

The small room comes alive as I switch off the light. Bugs crawl in the woodwork of the bed, lizards scurry and fornicate and call after their mates, the air-cooler throws blasts of desert air at my bed, which creaks in protest as I curl into a foetal posture. And suddenly, unable to sleep and ready to participate in this excitement of the vital force frothing all around, this profusion of presences human and other-than-human that dance around me, visible and invisible, brushed by gusts of air from the machine, I go up to the window.

A white hot sun has crept up from behind the railway station. Diesel locomotives cough like consumptive workmen waiting to be hired. Below the room, on the roof of a house, a peacock spreads his resplendent plumage and begin to dance. It is such an unexpected and wonderful sight that my hairs stand on end and, for a moment, the fog clears. It is Kapoor who has brought us here to Bhaskarnagar on this unplanned train journey. Planned or unplanned, he knows best but where is he now? Did he go out while I tried to sleep? The peacock dances for some more time, the sun vanishes behind a billboard selling holidays in Europe. Smiling women on a beach at the dead end of high carbon jet flights—Jean le Pins, St Tropez, Nice, the snow-clad Alps, a panorama of the Estérel, ski slopes, tulip gardens, high-speed trains, a funicular and the bubbles of joy for a chosen few—Paris, Lucerne, Chamonix, Mt Titlis, Jungfraujoch, Zurich. I clench my fist as I watch the shiny happy faces on the holiday ad. I turn my face away and step back into the room.

A knock on the door. I wash my face before opening it. A smiling boy has brought my breakfast. Breakfast? When did I order? But I am hungry and I don't know what it cost. I sign the bill and keep a copy. The boy leaves. The coffee goes cold.

Paris, Jungfraujoch, ski-slopes, Matterhorn, unforgettable, Interlaken, splendid, Bordeaux, excursions, Oktoberfest, adventure, Titlis, Titlis, adventure, adventure, PARIS, PARIS, JUNGFRAUJOCH, JUNGFRAUJOCH… the drone continues louder in my head and it hurts. It waxes and wanes, ebbs and flows, but never dies. Breakfast tastes bland. My head aches, aches bad. Deep inside my belly a rumble of nausea grows, building up slowly. A monster waking up, churning my entrails, kicking hard with hoofed feet till I rush to the washbasin.

I sleep for hours afterwards.

There is a power cut. The ceiling fan has stopped and the room is on fire. The vents of the dead air-cooler breathe fire, defeating the curtains, fire leaps at me towards the warm bed, the floor is hot, the ceiling is radiating heat, there is no water on the tap. I bark into the telephone and arrange for a ten-rupee bucket. The money is running out. Electricity is running out. This land will soon be left with no water. No power. I have to go home. I have to buy my return ticket. I have to run.

I step out after sometime. Just outside the hotel a rough bar with a gaggle of characters. Across the road—beside the railway tracks, auto drivers hanging in groups. Waiting. Rough country faces and broad muscular arms, their heads swathed in *gamchha*s.

Idris comes to my mind! Oh, my! Lowlife! What depravities have I sunk into? Those beautiful houses of Four Horse Street. How without compunction I had made it easy for them to manipulate the heritage committees, showing them the chinks in the armour. How did I sink so deep? My city, the handsome mansions flattened with sledgehammers and glass, steel and concrete monstrosities taking up their place. The dust of demolitions and from it temples of Mammon rising like sildenafil erections, where you buy yourself to numbness while screwing the planet for free.

'Go to the main station,' the clerk at the ticket counter says peevishly. This wouldn't be smooth. I climb into a bus, the cheapest mode of transport available.

Inside the belly of a giant cuttlefish. Strange smells emanate from its depths, bilious juices and acids rain from the rooftops searing the skin. The fish weaves through thick traffic and the singing ticket-seller calls out the stops—his sense of music untrammelled by the heat of a punishing summer. At the station, I am ejected half-digested, a blob of flesh and bones with a mind not my own.

Try to focus. You are at the main station. For your ticket back. Kapoor is not with you now. Of course, he has to return to his city but that's not so far. Besides, he is not your responsibility.

At the foyer I am accosted by a big man. 'Reservation?' Surely, but definitely without his assistance. I say I am here to receive someone and head for the grilled counter.

Lucky! I get a ticket for the next day but no reservation. So I will have to sit, maybe stand through a thousand miles. There is no other way; I have almost run out of cash. I will return and start afresh. With my journalist's training, there will always be something for me. But no more telling lies. Some honest work. I could write news stories about the planet. Even the flower boutique, that was kind of a good idea but never with Idris again. I will burn those bridges.

There's a sudden ruckus outside the station building as I go looking for a cheap food joint. A party of dreadlocked sadhus with bundles and pots have camped in the shade of a peepal tree. A group of hawkers selling magazines and cigarettes were quarrelling with them. Looks like the holy men have parked themselves in a reserved area. The exchanges grow louder and people stop by to watch the *tamasha*. The sun doesn't deter them.

I am very hungry now. The heat hasn't killed my appetite. There's a modest looking dhaba where I can eat cheap but the sadhus and the hawkers are fighting right next to it. A ring of the curious have formed. I am waiting for a passage but it grows worse. One of the saffron men snatches out a cell phone from his *jhola* and begins to make a call. The hawkers are rolling their sleeves, looks like they will remove them bodily now.

I step closer for my chance to slip into the food joint. The crowd grows thicker.

'Why don't you try the railway waiting room?' someone barks at the sadhus.

'The waiting room is closed,' replies one of the mendicants with a soft, kind face.

'Liars!' growls a hawker and begins jostling them, snatching their bundles and bags, flinging them on the street. The saffron group, suddenly electrified, charges at them with their tridents. A pitched battle begins amidst which a seller of bamboo flutes breaks into a Bollywood tune...*Dil deewana bin sajna ke mane na*...it went, that lilting, sweet melody, talking of a lovelorn heart that is never at peace in the absence of the beloved.

The crowd takes it up, more excited by this distraction, singing the refrain...*ye pagla hei, samjhane se, samjhe na—*

this mad one doesn't understand even when explained. The flute-man joins in with the music, the afternoon haze melts, the wind-blown dust brings with it the scent of roses of times long gone.

The jostling had stopped but suddenly fists begin raining on our backs. The crowd scatters. Six young men with saffron headbands pounce upon the hawkers with *lathi*s. I take to my heels, dashing into a side street, negotiating cloudy-eyed opium-eaters and camels in siesta. The *lathi*s of the saffron gang are thick and well-oiled. I run till I feel my lungs bursting. I stop, completely out of breath, and suddenly there is no one around.

This street is absolutely quiet. A faraway cigarette shop shimmers fraily. I am free to eat now. I have to find a joint. But there is none. Only an enormous hotel at the next roundabout. An intimidating glass and concrete structure, alien and brutal on this leafy street. I pass it by and go looking around the neighbourhood for a cheap joint. I have so little money now that I can barely buy a thali. I hope Kapoor was with me now; we could have eaten together. But I have hardly seen him since we arrived this morning. I will have to check out from the hotel early tomorrow to avoid paying the day's charge. Spend the whole day on the streets and wait for the midnight train home.

I trudge along for ages down those friendless streets clothed in petroleum odours. My eyes smart with the poison in the air, and I can feel myself grow old as I plod ahead. My untrimmed beard, which my ex-colleagues said gave me the aspect of a prophet—Jesus, they said—is stiff with dirt. What would they say if they saw me now?

I examine my face in a barber shop mirror. A feeble and tired man, with thick shaggy eyebrows stare back at me. My lean face, now thinner with scour holes on my cheeks, and my deep-set eyes now drowned in the darkness of fatigue. I try to straighten my drooping shoulders and notice the furrows marking my forehead. My injured hand looks odd in the reflection but it's not a part of my body anymore. It's in the belly of a fish soothed by digestive proteins. My eyes are crimson in the heat.

I wander into the walled city where, luckily, I find a place to eat. The boisterous music of a marriage party rises from outside. A procession of gaily dressed men and women walk with the music towards the House of Secret Delights. I gorge on the warm chapattis and dal fry that taste like heaven. I can't avoid the temptation of a *dudh-badaam*, but after the meal I begin to miss my Chinese toothpicks. I decide to take a bus to the hotel but don't know the routes. The headache has worsened. I sit down on the bench of a teashop. The dusty road packed with autorickshaws and camel carts, small buses and scooter-riders, bubbles froths and flows towards the gates of the old city, towards another time. A time of kings and courtiers. The glass door of an ATM kiosk reflects my broken face with merciless pleasure. I remember the misplaced cards, the refused transaction, the white slip of paper spat out at me by a heartless quasi-object. The ATM machine was doling out cash. Men and women came and collected their notes and went. A strong impulse came upon me to snatch a purse and run.

I touch my wounds. The pink burns look like they would burst in the heat. The Goth returns to haunt me. The giant pendulum…all that blood on the floor of the house. Sick, I feel very sick. Murder! Murder! I scream out loud and, rising from my seat, begin to walk very fast. The tea-stall man comes running. I have forgotten to pay him.

'Are you checking out tomorrow, sir?' the clerk at the hotel reception asks as I enter. It is past seven, but there is still some light at the edges of the summer sky.

'Yes,' I say.

'Can we send you the bills after dinner?'

'Send them in the morning.'

The clerk at the desk with the flowers doesn't seem to like it, but I ignore him and continue up the stairs to my room.

I switch on the lights and crash. One more night and I will be on the train home. It was reassuring to know, but what was waiting for me at the other end of the journey? I have a feeling that I had some kind of trouble with Idris before I left but I can't be sure.

I wish Kapoor would return and I could perhaps ask him. But how would he know? Was I mugged in Anantanagar, a blow on my head that has blurred the past forever? Where is the rest of the money I had on me? And as if in answer to my thoughts, the room service boy appears with his wan smile. I had forgotten to latch the door. He is carrying the bill for the room and asks, 'Dinner order, sir?'

I won't be able to buy that dinner. I say I am meeting someone and won't have dinner at the hotel. 'Leave the bill on the table. I will clear it tomorrow. I have already told this at the reception,' I add, glowering at him. 'Get me some water.' The boy disappears like a lightning bolt.

A Crocin had been fighting my headache which, like a stunned but powerful animal, is nursing its wounds. I study the room service menu though I can hardly afford to order. The letters go blurry as my hands are seized by a tremor.

I imagine heaps of rice on banana leaf plates and the aroma of fish frying in the wok. Mustard oil, that's what we prefer. But now I could even do with dal fry, but it is not for me. Food is not for me tonight. I am not for food tonight. I slide the menu below the carpet. There will be thousands all over this unhappy land who will go without food tonight, and

many more nights. I will join their ranks, this last night in the
city of kings.

A whistling locomotive tears through the sounds of the
evening outside my room. The cursing and bickering of drunks,
the hubbub of undergraduates buying guidebooks and papaya
juice at the rickety stalls, the intermittent mooing of a lost cow,
the stereos of passing cars and the sputter of autorickshaws
coming to life disappears in that great blanketing noise. The
room service boy appears with the water and a pot of petunias
identical to the one at the reception. He puts the petunias on
the table, smiles and vanishes.

I try to take a nap, to fight hunger, but sleep eludes me.
Then suddenly the lights go out. The orange sodiums from the
railway tracks filter in through the curtains. This sad orange
light congeals like ectoplasm as it finds repose among the
shadows of the lonely room. The heat becomes unbearable. I
step out for a walk ignoring the suspicious stares of the desk
clerk. He has apparently taken a dislike for me for not squaring
off the dues.

I take a long walk along the rail tracks. On my way
back, I find a booth selling milk. Men from all walks of life
standing in a long queue outside the booth, while others with
satisfied faces leaving the cubicle of a shop with plastic milk
pouches dangling from their hands. What were they going
to do? Will they drink all that milk or use it for something

else, like sweets or curd? Perhaps to feed some thirsty god? I wondered. On an impulse, I too join the queue of milk-lovers. It gives me a sense of being part of this city at last. A city I hardly know, which looks even more unfamiliar as the money runs out.

Drunks exchanging blows outside the bar. The autorickshaw drivers watching from a distance. The students all gone, the cigarette seller closing shop. I hide the milk pouch in my vest and climb up the steps of the Peacock, for the last time.

The electricity has been restored. I curl into my bed which is still hot and uncomfortable from the day's heat. I try to sleep, but the warm bed wouldn't let me. I sit up and pace the room. The drunken brawl downstairs is getting louder. My nerves begin to split open, firing bursts of chemical electricity in all directions.

Small bar of ayurvedic toilet soap on the washbasin. I splash on some water, take off the wrapper and rub my face clean. Sandalwood. The scent is refreshing and perhaps will allow me some rest. The fragrance of sandalwood is soothing in this warm darkened hotel room. I take the bar from the bathroom and, pressing it to my nose, flop down on the chair. And I press it harder and harder on my face and against my nose till I am choking. And I take a bite. A little bit first, then bigger. Crunch. And then I bite off half the soap slice. Smoosh.

And chew and chew and chew some more and feel elated and very pleased. But I cannot say whether it is the scent or the taste that has taken hold of my mind.

The sandalwood fragrance sharp again. A sunlit room of Mitra House. Light dappled by the leaves of an *aparajita* creeper on the window. Warm and friendly on my back. Sitting in my school shorts, sitting before the queen of Bhaskarnagar. Her hair tied in a bun, smiling eyes, looking at me. Her nose like those of marble statues in the houses of the rich. She is always there, talking with me, helping me with homework while father is often away from home, dreaming of taming rivers, estimating the speed of winds and storms, calculating the depths of gorges, discussing the strength of structures, and how science and technology will make the world better for us. Meanwhile mom, always close, always clothed in the scent of sandalwood.

I like to sit beside a girl in class. But she's not as pretty as mom. Though she has big eyes like the Goddess. I like the Goddess, she is beautiful but not as much as mom is. I know if there is a pageant, mom will win hands down. Mom's cheeks have a soft orange glow, while the Goddess' are too bright, slippery like oil and turmeric. Mom's not like that. She is soft eyes, warm smile and long fingers. She wears no nail polish, only a little black *teep* on her forehead sometimes. It was with that turmeric—that reminded me of the goddess—that they smeared her face when Mom left us. I was in class six. Mom had given me a clockwork policeman for my fifth. It is on my desk. The policeman is riding a motorbike; and on the birthday card, Mom had written:

Happy Birthday my hero!

— *Mamma*

I had saved that card carefully in my personal drawer. The policeman is a bit dusty and so I take it, brush off the dirt and read mamma's handwriting. There had been no presents from father. Father had been posted at an advance base in the north and seldom came home. Mamma had said 'he will be back on your birthday' but he hadn't returned. And then when I got the policeman, I had forgotten that he was not there.

With the turmeric rubbed on her face by my *mashi*, mamma leaves us. She begins looking like the Goddess, which I hate. They make her up with sandalwood dots but I can no more recognise her. Mamma leaves in a glass-box car. The house is empty and cold with solemn uncles I had never met before.

I spend the night with the policeman. Father returns late with friends and keeps a gloomy watch over the house. I think why the policeman is not sad about what has happened. That my mamma has died. Why is no one but me—and perhaps father—sad? Why hasn't the world, because mamma's gone, not lost a moment in its journey through the lonely skies? Why still the houses of Four Horse Street had lights at the windows, and there were people watching cricket matches. And I think about this for days, and I stop going to school and stop talking with everyone.

The bleating of a railway locomotive wakes me up. I was sleeping on the chair. The streaking sunlight strong. A bitter taste of soap in my mouth. I am feeling weak, my stomach rumbling angrily. I wash and gargle to clear the disgusting taste of organic oils.

A peacock screams outside. The curtains writhe and shiver from blasts of desert air. I drag myself up to the window. The summer of annihilation has arrived. The worst summer of many, a vengeful heat, a willful massacre. Down on the street, camels snort and pull goods carriages, turbaned men rise from wood benches and collapse from heatstroke. Exhausted *autowallah*s are still asleep in their autos while some in a group survey the road with predatory stares.

The giant billboard of the European holiday comes to life, bright as the sun. Glowing, aflame. But the more it radiates the heat of its dreams, the bigger it grows. It looms like a mythical bird. Pouilly-Fuissé, Macon, Champagne—it breathes and sighs long and hard like some lost animal: Paris, Versailles, the French Alps—Cyclops like it stares with one eye: Chamonix, Lucerne, Jungfraujoch—it screams, it wails, it caterwauls; then it grows eyes, two, then more, more and more, like fungi, till a thousand and one eyeballs beat me down and Peacock Hotel and the rowdy bar downstairs and all that was behind and around me…the sleepy camels of Bhaskarnagar, the students at the juice stalls, all and all! The waves of a blue Mediterranean ever so gently now, lapping against the white sands of the south of France.

A knock on a door somewhere close.

AMBROSIA

Reconstructed lab Notes of Vincent Dutta
Transcribed by: Inderjit

Client name: [Missing] [Many pages damaged by fire and oil stains]
Project: FELICITY

Introduction and Background: Entheogens can be described as a class of psychoactive drugs that are said to 'create' the divine within the user. According to a slightly different view, these substances—when ingested or used otherwise—cause God to be within us. Many religions of the world have used, and continue to use, entheogens in their rituals and practices.

From a scientific viewpoint, these substances among themselves affect the central nervous system, thus creating a wide array of effects—including psychedelic hallucinations, empathy, delirium, stupor, trance, dissociation and dreamlike states of bliss.

The flying ointments used by witches in ancient Europe or the drink *soma* mentioned in the Hindu scriptures were all supposed to be prepared from entheogens. The ointments which allowed witches to fly came from entheogenic plants like deadly nightshade, while *soma* may have been prepared from a mushroom having entheogenic properties. Ambrosia, the food of the Greek gods, was possibly a product of the mushroom, *amanita muscaria*. Many South American, African and Indian religious practices still continue the use of entheogens found in psilocybin mushrooms, peyote cactus, datura, ayahuasca, marijuana and other plants.

The effect of these substances on our minds have been widely studied and described by spiritual seekers, secular users and the scientific community. The Marsh Chapel experiment (Journal of Religion & Health, Vol. 5, 1966) and another study by the Johns Hopkins University aimed to investigate if such a substance facilitates religious experience of a mystical sort. The results of the Marsh Chapel experiment produced strong evidence in support of the idea that a mushroom (psilocybin) can, in fact, produce a mystical experience. The criteria for calling an experience mystical were also studied using religious and other sources, and enumerated for the purpose of this important experiment.

Guidelines and Scope: Design a perfect entheogen with special properties. Client requires a substance (we are calling it Felicity) that would work equally well every time. Tolerance shouldn't develop or be very low, and the substance should not leave any hangovers. 'The doors should open wide', the typed instructions said, 'The ecstasy has to be rich, deep and long-lasting. Just a peep into the other side will not do'. Moreover, 'the viewer should be able to gaze and gaze deep, and be part of the infinite world of light. He should be soaking himself happily in the *mysterium tremendum*,[1] and coming back every time more joyful, more satiated. It's very important to ensure that the effects will not die down with repeated usage; substance should be safe and without side-effects. Users should come back again and again, but not as wasted addicts. Felicity should make everyone happy. An unbounded joy should flow through every heart. Most of all, this bliss has to be such that people enjoy these holidays and come out fresh and recharged. They should radiate joy, *ananda*. Afterwards, they should immerse in joyful labour. To work, to work more and even more till we have created a true utopia in this country, and then on this planet too. Love your work, love your holidays, love your work again—that is what we are aiming for. This *ananda*, this carefully calibrated *moksha* will be packaged and sold from

---

1   A term used by Rudolf Otto to describe an aspect of the Infinite, the awareness of which humiliates and overwhelms.

stationers and grocery shops. It will have to replace cigarettes and scented tobacco. 'Let's offer them paradise in small boxes. If we are successful, another Golden Age awaits this country. Crime will peter out. Productivity will scale unimaginable heights,' the original brief says.

Procedure, Experiments and Analysis: I had begun by looking at the problems of some known entheogens, and started experimenting with dosages and blending with other substances. There are many infusions I am trying, of which the BZ series has proved promising. More about this below. I have experimented with analogues, synthesised a few new chemicals, and have turned into a top notch cook of banned substances.

Luckily, I have a helpful lab coordinator and good research assistants. We have one of the best equipped labs in the continent and a super-efficient supply line which gets anything I requisition, from anywhere in the world.

To address the objectives set out by the client, I often referred to the pioneering work done by Alexander Shulgin, and notes of secret experiments conducted by the CIA as well as the Russian military. Luckily, some of this work has been lately declassified. Dr Shulgin's scale to measure the degree of effectiveness and the nature of effects of a drug helped me to initially rate some of these substances. Being a follower of the great Barry Marshall, I mostly tested on myself and one or more assistants or volunteers, to narrow down the subjective aspects. Once some promising substance is synthesised or emerges, we take help of experimental methods as well as AI software and deep learning algorithms to predict the structure (if not already known), and binding affinities of the substance, its naturally occurring types, designed analogues and even genetically modified varieties. This will then help in further refining the substance and creating new appropriate designs using various methods. Next, we will be doing wider controlled tests.

[Many pages of descriptions of substances, their synthesis, chemical properties, structure, pharmacodynamics, notes about effects. Excerpts follow.]

SANTA MARIA:

The psychoactive constituent is a cannabinoid receptor agonist for both type 1 and type 2. Smoked pure from clay pipes using different amounts on different days. Enhanced sensitivity to sound and light. Slowing of time. No open-eye hallucinations. Hallucinations with eyes closed and music. Beams of primary colours on a black background. Colours more animated, beams curving into parabolas, circles, dancing curves. Everything happening to the rhythm of the music. Feeling of empathy.

Alternating meditative, introspective states and the ability to think about thought. Vision, taste, hearing sharper. Sense of time distorted. After-effects are mild to non-existent.

Comment: Some entheogenic properties. Could be useful in combination with other substances.

GANESHA:[2]

Synthesised this substance in the lab using Shulgin's method, starting with the aldehyde. Inhibits DAT, increasing dopamine availability for the receptors. Tried various doses, starting with 10 mg. At higher doses the progress to a high-level of engagement with the substance happened fast. It was not possible for the mind to ignore the effects of the substance any more—the most important effect being a surfeit of images. The images in case of Ganesha are more detailed, more complex compared to the easy geometry of the Santa Maria images. Some bodily sensations and mild after-effects.

Comment: Needs more experiments.

MDMA:[3]

Arguably the most famous of hug drugs. It is a monoamine releasing agent for serotonin, norepinephrine and dopamine

---

2   A compound with chemical name: 2,5-dimethoxy-3,4-dimethylamphetamine hydrochloride

3   A compound with chemical name: 3,4-methylenedioxy-n-methylamphetamine commonly known as Ecstasy

besides having other roles. Gives a strong sense of communion and empathy. This empathogen has been used by psychotherapists as well as by the US covert operations agencies in their secret MKULTRA project. I used standard 250mg tablets, half of its weight being the pure substance. Initial symptoms included a lot of teeth clenching and a flickering eyelid. Between half and quarter of an hour, the amazing powers of the substance began to be manifest, with initial feelings of love rising from inside my belly. Love like a warm blob of light glowing inside me and slowly emanating from my being, enveloping everything and everyone around me. There is a tremendous euphoria and I could feel my connectedness with everything and everyone around. Remembered someone with whom I had a rather nasty split and felt very sad for her, wanted to talk with her immediately and had visions of holding her and everything being same as before. The effects of MDMA lasted for more than a day.

Comment: Subject-object dichotomy is affected, giving an all-pervading sense of unity. One of the possible starting-off points for Felicity. Need more experiments with new analogues, more subjects, repeated dosage, combinations with Santa Maria(?), Psilocybin (?) and other substances.

DATURA:

A deliriant with medicinal and religious use—especially by shamans and in Tantric practices. The flower is used in the worship of Shiva. Also known as Jimson's weed, following an apocryphal story of a group of soldiers in Jamestown going mad on eating the cooked fruit; Jimson being a corruption of Jamestown. The active agent scopolamine, depending on dosage, acts as antagonist for muscarinic receptors for acetylcholine. First experimented by making a tea by boiling 50 seeds in water and drinking it from a beaker. In the next experiment, increased the dosage to 75 seeds. In either case, the entry into a state of hallucination was smooth and unnoticed. Noticed a crystal statue of a woman in the laboratory which hadn't been there before and tried to have a conversation with it. The woman didn't answer. Kept humming a song in Hindi, which was about a woman in a village seeing off her lover at a train station. More hallucinations. Continued to address the crystal lady on various subjects for a long time. Bodily symptoms included dilation of pupils and, because of it, everything looked very bright. Headache on the next day.

Comment: Seems to be an unpredictable substance from my experiments with dosages and subjects. Would be difficult to get uniform results.

PSILOCYBIN MUSHROOM:

Well-documented studies exist for this psychoactive mushroom with positive results for mystical experiences.

Psilocin, the active agent, acts as an agonist for certain members of the serotonin receptor family. Consistency of repeated doses have not been studied in detail for this entheogenic substance. Legality issues exist for this, and many of the other substances. Started with 15 small sized dried mushrooms boiled in tap water and drank the mushroom tea, chewing the pieces quickly. They don't taste good. In the next experiment we used 20 mushrooms as sandwich filling, and 40 dried mushrooms another time with drinking chocolate. Asked my assistant to play Enya on the speakers and rested in an easy chair. There is a gentle movement towards the high and initial nausea. Soon the world around comes alive in living colours and animated, pulsating geometry. These beautiful colours and the geometry of every small and large object is intense, musical and stimulating, so much so as to bring one close to an orgasm. Obvious synesthesia at this stage. But thoughts soon stop following linear patterns. The living walls and the living objects started to communicate with me and an intense joy coursed through my body, and the mind begins to play with the sense of time. Time itself moves back and forth or stands still until there is no time at all, and one is in this shimmering moment of golden-hued eternity that is also joy. The active ingredients of the mushroom took complete hold on me, yet it was a gentle, loving embrace. An overwhelming sense of the sacred washed over me as I stood at the centre of this glowing moment of past, present and future that is now. Euphoria continued for days.

Comment: We are close but more combinations, new configurations to be tested. Tolerance kicks in after repeated use (have to work on this). Work also needs to be done focusing on serotonin (note: this neurotransmitter is also linked with the chemistry of love). Think how desensitisation can be controlled so that effects can be replicated without loss. Mushroom tea preparations too idiosyncratic because of varying water quality.

ANGEL DUST:
A dissociative hallucinogen, acts as an NMDA receptor antagonist. Documented to cause violent behaviour. Began testing it by snorting later in combination with...

[Many pages missing, some badly burnt, there are a few semi-legible entries about the BZ series of infusions which use ibogaine and psilocybin, among other substances, but the entries have been licked by flames and there are grease smears on these pages. Then this solitary entry below]

My experiments continue but these are more of fine-tuning, for I think I have almost reached the end of my quest. In a few hours, I will be administered an enema of a carefully prepared extract of four substances with which I have been experimenting for the better part of a year. I will repeat the enema for the next two days and then if all goes well, I will try other methods of administering the formulation, keeping a note on efficacy. We have already done some control experiments and the results are hopeful. If everything goes as I expect, then in a month or two, I will have decisive news about project Felicity.

[Remaining pages completely burnt or missing. —Inderjit]

THE EMPEROR
IN THE GUTTER

'Who the bloody hell?' Kapoor swings around and walks to the door. His head reels as he unfastens the rusty latch with some effort. A thin boy with a stupid smile and an older man of medium build standing at the threshold.

'Check out time, sir. Please clear the bills for the room,' the man says in a business-like tone.

Kapoor stares back at them, irritation written large on his face.

'What?' Kapoor says.

'Check-out time is 11am, sir. We sent you the bills last night. We are expecting guests,' the man said. The boy's smile looked even more idiotic. Kapoor looks from one to the other. 'Where is that woman?' He growls at them, stepping closer.

They look surprised but hold their ground, 'One thousand fifty six, for the room and food,' the man sounds impatient.

There is a flicker of incomprehension but then he grins and clears his voice. 'See here Lilliputians, I am not checking out now. If a woman comes looking for me, just note down her message. She has a waterfall of hair, black like the raven's wings,' he glances at the flimsy desk calendar and grimaces. 'Now don't bother me and carry on with your work. I am here on important business and I've already lost time.'

'Please, the bill, sir,' the man insisted.

'Tch, tch! I told you I will pay later. Now get back to your jobs and let me rest,' Kapoor says.

The man clenches his jaw, 'Check-out time is 11am and you pay one day extra.'

Kapoor raises his voice, 'Listen, my dear fellow. Go take care of your guests. I have no plans to check out and will be back tonight. You charge whatever you have to.'

Something in his deep voice and the commanding tone makes the other man, who could be the manager, unsure. He thinks for an undecided second, and that is the moment Kapoor speaks again, 'My dear man, see to it that this room gets tidied and change those flowers over there,' and without another word he swings around and marches into the bathroom to wash his face.

'Please clear part of the bills, sir…hotel rules,' the manager mumbles before leaving.

'Okay, okay, tonight.' Kapoor continues splashing water on his face then noticing there is no soap, asks 'Now where's the soap gone, don't you put fresh toiletries in your rooms every day?'

The manager eyes the boy with suspicion as they retreat down the steps.

Kapoor studies himself in the spotted mirror. His skin looks clammy and he hates what he sees. 'Damned dosshouse mirror,' he mumbles. His plump cheeks are layered with dust, grey filaments of it covering the dirty and unkempt beard. He has always preferred a clean-shaven look but now he can't visit a salon. He keeps rubbing his face vigorously with a wet towel, for the soap hasn't arrived. He has to go out. He counts the cash and change. Hardly anything left. His money must have been stolen but he has to finish his work. He will have to call his office, or maybe that girl from the train. Sujata. She will be here for some days, that's what she had said. She had agreed to be the face of the chocolate campaign. Choco Raja. His lips cracked into a smile. Now he has to go find her. No problem in a small city. He will definitely find her. Locking the room, he hurries down the stairs. There are no taxis visible. He buys a pack of king-size cigarettes and hires an auto. The driver cuts a hard bargain and that irritates him. Clearly, he detests arguing with the fellow but the money situation looks bad. 'This attitude of *autowallahs* is natural for a city growing on tourist money,' Kapoor tells me. I hear him and make no response, but he doesn't mind. I know that he doesn't.

Kapoor decides against calling his office for help. Through clouds of cigarette smoke, he says, 'There has been a conspiracy, and that fake man has somehow taken over. I don't know which of my men helped the impostor. So I need time to organise, get my trusted lieutenants around me, before throwing him out. But I have to find out who this fraudster is. I will skewer the bugger on a slow fire, but first, I need to find that woman. She seemed genuine and I need her help to launch Choco Raja.'

I quietly say I will help him find her.

But she wasn't easy to find. Kapoor uses up most of the remaining cash looking for her among the dusty roads of the once-beautiful city. Kapoor says that she had mentioned that her office was beside the main post office, or maybe it was called the general post office, so he takes the auto there. But I'm not sure he remembers it correctly.

Opposite to the post office building is a garden with flowers and birds, but there's no office in sight. For some time, he sits on one of the benches in the garden. The sounds of the street get filtered by the big trees along its perimeter. A green-coconut man comes, and he buys a coconut and drinks the water. There are birds in the trees, squirrels playing detectives among yellow and orange flowers. An ornamental fountain is going lazily; he is thirsty again, and he drinks straight from the fountain. A cuckoo begins to sing in one of the trees. He listens to the bird for a minute before picking up a stone and throwing it into the tree.

Kapoor is asking the man at the General Post Office enquiry counter, 'I'm looking for an office beside the post office.'

The clerk is absorbed in a cricket match on TV and looks annoyed by this intrusion.

'This is the post office, there is no office here,' he says.

'Is it? But where is that post office with the office on the other side?' Kapoor goes on.

'You can post whatever you like, no questions asked, but no office, and no sides,' the clerk replies peevishly.

'I need another post office which is taking sides I, er…no, not the post office or maybe…but it, the office should be there.'

'All the offices are in Q circle; you come here to post only, if an office was there it must have left,' the clerk says.

'But there should be a frigging office!' Kapoor barks.

'There is one, no many, but this is not the office or the post office, and neither it is what you are looking for, which is the office on the side, the office that takes sides, but no sides here, neither batting nor fielding, no directions really except for the bus to your home, which goes south and there you should try,' the man said with a glint in his eyes.

'The office that sits opposite to a post office, that goes south?'

'I am not allowed to tell you more,' the clerk says. The batsman hits a sixer and the employees of the post office burst out in applause.

'Find her I will' Kapoor says leaving the counter. 'Good luck, but don't take sides, not right nor left nor east or west, only south, remember only south,' the clerk turns away to watch the game, back to his world of stamps and envelopes behind the unclean glass of the enquiry counter.

Marching on through the heat. Smoking more and more cigarettes. Through the day, meeting some more like the clerk sending him south, more post offices, big and small, and a few offices too. The men in those offices give some suggestions but the elusive lady is not be found… By the time he gives up, he is nursing a terrible headache.

The injuries are not looking good. The raw pink scar of the burn went right up from the palms, touching the elbows. On the palm of the right hand near the Mount of Venus and up the thumb, the fire damaged skin was marked by rows of lacerations, like some crimson moonscape violated by a caterpillar-tracked machine. Kapoor tries to pull out dry skin but it breaks, spilling drops of blood. He buys some paracetamol from a medicine shop.

There is a bar next door. He rushes down the stairs to the basement. Kapoor checks the menu but he cannot afford his favourite Stoli, and has to settle for a local beer. It is a gaudily decorated watering-hole with prints of the beautiful Bani Thani and dancing women of the desert on the walls. The lights on the ceiling are bright and ugly but the AC is running at full steam and that's all he cares about.

'I'll have to return to Aukatabad fast. Sujata, that woman on the train, has vanished...I have lost her. But I have to reclaim my corporate empire,' he tells me between sips.

I nod in agreement. I know his thoughts, often I do. Wasting time looking for that raven-haired woman made no sense to me. There are a hundred pretty faces to launch his campaigns. But I think she somehow struck his fancy...which can only mean trouble.

The late afternoon beer stupor, heightened by the blast of air-conditioning, casts a dreamy spell and we hang back for some more time in that refuge.

It is a steamy summer evening outside. Kapoor has spent almost everything. 'I can't recollect the name of my secretary,' he says, adding 'I thought I will ask him to clear the hotel bills and get me a ticket for the journey. But what if he too has switched sides?'

'That's quite possible,' I tell him as we look for an auto. I am beginning to get scared.

'My chopper is parked up in Aukatabad, and is of no use now. The Gulfstream is in Europe on business, the other jet down in Daulatpur on the Arabian Sea, all too far away. I am sure that impostor has been taking joy rides in my birds. I could get someone to give me a lift perhaps. But who should I trust when my closest people seem to have switched sides?'

I told him he should contact someone from his legal team. Perhaps they could get help, and also expose the impostor.

'I don't remember names, and my phone is gone too. I'm sure they have hacked into my email and stolen what they could by now. I hope my cat is safe. If those Nazis or whoever is propping up the impostor harm Prana, I will cut their balls off and put them on display outside the chocolate museum. And what happened to that bugger Sharma, was my secretary Sharma or was it Surana, or, is he a Bengali? No, there are very few Bengalis on my personal staff. I don't like the mushy softness of that language, not in my office in any case.' He is unmindfully nursing the injured hand as he speaks, caressing the bite wounds as if those are love bites, and his expression doesn't betray the pain.

Luckily there's a cybercafé in a hotel right next door to the bar, and Kapoor dashes off a message from the Atman group website. 'Sharma or Surana or whatever your name may be, gear up and be prepared to act fast if you have any love for your job,' he mumbles as I watch him type vigorously. When I ask him, hard as he tries, he cannot remember the numbers of his personal staff.

The streets are emptying out. Kapoor has been walking aimlessly for hours. Old *haveli*s here. Grand mansions, he stops and studies a few. 'I should buy one of these properties and convert it to a hotel,' he tells me.

'Good idea,' I say. But he is looking crestfallen. He couldn't find Sujata, and now the manoeuvres of the German competitor Ritz and the fake man in Aukatabad are on his mind. The beer buzz has faded and knots of pain from the hand injury are surfacing. The peal of bells from the small temple which was right next to the hotel alerts him. And then he is right at the entrance. The man who had come up to the room with the boy and two thuggish characters are huddling over something in the reception area. 'Sir, the bills are due for two days. Please clear the first day's dues,' one of them says in an icy voice. He has a thick handlebar moustache and the rough sinewy arms of someone used to hard labour.

'I will clear everything tomorrow,' Kapoor says in a firm but polite tone, gauging their displeasure. So he does have money after all, I feel relieved.

'No, sir, you have to pay now,' the thug raises his voice.

It's clear, they are not going to make adjustments this time. Why doesn't he pay up and get it over with?

Kapoor fishes into his trouser pockets, brings out a handful of crumpled notes and flings them on the counter. The soiled notes flutter in the fan breeze and settle down at the edge of the thick guest register.

Four hundred rupees. The bill will be five thousand.

'You duffers should understand that it's beneath my dignity to carry cash. Stop begging and let me sleep. I'm tired, tomorrow…' but before he can complete, one of the thugs lashes out angrily, 'Get out!' he orders.

'Get out!' he thunders again, his breath hot on Kapoor's face.

'No! Call the cops!' another says, 'let them beat the shit out of him!'

'Yes, call the cops,' the third one joins but now the first man pounces on Kapoor. Holding him by the collar, he shoves him against the wall and throws a beefy fist. Kapoor barely manages to parry the attack.

'Begging, huh? You think this is a *dharmshala,* no money, no problem! Thought you could get away with it!' a hard slap stings his face. Kapoor loses balance but manages to grab a window grill at the last moment. Fear and fatigue has given a strange aura to his face.

'No, no, don't hit him. Let me call the cops,' the man behind the counter screams. He begins to dial a number.

But the other two join in pushing and hitting Kapoor. Kicks and blows rain down on him.

'You'll pay dearly for this,' Kapoor warns them repeatedly with a failing voice. They keep on hurling abuses and continue shoving, striking his face with their open palms.

Kapoor's eyes take on the glazed look of defeat, making the attackers even more aggressive. A thin stream of blood is running down his nose. Suddenly he veers left and sees the door. The empty street is just a few steps down.

He twists away from the thugs and leaps, clearing the flight of stairs. He lands awkwardly and falls, but is up on his feet immediately. He dashes away towards the railway tracks.

The duo comes sprinting down the stairs. '*Pakdo pakdo,*' they yell after him in the darkness. Kapoor scrambles through an alley and a side street. Then across the tracks to the other side of the station.

The men can be heard cursing and running about near the stalls selling exam guides. There's a high wall flanking the railway tracks, and his pursuers are not too far away. He will have to survive this night. He reaches for the wall and heaves himself up. He leaps into the darkness, crashing into weeds and thickets. The steel tracks are just a few feet away and there's another guard wall on the other side.

Kapoor thrashes among the undergrowth to scare away snakes. There are desert scorpions in this city, which have been displaced from their sandy habitats by the weird weather. Fear drums his chest. Nothing moves. With his chest heaving, Kapoor leans against the darkness of the guard wall.

The curses of those two thugs can be heard no more. There are drunks loitering about somewhere close. He can hear their gibberish and tries to locate them. But they remain invisible. 'I'll bury this hotel,' he mumbles to the darkness.

The whistle of a diesel locomotive follows the siren of a police patrol. Surely the hotel has called the cops. The police jeep drives slowly past the guard walls. Kapoor slinks deeper into the darkness. A diesel engine's headlamp flashes, chasing phantom shadows as it charges up the tracks hauling a long distance express train. The thud of heavy pistons, the screaming of wheels on the tracks, the loud rumble of the coaches, the hammering of steel on steel, shattering the world apart. The policemen speaking in low voices, and now one of the drunks is right next to Kapoor.

Hands freezing to stone, the drunk looking familiar, throat parched like sandpaper, the drunk looking like the thug from the hotel and deeper in the night, silence losing its battle with the pounding of his heart.

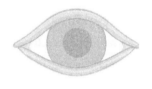

VISIBLE AND
INVISIBLE

OWL AND HURRICANE

It used to be the Lonely Owl but with the weather getting wonky all over and the rising box-office popularity of disaster movies, the club was renamed to Owl and Hurricane. But because bad weather is hard to paint with words, they used a larger-than-life model of a dimly-lit hurricane lamp and an eagle-owl on the grated wooden door, which coughed and creaked like a consumptive as guests went in. Tuesday was ladies' night at the Owl and Hurricane.

She had returned from somewhere and had gone to the parlour. Her legs were waxed, and she relaxed as the beautician gave her a long and nice massage. They cleansed her face with a scrub of tangerine and Dead Sea salts, and covered her up with a mask prepared from the milk of the blue bull. Finally, her hair was cleaned with a shampoo from Arabia and her nails painted a bright amber. Then the young beautician excused herself, and the mistress of the parlour tiptoed in and applied a cream on her face made from snake venom.

By the time she returned to the house, it was pitch dark in that neighbourhood with abandoned transport godowns and under-construction commercial buildings. Though relaxed after the parlour session, she still needed to unwind, stressed as she was with many conflicting thoughts circling her mind.

She paired on a black tee with black denim boot-cuts with a laser-engraved paisley pattern. Next, she put on her square-toed ankle boots with heels and wore a blood red lipstick made from crushed female cochineal parasites. When she gathered her hair with a butterfly-clip, the squiggles and ringlets hissed with electricity. Throwing on a black corduroy jacket and a sienna coloured beret, she stepped out.

She unlocked the garage and eased the black Jeep Compass down the driveway, littered with dry leaves. The rusty iron gates creaked and shuddered when she opened them to let the car through. She drove through dark and empty streets right up to the bypass, and then seventeen miles to the edge of the forest. The posh resorts and nightclubs were along this stretch.

The grated wooden door swung open, revealing a shadowy passage lit by electric candles. A rough-hewn door with metal clasps led into the cavernous interiors. Not many come all this way, and the crowd was thin. A few women with glowing faces, boyfriends in tow, two girl gangs of four or five and one middle-aged couple at the far end. The lights had been dimmed but the eyes of the eagle-owls perching in strategic locations were burning with fire.

A woman of indeterminate age was swinging to the beat on the dance floor, a slightly bulging man in her arms. The DJ was playing rock numbers from another time.

She found a low sofa in a nook covered with posters. Two women were sitting at the other end of the sofa, one dressed like her, and the other in a flounced white skirt and a multi-coloured top. A man sat opposite to her but his partner was nowhere around. He was well-built with wide shoulders. He looked much older and his steely eyes brushing against her gave her a slight discomfort. She got herself a vodka and turned towards the stage.

To her right was a niche in the wooden wall with a black porcelain statuette of a cat. A thin cat with long, pointed ears; it sat straight, staring at her. Beside the cat was a wooden pillar with a lightbox advertisement. The model—a man with strong jaws and hairy hands. The display lights lit up the face of the man, wearing a red jacket over charcoal black trousers. His hands hung by his sides, fists clenched, and he was giving her a toothy smile. Didn't he look like the man on the sofa? She stole a look in that direction. The man had vanished and a young girl with a doll's face had appeared, sipping a Cobra.

She sipped her vodka and watched the clients. Mostly women of her age, some even younger. They wore faux leather topped with antique embroidered shawls, miniskirts with oversize red leather jackets, sported fluorescent headbands, chunky accessories, and dark smudged eyeliner. Their smouldering eyes reflected the fiery gaze of the owls that kept a constant watch. They looked confident, carried themselves well and spoke in sighs and whispers—their black nail polish gleaming under the pirouetting strobes of the dance deck.

Some flashy young men. Expensive watches, imbecile-like laughter. Few older men with toothbrush whiskers and lecherous eyes. The ambient light changed with the music, weaving phantasms, mysteries locked in embrace, matryoshka dolls of secrets, one reflecting another, right till the end of the world.

'Zeeta,' said a gruff voice, 'has been killed.'

She sprang from the sofa. 'What?' escaped from her lips as she turned around to see who had spoken; but there was no one behind her, only the posters on the wall. The soft rock had segued to blues. Her eyes fell on the poster of the model in the lightbox. His face looked grim now, his jaws moved slightly, 'Zeeta is dead,' he said heavily.

She was shaken but she looked straight into his eyes. 'Who are you?' she whispered.

'Didn't they tell you about me?' the man said. His face was stern now.

'I don't know you. What are you doing here?' she asked, her expression more composed, the initial flush of surprise having disappeared.

'Well they call me Perfect Man,' he wavered between grimness and movie star airs.

'Eh? That can't be your name, what do you do here?' she asked calmly. Nobody noticed this conversation. The club slowly filled up but the crowd funnelled towards the dance floor. Sparks lit up work-weary hearts. People danced.

'As you can see, I'm selling caps and wallets,' he said.

She hadn't noticed this before and read the advertisement: *Perfect Man, Handcrafted Accessories,* it said. Is that so, she thought. 'So you are not modelling for that dressmaker anymore?' she asked.

'Dressmaker? Never. Have been selling caps, wallets and belts for more than a century,' his face was stern again, and his gaze turned inward as he spelt out the words, 'your life is in danger.'

'How do you know me? Why should I be in danger?' she asked him. She was not exactly scared; she was tense, also slightly amused.

'That's my job. I carry their messages,' he said.

'Is it?' she looked straight into his eyes. The live band had begun to play. People left their seats and moved forward, towards the stage, to feel the music, shake hands with the musicians.

The lightbox shuddered, as if to the beat of the drums, and then Perfect Man made a sign with his fingers. She stood up, touched the box and sat back on her sofa. A young waiter, a new recruit, noticed something. He walked up to her and asked if everything was okay. But when she looked up at him he froze for a moment, scratched his hair then hurried back the way he had come. 'Absolut and Coke for me, please,' she went up to the bar and ordered her drink before returning to her seat.

'Didn't they tell you about me?' the man in the picture spoke again.

'Who? No…not me… I have heard about you, of course. But, but how did she die?'

'It looks like an accident but we are not sure yet. You should be on your guard,' he warned her.

'I'm okay,' she said. What did she have to do with the death of the woman? Why would her life in danger? 'Do you have a suspect?' she asked.

'Kapoor's men, of course!'

'Jayant Roy Kapoor?' she wanted to be sure.

'Who else!'

'Oh!' She swept her gaze quickly along the club. The rush of blood in her cheeks under the bluish focus lamps transformed her fine face into an eerie apparition. The doll-faced girl on the other sofa gasped and slinked away towards the dance floor where the crowd was singing with the band.

Grateful Dead.

They swayed, they danced, they screamed shrill requests for more, for more of the rolling, easy-going medicine.

'Don't worry too much sister, the powers are protecting the conscientious worker for the cause. Just be a bit careful,' the man said in an assuring tone, adding, 'Focus your energies on the work at hand.'

'I'm doing just that, I am always working,' she said.

'We can't afford any more mistakes,' he said.

'Hmm…' she didn't know where this conversation was going. It wouldn't be easy to explain, for her thoughts were not clear at all. They wavered and faltered. Clouds had begun to float in, assuming strange shapes, some terrifying, some soft as rabbits.

'Don't stray from the path, sister. We have to stop Jayant Roy Kapoor and we have to stop him quick as we can! I know your man is here but he is not strong enough,' Perfect Man said.

'Did you say I did something wrong? How is that possible?' she said finally.

'But we didn't want it like this. We planned it differently. We wanted Jekyll and Hyde but we have got a man who thinks *he is* Kapoor! We needed a sleepwalker who could stop Kapoor for good and then come back unscathed by the mental impact of the deed, but instead we have a false copy of the tycoon who wants to take his place. That's a setback. How could this happen? Will he ever muster the courage that is required to get rid of the business captain? And a journalist to boot!'

'How does a being a journalist hamper this? Besides your information is not up to date. He is a florist now, left the journo's job,' she said defensively.

'Whatever be it, Jayant Roy Kapoor and his wicked plan has to be sabotaged, wrecked for good!' Perfect Man said.

'I know, I am… but can I…can I ask you a question?' she felt a little tipsy now.

'Yes,' came the curt reply from the lightbox.

'Has all of this you are telling me, standing there, got any connection with your caps and leather wallets?'

He looked offended at the question. 'Don't mock the wisdom of the Nine,' he snapped back, 'everything will be revealed when the time is right.'

'I will remember that,' she said, and knocked back her drink.

CORPSES HAVE
NO ANSWERS

Very few people of Aukatabad have seen the house except in pictures. In any case it was on the perimeter of the city where low brown hills meet the plains, and hungry leopards roam about at night looking for easy kills. The high granite walls around the mansion are topped by electric fencing and the only intruders who might have had a glimpse of the Palladian façade of the building are the dead Himalayan baboons, whose blackened corpses are often found tangled with the electric fencing which spark with blinding blue flashes whenever an animal is snared by its tongues of death.

Inside the walls are carefully maintained grounds, with rolling grassland and stands of trees, at the centre of which is a ring of amaltas forming a natural barricade around the building. Behind the mansion, the grasslands stretch for half a kilometre, meeting the boundary wall at the edge of the old hill. Throughout the property are stands of kadam, shady debdarus and patches of desert roses whose scent hangs thick all along the curving path that leads up to the house.

It is still the small hours of the morning when the medical van meant for transporting animal carcasses drives through the gates. Its headlamps are switched off as it winds up the path to the mansion, coming to a halt on the concrete apron behind the building, which is also used as a helipad. The engine idles as two men jump out of the cabin and rush to the back. Their faces are covered with surgical masks and they are disciplined in the way they unlock the carrier as one stands back and then the two vanish inside it for a few minutes, after which they emerge, easing down and rolling out a gurney covered by a black sheet. They lock the carrier and walk through an open door at the back of the house.

Jayant Roy Kapoor appears through the kitchen door in a well-cut business suit, his shark eyes watchful as the two men wheel the gurney right into the scullery. The gleaming white crockery stacked in rows paint their faces a startling white, and it would seem the two men walking in had all the blood drawn from their bodies. Bullet, the buck-toothed tough, his face criss-crossed by knife scars, stops a few feet from JRK and bows respectfully without speaking a word.

He studies their faces and dismisses one of them with a wave of his hand. 'Did you get the stuff?'

Bullet shakes his head, fear writ large on his face, 'We looked carefully. The crash complicated things, we had to bribe the police but we couldn't find anything on her.'

'Did you look everywhere?' he eyes him meaningfully.

Bullet nods.

'It can't just vanish. We definitely know she made off with some samples. Now about the accident, don't believe everything you are told. It could be an inside job too; whoever these people are, they can be ruthless,' he snapped, suddenly losing his temper, 'I don't have to teach you that!'

'I'm sorry master, we've put our networks on both sides of the law to work,' Bullet mumbles, half-eating his words.

JRK slaps the counter-top loudly and says, 'You told the whole world that they were handling drugs in that lab?' How could he even explain the risks to this dimwit? What could happen if this stuff falls in the wrong hands, especially the formulas and who knows what this egghead had come up with. How close he was to the finishing line.

He takes a step forward and, with a violent tug, removes part of the covering to reveal the battered face of Zeeta. Blood splattered, bruised and long dead. The musculature of the face had changed and the eyes had burst open in the final moment of agony. Bullet gulped and stepped back. Fresh blood was his business, not dried rust. He felt queasy in the presence of the long dead, which is why he had asked his partner to check the corpse thoroughly when they stole it out of the morgue.

'Do you think this was an accident?' JRK asks as he continues to stare at the face.

'The *policewallah* says the driver tried to save a jaywalker and swerved and hit a tree,' Bullet answers.

'And the driver died, so no way to find out what happened to her things,' JRK says with rising disappointment, adding, 'Where is her phone?'

'Missing. She had a head start and the milk crowds slowed us down, otherwise we would have got to them before this happened,' Bullet says haltingly.

'Milk? What the cock are you talking about?' JRK asks, giving him a dark scowl.

'Sir, the devout offering milk to the God, it stopped all traffic and...' he half mumbles, appearing as if he would piss in his pants.

'*Behenchod*, what have you been smoking these days? Or have you been screwing this dead cunt on your way here that you lost your mind, giving such excuses!' Blood pumped through his temples, and he yells, 'Get out! Get out right now or I will have you sent to Congo right away and...'

Bullet scurries away and the door swings shut after him. JRK bends over the gurney and yanks the sheet off the dead woman.

She is quite a sight. A deep gash runs down her chest that had slit open one of her breasts, and it was hanging at one side like a distended balloon of fibrous tissue caked with rusty blood. The impact had killed her while the glass wounds had drained away the blood. Glass shards had made deep punctures all over her face and arms, each like a volcano that had erupted red lava that was now dried in rivulets. As he watches, anger rising in him, she moves. A muscle of her face twitches and the head slants to one side.

'Where have you hidden it, bitch?' JRK had begun to breathe rapidly and the words escaped from his mouth like overheated steam.

No answer, only her mouth gives a slight twitch as if she was trying to speak but failing.

In a fit of rage he rushes to the wall and snatches the meat cleaver from its hook. He holds the blade to her throat. 'No more games, tell me who sent you? Where are the formulas? How did my scientist die?' His temple throbs and he feels his head would burst.

All through his rise he had been plagued by the fear of enemies; and indeed, there had been many along the way. But he had worked hard, and all designs against him had failed. Recently things had begun to get messy again. The German challenge to his chocolate operations had been stiff…and now this invisible adversary who was clearly targeting Felicity—his pet project. The fire in the lab, unexplained accidents, and now the chief scientist poisoned and this girl dead.

'Who sent you to screw up my lab?' he screams and bangs the rails of the gurney with a thick fist. She lurches from one side to the other as a deathly gasp escapes from her mouth. The whole mansion shivers at this unworldly sound which grows louder as it rushes through every room and passage, up the stairs and into the bedrooms, freezing the occupants in their sleep.

Bullet hears it and comes rushing through the door; and the meat cleaver, carefully aimed, flies out of JRK's hand and whizzes at him as he ducks right in time. It hits a set of crystal champagne flutes, tearing up the night with ear-splitting music. Zeeta's corpse sighs loudly as JRK storms out of the scullery through the backdoor, leaving the dead woman with Bullet, quaking in his shoes, amongst a heap of broken crystalware.

WINGS OF ETERNITY

A wide road flanked by a low hill. If the sun had just set, one would see a stone castle floating in the sky, dazzling in the red and burnished gold of the last rays before dusk. If our gaze lingers, we will see the steep climb to the top, a narrow path hanging by its teeth from the craggy rockface on its way up to a castle built in Scottish style. There were many stories about this estate. Stories of royals and spies and hidden treasure—and inevitably, of politics and power.

When Sujata was returning from the lawyer's office that evening, she looked up and saw it; and because the clouds were low, it seemed the stone structure—glowing in the rich light— was indeed floating among the clouds. Like a reflection of the real in another dimension which has been suddenly revealed to her. It remained with her, the vision of the magic castle floating in the darkening horizon like a pennant of light, flying into the evening of escapes yet anchored firmly in the real. And she wondered what it could have been telling her—bathed in the orange of the evening, always and ever prepared to take flight, to ride unknown winds or circle back home, where she finally wanted to return. 'As above, so below,' the wisdom of the ancients flickered through her mind.

She had been running against time with her work. There was no one really that she could blame, no one at Grey and Govindan, the law firm which was her address in this city. It was against the rules. Something was distracting her but she couldn't put her finger on it yet.

The day after she had arrived in Bhaskarnagar, they said that one Mr Kapoor had come looking for her. That must be him. But more important matters had intervened, and she had let it slip for a while.

He had saved her life. Perhaps she could have dealt with the situation herself but how does one forget his bravery? She remembered the snatcher on the train, and the fight that followed. Who would have taken the risk to help her? He was a kind soul, a lionheart...and she didn't want him to get into unnecessary trouble. From what they said it seemed he needed help. 'He looked like a ghost, bloodshot eyes, unbrushed hair, dirty clothes,' they told her. She had given him the name of a cheap hotel. She hoped he would be there. Should she go now and find out? But she had been indecisive and there were other things to attend to.

But today, she had decided to make that call. She had been thinking of him before she'd fallen asleep last night.

Mr Kapoor…Chanchal Mitra…he had a weakness for *ladykenis*, that was for sure, she smiled to herself. And Mr Kapoor had been cursing the German competitor. Last night she had felt a strong urge to call up the hotel and find his whereabouts, but she had been too exhausted. Now, she dialed the number. 'Oh! So you are related to that thief?' The rudeness of the man on the other side of the line was shocking.

'How dare you speak to me like that? What's your name, give me the manager!' Sujata shouted back.

The man from the hotel raised his voice, 'I mean what I say. That slimy two-faced thief fled without paying the bills!'

'That cannot be. Where is he now?' her voice faltered.

'We are looking for him and if we get him, we will teach him what it means to cheat us,' the man said menacingly.

'Now, please listen, he is unwell, I will take care of your dues. If you find him, just say I will be there in an hour with the money,' she gave them her name. She had to extricate him from this mess.

'Ah! If you mean it then come over immediately. The cops are looking for him,' the voice had lost a chip of the menace in it.

'Give me an hour, I will be there.'

'*Jaldi*,' the man said and banged the receiver.

She reached Peacock Hotel inside of an hour and spoke with the manager. Where did he go, she asked them again but they said they had no idea. The bill was paid along with a fine.

She had to find him. Should she go to the police? Weren't they already looking?

She took an auto which would be faster in the peak hour traffic. She asked to go to the police station but they got stuck at the railway crossing. The gates of the level-crossing were closed, and a long line of vehicles and camel carts had formed along the road that crossed the tracks. She felt restless; she had to find him. But this waiting for the train to pass was killing her.

No, this won't do. She will cross by foot to the other side and get another auto. She paid the driver and stepped off. She looked up and down the moss-covered guard wall of the rail track that flanked the road.

A hundred feet or so down the road, there was a breach in the wall. Bricks had been removed, leaving a space through which an average person could squeeze through. People used it to cross the tracks when the level crossing gates were closed. She slipped through the narrow breach. It was a dirty crossing. Garbage and excreta strewn on both sides, and clumps of weed everywhere. She looked up and down for the train and began to cross, and then something caught her eye. On the far side of the tracks against the other wall, almost hidden by the undergrowth, a man lay slumped in dirt. A discarded rag-doll. His face turned away, his clothes covered with grime.

A drunk perhaps. But something drew her towards this figure. She stepped closer, bent down and shook him. He moved a little but couldn't raise his head. She poked him with a finger. He stirred, turning slowly, his rheumy eyes refusing to open. At last, he blinked at the fading light.

The gaunt face caked with dirt would have been difficult to recognise, but how could she forget. Those thick eyebrows, the deep set intense eyes, now tired and unfocussed. His overgrown beard, like a dusty cobweb, formed a sad halo around his face. He kept blinking; there were black bruises under his eyes. His breath smelled horrible.

'Bastards!' she hissed under her breath.

'Sujata? Pretty woman from the train?' his lips moved with effort.

She almost smiled but she couldn't recognise the voice, burdened with defeat. A whisper exhaled from a lonely cavern. He sighed and raised a feeble hand as if to examine it. She held his hand. Her grip was like tempered steel, uncommonly powerful. He felt that power in her grip and looked at her, surprised.

'What happened?' she asked. He shook his head slowly from side to side. He didn't remember.

Sujata was moved like she never had been. The curious onlookers who were waiting for the train to pass didn't notice her transformation. Nor did she herself know how in those few moments, rare moments when perhaps time also stops playing its games with life, she was once more that castle of secrets which could fly in the glow of an amber dusk.

And that great moment of distilled eternity wrapped around her, and him too, yoking them together, sending off the curious onlookers, stopping the train at the station and clearing the road on the other side so that they had passage, so that they could fly, fly on its wings.

The tyres burnt and hissed on the asphalt as they raced through the sepia streets of Bhaskarnagar, down avenues of gulmohar now breaking into flaming blossom, past splendid havelis and smoking crematoria, beyond towering shopping malls and across the dismal quarters of elephant-trainers, beyond slums and sandstone palaces, all the way through the blue-grey dust of that evening.

She helped him through the gates of the guest house.

He dragged himself in, slowly, looking this way and that, and flopped into a couch in the front room. The wind had blown away some of the dust from his face.

'There's a washbasin over there. Wash your hands, I will get you some tea,' she said.

He looked around suspiciously. 'How do you live in this shoebox?' he said.

Sujata was taken aback. As much by the unexpected comment, as by the deep gravelly voice. But then her marble black eyes crinkled with stolen laughter,

'I manage,' she said.

THE EYES IN THE LOBBY

I had gotten myself into trouble. I'm no more at that hotel, but neither am I back in Anantanagar. I definitely remember buying my ticket home. Had Kapoor been up to something? He might have kept the ticket by mistake. But the train, wasn't it scheduled to leave last night? So I have missed the train! Now what is this place, are we still in Bhaskarnagar?

I ask the woman, Sujata. She is here too. Now this is interesting.

'Yes we are in Bhaskarnagar,' she says.

I have fresh cuts and bruises on my face, the burnt skin of my hands was healing very slowly but looked better than before. She gets medicines, bandages and all that. Antiseptic smells of childhood on days that were unduly white, white linens of hospitals. Very kind of her, no doubt. Should I borrow money from her and get another ticket for home? But I was weak.

'Give it a day or two,' she says.

But I want to get home.

'You're not fit yet,' she counters. I learn from her that I had an accident, which explains the bruises on my face.

But what accident, was I roughed up or something? Looks like it, but I don't ask her. It's too embarrassing. Night is endless and empty, and so is the day that follows. The hours seem interminable, a relentless drumming of false beats. A pendulum, imprisoned in a clock chamber, swinging back and forth without escape. In these false days of emptiness without a shore, I am always reading a book. *The Great Derangement.* It's a book about madness. The book was lying about in this house and I picked it up. But it wasn't about the usual kind of madness, rather one that has gripped us all. Me and you, and Kapoor too, I suppose; and those who believe we are better than others, so we needn't bother about what happens as long as we are okay. I suppose, that's what the book wants to tell us though I have read just a few pages. But where's Kapoor? I haven't seen him in this house yet.

Today, I am tired without reason. I get out of bed late. Perhaps I need a day or two more before taking the train. Though I hate to do it, I write a letter to Idris.

Luckily, I can remember his address…at least the street name is okay. Not so sure about the house number. I don't tell him much, just that I am in a jam and need help. Can he send money?

Now I am lounging on an easy chair in the verandah and reading that book. I doze off a few times, finally waking up to find the day had died. Is this the same day that I wrote the letter to Idris? There is no answer to such questions.

I am strolling in the lawn, watching gulmohar blossoms spray-painting the grey road a fiery orange. Right at this moment the sepoy bulbuls are flitting about among the rosewood branches and I'm trying to speak to them. The leaves of rosewood are wet and glistening, which means it must have rained. And now I notice, my shirt is drenched too! So I must have been out on the street in this unseasonal rain.

And this night, it's on TV. Cloudbursts. Torrential downpour in the desert further west. The erratic weather which helps no one. The land unable to quench its thirst because a deluge, like a drought, is nobody's friend. Water that flows away without going deep under the ground. The water that Sujata is talking about on the phone, with someone, maybe Kapoor? But I cannot be sure. Kapoor wouldn't be interested in such things, his measures of the world are quite different.

I am sleeping in the room next to the kitchen while Sujata sleeps in the other wing beyond the dining and sitting. There are two more rooms, and Kapoor must be using one of those. All of us have got keys.

'I'm fit to travel,' I tell her another morning. I am feeling uncommonly energetic. The scar tissue was healing and the bruises are also suddenly looking better.

'I am not sure. Let the bruises heal,' she says.

'This isn't a picnic for me. I've important work at home and need to rush back as soon as possible. Besides, there is news of heavy rain in the districts; and if there are floods, I will get stuck,' I say.

She looks alarmed. Still, I insist.

'Everything can wait. You have been through hell and I can't let you go like this. You are weak and on antibiotics. Please try to understand…' she says while fastening the latch of a window facing the garden.

'Am I being kidnapped, huh? Thanks for everything but I don't need your kindness,' I tell her and march out of the house.

I am at the garden gate. She comes right after me. 'I won't be responsible if anything happens…' but she doesn't finish the sentence. She looks up and down the street and steps back into the house.

I don't know what to do. Perhaps I can leave this weekend. But she continues arguing and I have to shout at her. The tension is quite horrible after that.

Next morning, she looks happy. She smiles mysteriously and holds her gaze when I ask her if there was a train that I could take this weekend.

My body is humming with energy today. There is a buzz of joy in my head, a bracing feeling, like sea breeze sweeping over me. But the joy is laced with ambiguities. This, I think, has to do with a dream I had last night.

I was with a woman on a boat. Couldn't recognise her...but still, she looked familiar. She had soulful eyes and the sailboat had a wide deck—just the two of us. It was in the middle of a lake, the water sapphire-blue. The hour was twilight. But the lake was not still; there were ripples. We were talking sitting on the deck, and once a water taxi passed, cutting out our conversation. And when I had nothing to say, she started singing a song. One song, then another...and from the depths of the lake rose a beautiful music to accompany her singing till a time came when I began to feel really light-hearted and happy. I pulled the deck-chair closer. We were sitting very close now, and then we leaned closer and kissed. Her lips—plump, wet and soft. Obviously, she had stopped singing, and now there was only the music from the depths of the lake—a hidden orchestra, and the boat was bobbing gently.

I took her in my arms and began kissing her, all over—my hands cupping her warm breasts then pressing harder. My hands then reached under her mirrored skirt which had the colours of the rainbow. She gently caressed my temples with an ostrich feather that had been lying beside her. I looked back and there it was, the dead ostrich...all bloody and injured.

I screamed but she pressed her palms on my face. My head reeled as she pressed herself against me.

We kicked the deck chairs away and they flew into the water, turning slowly over and over again, tumbling noiselessly into the deeps. We were on the deck now. And we were both moving, slowly at first, then faster, then slow again—and it went on like this. The deck was bloody with ostrich blood, and our naked bodies were painted red by it like pantomime artists playing the dance of devils.

The music went on, sometimes in rhythm with our bodies, then at a different tempo altogether. This continued, seemed to go on forever—the music rose, it billowed and pulsated with energy, a scherzo it was, then higher to ever higher notes, to frequencies beyond the ken of common instruments, and soon the joy coursed through our flesh, I groaned, she kept shivering with pleasure, the dead ostrich's head was dangling from its broken neck over the blue ripples. The dream still haunts me while we have our morning coffee.

'There is a train but you won't get any reservation. I've checked. Besides, the tracks are flooded and the rail service is uncertain,' she says.

She doesn't object to my plan to return home, but she doesn't help either.

'Oh, so there are floods already?' I ask, not sure if she was making it up.

'All around. No one has heard of floods here in decades. This time we had these abnormal summer rains, and they had to open some river barrages to release water,' she says.

It had rained heavily the night before. There is water standing in the lawn and the leaves are glistening fresh. 'There is continued forecast of bad weather, so please hang on,' she adds.

I don't have a good argument. Perhaps she is right. I finish my coffee and drift away. Soon, the situation turns bad in the city too. It is no surprise, for the weather has been getting weird everywhere as we piss our dreams up into the heavens.

Then suddenly the rain stops one evening, and there is a ferocious dust storm—like a break in the story to allow one singular actor, like a portent, to appear. The *aandhi* rampages through Bhaskarnagar for an hour, howling down the streets, and covering every tower and tomb with inch-thick dust. And then, around midnight the rain is back. The rain returns and never stops. It rains torrents all through the night.

The front lawn is now completely flooded, and the tin and pasteboard dwellings of construction labourers further up the street have been flattened by the fury of the wind. Whatever could have been salvaged is now drowned in rivers—that's what the streets have become. The workers have taken shelter in the upper floors of a five star hotel coming up a little way down the road.

It's in the darkened lobby of the hotel that we see it that night. Not sure, whether it's me or Kapoor who sees it first; we don't talk so much. I guess he doesn't like my company anymore. But both of us notice those eyes shining in the pitch dark cavern of the reception area, and then that chattering laugh which chills the blood of even the most seasoned hunters.

I panic and try to run, but the water is knee deep in the lobby and it isn't easy. Waves of dirty water swish around us as we rush towards the gates, struggling to keep ourselves steady. When I manage to switch on the torch and sweep the beam across the enormous lobby, the faint beam doesn't pick up anything.

The labourers are sheltering in two upper floor suites of the hotel, and we have organised cooked meals for them with the help of Sujata's law firm. The young lawyers have chipped in with money and a local NGO, Prakash, has taken the initiative to cook—and also provide dry food, medicines and other disaster ration.

'Did you see something downstairs?' I ask the stranded construction workers.

They look at each other and their cloudy eyes tell us nothing. They take the packets of ration, join their hands in a namaste and walk away quickly, their wan faces withdrawing into masks. We have managed to get some solar lanterns, and they eat their rice and dal with this blessing of the sun throwing whispery light across the cavernous suites of the unborn hotel.

The water has risen chest high in the lobby, and it is no more possible to walk through it. The volunteers from Prakash, who have fashioned a makeshift raft out of empty jerrycans to ferry the relief, think we shouldn't scare the labourers with questions. They are smart people with a lot of experience working in disaster-affected areas.

But the volunteers don't turn up the next morning, so the NGO sends two medical graduates with some supplies. But it's never enough. The rains continue, and without the rafts it would have been impossible to reach the stranded people.

As we are at the edges of the city with hardly any residential houses, the government relief effort and disaster relief personnel have not arrived here yet. Behind this unfinished hotel, wooded hills mark the city limits, the slopes looming like a thicker curtain of black rain. Tears of the world slowly falling, transforming into great chunks of slate grey.

That night we hear the blood chilling laughter again, and then an ear-piercing cry. Kapoor rushes out of his room cursing, I can hear him trying to open the front door.

I jump out of bed to stop him but there is no one outside. Sujata is there too.

'Should we go out and check?' I ask her.

'No,' she says firmly. The piercing cry, puncturing through the rain and lashing at the windows, remains with me till I fall asleep once more.

They find the mason's body, torn to pieces and floating in the lobby near what would be the black granite reception counter of the hotel. The blood marks on the stairs seem to suggest that he was attacked there, and then dragged down here along the elevated floor skirting the lobby. Otherwise the rising flood water may have floated the corpse all the way to the reception area.

I remember him from the other night because he had helped us unpack the meals. Parts of his face were eaten and his heart had been torn out. We find the labourers cowering in their suite as we approach with the cooked meals.

'It's a *kaftar*, living in the reception,' one of them says, trembling.

'What's that?" I ask the young doctors.

Sujata is right beside me. She makes a grave face, 'Half-hyaena and half-human. People here believe evil magicians transform into a hyaena at night and take away young children.'

I was amused but couldn't laugh; the corpse was bobbing in the water at our feet. 'We have to call for help,' I said. I think I know where the hyaena might have come from. But they rarely attack people.

'We cannot have a hyaena living in this hotel and stalking our workers,' the pot-bellied contractor, who appears that day, says.

I keep quiet. I'm very much in a mind to feed him to the starved animals. But I am getting dead tired with all the work for the relief effort. Now the volunteer group is planning to extend their reach further. They will be going to outlying villages with relief material, and also performing skits to create awareness about health, hygiene and changing weather.

More people have come forward with money. I am happy to be of use but fatigue has been killing me. There is still some good left in this world? I ask myself as I settle down in my bed for the night. That night I see the hyaenas. Two adults prowling around on the high ground, on the other side of the road. I had been to the toilet, and then I heard that eerie laughter which sends shivers down the spine of the bravest. I open the main door quietly for a better look. Who can resist the unknown?

They fix me with their stares. They've seen me. How easily you hypnotise me, reminding where we came from. That we had never been without each other, whatever they might have told us. Between them and me, this gurgling river of storm water and a low picket fence.

I try to step back but my legs have turned to stone. I stare into the darkness all night. Their eyes burn up the darkness and a scent of fire, somewhere close, begins to gather around me.

WEIRD WEATHER

The storm brings desert dust to the city, from where it will travel eastward, spreading a grey blanket across the northern lands. It will journey to Aukatabad, Meherganj and Ramrahimpur, and cities further still, smothering people and towns with its asphyxiating shadow. Dressed thus like spectres, the monster metros and their inhabitants will live on with their rasping coughs and sleep-inducing bronchodilators till the air heavy with misdeeds will send them all beyond the shiny bright tomorrow that was about to appear. But here, it is still raining.

Kapoor is looking irritated. He disapproves of everything about the shoebox he is living in. His bedroom is small and cramped, and now the roof is leaking as the rain grows heavier over the days. He mops the floor and puts a plastic bucket where the water is dripping from the ceiling. 'Doesn't this house have a single servant', he complains; and now this woman, her eyes black like the witching hour, was getting on his nerves.

'No, you rest for a few more days…' she says as always, pausing midway, lost in thought, her expression changing to severe, adding, 'Then we will see.'

'Rest, rest! How much rest do I need? And all this rest while that fraudster, that bloody fake, fattens on my wealth. God knows! Maybe by now he has sold off my vacation home on the Riviera, liquidated much of my shares, hawked my Gulfstream; he would turn it all into cash and run. He will scoot, I know that for sure. How many days more do I have to fester in this hellhole!' He bangs the table loudly and rushes into the kitchen, a half-eaten omelette on his plate, the mustard-dripping chicken sandwich untouched.

Sujata remains quiet. 'Okay, go!' she says finally, raising her voice, 'go and wring the neck of that impostor.' Then in a more even tone, 'if that will help everyone.' She scoops out marmalade and spreads it on her bread, white as driven snow. 'Okay, go! Okay, go!' her eyes are suddenly wet with tears. Kapoor stands at the door to the kitchen, an apple in his hand. He wavers between sadness, seeing her cry, and the stinging electricity of those words, 'Go and wring his neck…'

Her tears hold him back, one more day, as the outside is slowly shut out by the rain, and the hills behind the house disappear into grey nothingness. He seems to know that he is stuck with her for some more time.

Kapoor rests. He rests and plans his comeback. He discusses his pet project Choco Raja with her when he is in the mood.

He has thought it through, he tells her. She will be the face of his campaign. He cannot think of anyone else in that role, he adds, but now they are in bed together and I have to retreat from that room.

These things happen without warning and one gets little time to step back. This moment they are having a fight, and the next, they are all over each other on the couch, and the moans and sighs fill the hall and I have to literally run out into the garden to find Darwin's finches feasting on flowers with glee.

I reckon the two are in love, or some equally crazy shit's going on between them.

I suspect this Kapoor has a crush because this evening I find her sitting on the wood and cane chair in the middle of the living room, munching handfuls of cashew, while Kapoor is walking in circles, slowly around her, talking with her, touching her hair that trembles near the floor.

But the news from Aukatabad is bad and that spoils his mood. Kapoor doesn't get any response to the messages he sends that day. His staff doesn't reach out to him. 'The impostor is well-entrenched,' he says despondently, while scribbling notes on loose sheets at the breakfast table. 'I have to change strategy with this bugger.' He pulls out another cigarette from a crushed pack and lights up. It's early morning and he is already smoking like a chimney. 'He is calling for a frontal attack and that is what he will get,' he declares and pushes the chair back before vanishing into his room. He sits there writing, making lists and planning endlessly.

'You look like a soldier with your beard gone, and that thick moustache,' Sujata tells Kapoor the next day, while they are loading dry food packets meant for the stranded construction workers.

Kapoor raises his eyebrows and looks at her sideways, 'But I never grew a beard. God knows how it appeared, I had been careless. So I shaved it off,' he looks irritated now, 'and I have always sported a moustache, everyone in this country knows. Were you living under a rock or something?'

'Perhaps, I was…' she began to say, unsurely. But then more volunteers from the NGO arrived and they got busy ferrying supplies to the stranded people.

Soon they have another fight, and this time it is about the book.

'Who reads this book?' Kapoor asks her, flicking through the pages of *The Great Derangement*.

'A friend,' she smiles and says.

'Why's it on this table? Why here? Why do you need to have other friends when I am around? Don't you realise the risks? And…and you know, I don't like it,' he brushed her with a gaze, snapped the book shut and shoved it into a drawer.

Now, turning around, he faced her. 'Who's this friend?' Kapoor glared at her, his voice sounding ominous.

'How does it matter, someone was reading, that's it,' Sujata was taken aback by the cold rage in his voice. To change the subject, she asked him if he really thought there were hyaenas sheltering in the five star hotel. But he wouldn't get diverted.

'You're lying. Now I know,' his voice climbed higher, drawn by rising anger.

'What do you know?' she stood up forcefully and began to draw the curtains, darkening the living room.

'You're sleeping with that fake, that impostor. Everything fits, yes everything's crystal clear. And you can switch on the light, there's nothing more to hide,' Kapoor said.

'What do you mean? I love you!' she said, adding, 'We don't need lights, we are going out in a short while and I have to save electricity.'

'What! Love? Electricity? Ha!' he laughed loud and hard, 'Love…yes surely, love it is! That's why you took that train with me, offered me sweets. Of course, because of your love, you realised I needed someone like you for my campaign. You took full advantage of my situation. My money, my cards just vanished! And that hotel, you suggested that doss-house. They are also with that fake. You're all in on this. You put me through that shit so that I become completely dependent on you. Yes. Haha aha, ha! Love it is! *C'est l'amour*! Now everything is as clear as fucking daylight,' he spoke in a frenzy.

'Sorry, Jay, but you're making a mistake. I'll explain everything, another time. Now we have to help with the flood relief effort, and there is much else to be done,' she said. She looked genuinely alarmed.

'Aha! Jay? Use my proper name, it's Jayant. Isn't it true you're in cahoots with that man in Aukatabad? You trapped and seduced me, so that finally you and your stupid partner in Aukatabad can frolic in the Mediterranean, on my yacht. So that you and that fake can waltz on my ashes. I know you are preparing to finish me off, put me in grave danger from which I won't be able to come out alive. Right? Is he here now? I have a hunch that he is around. Tell me where's he hiding? He's here, isn't he? I know. I can smell the poison of his sweat glands. I can smell his rotten breath hanging around you like a garland. I'll smoke him out, I'll set fire to this house and barbecue him alive. But I'll get him before he gets me!'

Tears rolled down her eyes.

His voice went a notch down but he didn't stop. 'I know who you are. You've been exposed. Never come close to me, never, or I will strangle you. Keep off. Okay! Keep well off. I know how to deal with you and that wanker beau of yours. Wait, wait one more night!'

Sujata rushes out of the room and bangs the door shut. Kapoor is quiet for a while but soon begins to groan with a massive headache. He tears his hair and tosses about in his bed. When someone from Prakash arrives later in the day, he gives him an analgesic and they leave for the office from where flood relief was being organised.

Back from that office, Kapoor disappears in his room and works on his plans to expose the impostor. He designs a new card with an outline of Prana, the cat. He makes more lists of names, scratches them out and makes another list. Later, he eats rice and fish, cursing whoever had cooked it. He says that he has never eaten fish all his life.

The skies are always so dark that lights burn in houses all through the day. Parts of the city are still flooded, and it rains heavily and without interruption, an endless torrent. Kapoor looks around him. He is in that dingy NGO office once again where one group is gathering relief material while another is rehearsing. They are actors rehearsing a performance. One of them with a bushy moustache, a character he instantly dislikes, asks him, 'Are you comfortable playing this role?'

Friggin' heavens! Has he been manipulated into an awareness building team of social workers? He feels like punching this man in the face. What does he mean by 'playing this role'? He tries to remember what part he was playing and where the stage was supposed to be. The other man keeps waiting for a response. And then, like a thunderclap, the horrible headache strikes again.

Kapoor thinks it's a dream. A nasty joke someone has pulled on him. But it clears in seconds, for those lights are bright and painful in his eyes. Without warning they light up these ragged people, these kids in tatters, these men around the unfamiliar courtyard, as if they were drawn out of the moist desert air. The low clouds roiling above, and hundreds of expectant eyes focussed on him.

Kapoor has no idea what he was supposed to do. A tune playing on a speaker over an amplifier past its prime. Old Bollywood melody sputtering from cracked solder joints. Oh! What is he doing here, why is he dressed like countryfolk, and with this spirit bottle in his hand? What is he expected to do… what? Hard as he tries, his mind returns a blank.

They are getting restive, the hundred pairs of eyes, and he notices the two men and the woman at the centre, standing before him. Dressed like him and one looked like he'd painted his face. Why? It seemed they are waiting for him to speak.

All of them. The survivors, those living on high ground, those whose villages have been saved by a whisker. They are all waiting. Thunder growls overhead and a shiver passes through the gathering. A silent reptile slithering over naked flesh, freezing hearts, a hyaena's laughter in the dead of night.

They still wait for him. Their eyes turning white with fear at the anger of the skies. The water's coming closer each day. Now the music leaps up a few notes, people crowding nearer to each other for the flimsy assurance of human warmth. The circle around him gathering like a noose. The beckoning darkness behind the circle is so close now. He can reach it by jumping over their heads. One long leap. A knight of old, a phantom in flight.

Faint shapes of camels in the distance. Ship of the desert, ready to sail through the blanketing clouds! He races in that direction. A roar rising from behind him. The clapping of amused children. Shrieks, hoots and swearing follows him. But the darkness is safe and warm with death.

He dashes across the distance, his shoes throwing up wet sand. Bewildered, they come after him but give up. What's the point? The camel is fast. Faster than any creature on land that night. It takes him through kingdoms of water, passing abandoned villages on the way, across a swift flowing aqueduct, the water roaring angrily below and then through miles of darkness. Up on a high road and then ahead further where, like an impassable barricade, night stands its lonely guard.

A FIERY WARNING

It had been two days since he had disappeared. A volunteer from the NGO, a stringy adolescent who acted in the street play, had brought Sujata the news after they returned from their relief and awareness trip to outlying villages. He had vanished into the rain and darkness.

Lonely and tired in her room, she slowly realised how much she missed him. What had gone wrong? She shouldn't have let him get involved with the relief efforts. But it was he who had shown interest in helping the stranded labourers, and then the disaster preparedness and relief effort. But she could no more be sure if he was speaking his mind. She should have accompanied them. Sometimes, she feared the worst. What should she do now? Her energy had been sapped by the weight of his absence.

She switched on the TV and surfed channels aimlessly. Police was playing Synchronicity. The distilled sounds of rock at its zenith made her close her eyes as she leaned against the headboard. Music speaking through contrasts, through the shades of its monochrome. Music that knew much but said little.

As the song faded she went to the kitchen and put her dinner to warm; she waited for the microwave to beep. From the room came the strains of another Sting song, 'Every Breath You Take'. That touching melody that lost love would be humming till the waters rise high above our heads. What the song told her was so much what had been happening to her life. 'Every Breath you take...I'll be watching you'... Why did the channel have to play this song now? Was someone watching her right then?

She remembered what she had been told, and a cold chill went down her spine. Could she run away from it all... run away with him and disappear? She wanted to give it all up and be close to him. They could tune their lives to the same key, and she could take him to those places which only she knew about; places where no one could reach them. Outside, it was a wet night. Bhaskarnagar breathed heavily in the steamy darkness, the city fast asleep. Only near the northern gates, in the district of transporters and repair shops, there was frenetic activity—loading and unloading of crates, hollering of porters, blows of hammers and the snap of wood cracking under crowbars, cartons being unloaded, bolts being noisily unfastened, orders being relayed at the top of the voice. From somewhere in that shadowy neighbourhood of sweat and oil, they had set off for her address.

It had rained again in the afternoon, and parts of the city were still flooded. At the centre of town, the art deco lampposts cast fluid reflections on the wet oil-slicked avenues, revealing the hidden city that only a few have seen. A show that transformed with the slightest wind or the passing of a cab. Here and there, light towers with stylized domes and the chill of fluorescent. Inside these glass menageries, enchanting women—sultry-eyed, high-cheekboned, lips painted crimson with the scales of the cochineal parasite—were selling European holidays or anti-ageing cream, hyaluronic acid and 5G sims. The hired Scorpio went rumbling along this vista of illusions where orange sodium weaved deeper phantasms, preparing the stage for the visible and invisible worlds to collide. Perhaps the hidden passengers of this automobile, weaving through the empty streets of Bhaskarnagar, were bringing with them rage that bordered on madness.

A little while back, Sujata had switched off the lights. She was lying on her bed watching TV, late night news. The newscaster went on in her tone of thoughtful nonchalance. The headboard creaked, or maybe it was the bed. The furniture of this private guest house often tried to tell the current boarders the secrets they had gathered over the years.

She was still thinking about him. Then she felt he was out there in the living room and wanted to go and check; she had heard something. A faint rustle from somewhere. Could it be that he had returned? Or was it the rats?

The rats were ancient inhabitants of the city who lived an undisturbed life. People had their food stolen by them, their books destroyed, their provisions pilfered but they didn't mind. The only proactive counter to the rat menace were the prayers offered to Ganesha, for the rat was the mount of this revered deity.

While she was wondering if it could be a rat, the noise she had heard before had changed. This could not be rats. Perhaps some bigger animal? No, those were footsteps on the verandah. Then the sound stopped. She held her breath. Was someone trying to break in, or could it be him? Had he come back, but how would he enter the grounds? The gate was locked; however, one could easily climb over the picket fence.

Couldn't be him. He wouldn't try to climb over the fence. She had the keys to the front gate. Sujata dug into her knapsack to check the keys. She swung off the bed, tiptoed towards the window and peered through a gap in the shutters.

An open verandah skirted the house, widening into a porch at the front, beyond which was the lawn and the main gate. The flood water had drained off but the lawn was wet and mushy, and strewn with detritus that the water had brought from the street. It was enclosed by the chest-high picket fence and lined by thorny bushes. Along one side was the driveway. Two sturdy gulmohars stood at one corner, right at the edge of the lawn where the fenced boundary turned sharply and disappeared behind the house.

It was dark outside but for a faint yellow glow hanging like a cobweb around the gate lamp. She saw two figures moving stealthily, sneaking up the verandah. They were coming in her direction. As they approached the façade of the house they scanned the wall, and then the pillars.

The two men came right up to where she was hidden behind the window, and one was pointing above their heads at the exterior wall. He was well-built, about six feet, and wore a long raincoat speckled with rain and a cap with a chinstrap. He had something in his hand which looked like a crowbar for jimmying locks. The other man, much shorter, had a thickset brutish face, and he had such a cruel look in his eyes that Sujata gasped when she saw him standing so close. He was carrying a jerrycan. This guy had a vermilion streak on his forehead, and his bucktooth was shining in the faint light.

Will they try to break in? She could call out for help with the hope that someone would hear. But the nearest house belonged to a private school, and there would be no one there except for the caretaker who would be dead drunk. The hotel further down the road was still waterlogged, and the labourers—even if they heard her—won't be able to make it here in time. Too late to call the police, and then there would be many questions.

The shorter of the two opened the jerrycan and began to splash some liquid on the walls and on the chairs kept outside. Petrol! His partner pulled a tool from his pocket and reached up to the wall. The electricity metres were just above his head. What! They were trying to short circuit the electric wires and start a fire! That's what she thought they were upto. And when she rushes out, they will shoot her and dump her body into the flames.

She went stiff for a second but was alert right the next moment. With a swift movement she swept away the curtains, pushed the shutter and stood straight in front of the window.

The thuggish-looking character with the jerrycan took a step back at the sound and then he saw her. He gave out a low whistle to warn his companion while trying at the same moment to draw his gun. But whatever happened after that was too fast for him, or anyone for that matter.

It is impossible to provide an exact record. If someone was watching, they would have seen her cross her hands after she swept away the curtains to face the hired hitmen. She joined her hands, crossing her arms in that millennia-old swastika mudra—which they say can even stop the devil in his tracks.

It could have ended there but didn't. As she made the hand gesture, buck-tooth whistled but he couldn't draw his gun. An ice shower from another world froze his muscles. He turned to stone, buried as if under an avalanche of ice.

Through that daze he saw the curls of her hair writhe and twist, having come to life, animated and growing longer. Sinuous dark ribbons hissing their way out through the window, hoods raised, fangs exposed. Till there was no one on this side, only these swarthy hissing messengers of death slithering into the verandah.

The taller of the two hearing the other whistle, cursed under his breath, 'Damn! What is it *yaar*?'

He glanced to his left but it was all too late. All that Sujata heard as she stepped back was a blood-curdling cry of agony as a blue tongue of fire leapt out from the metre box lashing at the two, flinging them back. Both were knocked out cold. It was only left for the fire to do the rest.

A hot train of sparks charged ferociously through the wires and licked the petrol doused wall. Within seconds the lawn lit up with this eerie blue light. Blue changed to white. Flames shivered like teasing tongues. Now they leapt through walls and doorways, and were streaking across the ceiling of her room in angry crimson arrows.

She threw on her jacket and rushed towards the passage for the kitchen exit. Amitav Ghosh's book about climate change still lay open on the couch where Chanchal had left it. She stopped, scooped it up and stuffed it into her knapsack. A book is always a good weapon, hardbacks are even better. Below the book was a half-eaten bar of Atman dark chocolate; she had given it to him.

She took a bite and jammed it into her pocket. The curtains in the passage had caught fire from the radiated heat coming from the next room. She made a dash for the kitchen. If it got hot beyond a point, the gas cylinder would explode. Not another moment to lose!

But the kitchen door leading out to the backyard was jammed. She struggled with the oil and grime-caked bolt, losing precious minutes. Is this how she will go then? Scorched beyond recognition in a guest house of Bhaskarnagar with two corpses in the front lawn? Though she was still alive, she knew those two didn't have much of a chance. The fire breathed heat into the kitchen, an angry intruder waiting to be let in. Crackling as it devoured wood and brick, almost genial, almost merry. Sujata struggled with the bolt as the kitchen became brighter with the glow of hot orange against black.

OUROBOROS

AN OLD SALT

It's a lot of work for Kapoor, getting out of the flooded desert. That panic attack, the red hot gaze of the audience at the school, the survivors closing in around him like a noose, he had to run. He leaps over their heads. He sees the camels in the distance. Darker shapes against the night. A helpful camel-driver was at hand.

Sikander is from one of the villages of the desert that the rains had flooded. Though the water doesn't stand for long in the desert, it does enough damage for the time it does. Sikander is happy with what Kapoor offers and off they go, the powerful animal taking them away at great speed. Real fast—through sunken villages and submerged roads all across the barren emptiness—pounding along through the darkness towards the closest town where a night bus might be available. It begins to rain again, and having no cover of his own Kapoor begins to get drenched when Sikander offers him a piece of plastic, which is not of much use either.

The bus to Aukatabad has already pulled out of the terminus but thanks to the intrepid Sikander, they are able to stop it with a risky manoeuvre which could have injured the camel-riders and the bus passengers. The driver jams the brakes and angrily blares the horn. Whoever is out on the road on this rainy night at this municipality town would see this curious sight of a camel blocking the way of a long distance bus, followed by an angry exchange of words, and then the camel lowering itself and the bus conductor opening the passenger door.

The night bus to Aukatabad resumes its journey. A rickety box on wheels with soiled curtains and gutted upholstery. The aisle clogged with bags, bundles and suitcases, and it's almost impossible for him to reach his seat. Crawling and skipping, he manages somehow but it's hard on someone used to luxury cars and private jets. Not easy by any stretch.

Kapoor tries to sleep but the bumpy ride makes this impossible. However, everyone else seemed to be sleeping soundly. The loud snoring of co-passengers feels like being whipped all through the night.

What an uncomfortable ride it was! Hours upon endless hours through desert, villages and one-camel settlements. But the city was reached at last. Sprawling endless Aukatabad getting ready for a new day.

A faint glow in the east. The wide road curving into the city, past the blurry outline of a corporate tower standing in the brown land stretching for miles. The smell of burnt leaves in the air, the breath of benzene and petroleum. Keekar trees like spirits hovering aimlessly at the edges of the nebulous grey wrapping the world. A shape-shifting demon enveloping the city of blue and white signs, and centuries-old forts.

Past sturdy office blocks and residential complexes almost invisible through the smog and over snaky flyovers coiling through the gloom. Then at breakneck speed down avenues of rosewoods, overtaking murderous buses proudly advertising their environment-consciousness, and finally the terminus. The driver parks the bus in its bay and passengers are getting up, stretching their tired bodies, down the tinned steps with their bags and bundles. Kapoor gets down and looks around.

He is back home at last! After that sordid misadventure of Bhaskarnagar. Back and ready to expose that fake. Have him hung from a tree upside down and whipped on his toes. But that would be too gross; he has better ideas. He had planned it all out while being held up at Bhaskarnagar with that treacherous woman. No, he still couldn't trust her. But he knows what is to be done with the impostor.

The terminus is crowded even at this early hour. People had wrapped handkerchiefs over their faces to keep out the smog. Kapoor's eyes are watering, his legs are aching and he badly needs to use the restroom. Luckily, there is one.

Afterwards, he eats a vegetable patty and drinks a milk shake from the counter. Most of the passengers from the bus had left by the time he is done. Only two cops toting submachine guns and wearing N95 masks stand near the bus bay, watching him. He looks away and walks out into the street.

Kapoor takes an autorickshaw to the railway station area where there are many cheap hotels, shops and hordes of backpackers. No one will recognise him easily. He is planning to put up there for a few days while meeting trusted people and launching a direct assault to unseat the fake. The obvious way would be to extract a confession from the impostor and share it with the world. But to record a confession, he has to get him in his hands first.

The traffic crawls. The yellow haze hangs over the city like love gone bitter. *Memento mori.* Dust of distant storms shrouding the metropolis. Dreams of endless prosperity gathering on alveoli till the genes go mad. Multiply, multiply! Cells dividing without God to watch over it. The god of ends has infiltrated the city. A traffic snarl clogging Citizen Place. People fearing they would miss their trains are getting off their vehicles. Kapoor pays the driver and alights. Beyond Citizen Place, a road curves eastwards towards the station and he takes this, beginning to walk at a brisk pace. The walk refreshes him a bit. That's when he sees him.

Perhaps his solid frame and towering height attracts his attention. That he is missing his left leg, or perhaps that penetrating gaze with which he is observing the endless procession of people, could be the reason why Kapoor stops.

His face is big as a copper pot with bright and intense eyes. He strokes his chin gently as their eyes meet. He is shod in dirty blue jeans, a leather side bag slung across his shoulders and his brick red kurta has sweat maps all over. The man, who seems to be in his late fifties, is sitting under a gulmohar tree on the side of the road, eating from a paper bag. A wooden crutch is kept by his side and the fiery blossoms have fallen all over him and around him, lighting up this spot.

His lips curl into a lopsided smile. Kapoor scratches his hair. This man looks familiar but he can't be sure. He fears the killer headache will return if he tries too hard to remember.

The man rises, waves his hand and, swinging smartly on his crutch, comes forward.

'What a pleasant surprise, comrade!'

Comrade! Haha! Kapoor struggles to remember if they have met while the man comes up and shakes his hand vigorously. Nothing surfaces in his memory, so Kapoor gives him a blank stare.

'Hello mate, are you all right, what brings you back to Aukatabad?' the one-legged man in the brick-red kurta pushes on.

'What do you mean *brings me back*? I have lived here since I finished my studies!' Kapoor almost snaps back. He is taken aback but keeps holding the stranger's hand. The man with the crutch offers a coffee, and so they make their way to a kiosk nearby.

It turns out the stranger is originally from Anantanagar. His name is Lohit but he prefers to go by his initials LJ—J being his surname, Joardar.

'LJ...that sounds like a product code. Couldn't you think of anything better?' Kapoor says, taking a sip of the hot coffee which burns his lips.

'Up to you, comrade, what you call me but, back in my hometown they all went with Comrade LJ.'

'Not comrades, understand? I'm not a bloody commie and I'm no comrade of yours either. You do look a little familiar though, but maybe it's from some movie I watched or a book I read. But don't consider me a commie. I'm an industrialist, which doesn't make us friends by any means,' Kapoor says.

'Oh, I see,' Lohit says, taking a sip from his coffee and caressing his chin. His eyes gleam with faraway thoughts.

Originally from Anantanagar, he had been with the merchant navy for some years before studying law and switching to a new profession. As a criminal lawyer, he was working for the Grey and Govindan Law Firm in Anantanagar. Grey and Govindan, the name rings a bell. Kapoor pricks up his ears. Weren't these the same people who had hosted Sujata in Bhaskarnagar. Could it just be a coincidence, since this firm was big and had offices everywhere? 'So you shifted to Aukatabad quite recently?' Kapoor asks him.

'Long story but the gist is: I was fighting a case for a shipping company; they have their offices here. One of their ships had sunk off the Skeleton Coast and there was a long-drawn legal battle going on with the insurers, so I was camping here in Aukatabad most of the time. When the case was disposed of favourably, the shipping company boss was very pleased, and he offered me a position on the legal team of his group company. And you know what, this guy gifted me a talking parrot who they called Commander. Some old salt had given up the ghost, leaving the bird without a master…and I took Commander gladly,' he said and emptied his cup.

'A talking parrot must be good diversion for a lawyer. So you left that Grey and Gobbledygook and joined the legal team of the shipping company?' Kapoor looked inquisitive.

Lohit sighs loudly and his smile vanishes. 'It's Govindan. Here at the shipping company I'm on familiar territory because I am a seaman at heart. But I can never go back to sea now. Anyway, I grew very fond of Commander, though he was slightly abusive. He had travelled the seven seas and knew many sea songs by heart—including, you know that one about the dead man's chest…but then,' his coppery face began to turn soot-black like a pot kept too long on a fire, 'he just flew away one day. Since then I have been looking around for him. I have scoured this town and the next, but no luck till now. It gets very lonely without Commander around.'

'No wives?'

'Who will marry an old sea salt who walks with a crutch?' His lips crinkled into a smile.

Kapoor keeps quiet and considers his answer. This man seemed friendly. A little while ago Lohit had mentioned that he had a nice place here in Aukatabad. Kapoor needed a base to prepare for exposing the false JRK, and maybe this guy could be of some help. Lawyers are always very resourceful.

'Can you recommend a cheap place for me to put up for a few days?' Kapoor asked tentatively. Without a moment's consideration, Lohit Joardar offered his home. Lucky, because there was hardly any cash left after paying for the bus ticket.

A PRISONER

'Bring him in!' barked Jayant Roy Kapoor into an intercom, and hit a panel button, switching off all the lights of the boardroom except the one spraying the area below the screen in a pool of garish yellow. They had all left a little while back, but someone had forgotten to turn off the projector; the last slide from the presentation danced across his face, and on the screen behind him. The words 'Choco Raja' were printed in bold at the top, followed by marketing plans, names of PR agencies, slogans for the campaign. The background of the slide had pictures of luscious chocolate bars, chocolate hearts, soft and gooey fondue, and tempting cacao nibs. The pictures and words lick his florid face, tattooing him with light. His shark eyes gleam through the projector beam as he flicks open a laptop and begins typing in a password. The new chief scientist, a professor from Tel Aviv who had taken over after Vincent had reported some progress, and he wanted to check out his report again. The partnership with the government would be formalised in the next quarter and he was hoping that by then there would be some concrete news from the lab.

As he begins to study the scientist's report, his grey smoke cat, Prana, appears under the table and begins to rub his head against his legs. Then he settles down close to his feet and closes his eyes for a nap. The projector makes clicking sounds punctuating the silence of the room.

Suddenly, a side door bursts open and a man swathed in bandages enters, wheeling in someone on a chair. The person sitting on it is Sharma, who used to be his PA. He is in his early sixties, with a thin moustache, and a balding pate ringed by a fringe of white hair. Sharma is lashed to the chair with nylon ropes. His feet are also tied. He looks emaciated and pale. He is breathing heavily and looking down as the bandaged man gives the chair a kick and it rolls straight towards the screen, bangs against the wall and comes to a stop with a shudder. Prana meows loudly and pads away through the half-open door.

'Bullet! You'll damage the walls,' JRK snaps at him, looking up from his computer screen, 'Now close that door!' It is hard to recognise the bandaged man as Bullet, except for those eyes dripping with malice. Part of his face has been badly burnt, and the red blistered skin can be seen peeping out from the edges of bandage near his neck as he goes back to close the door.

One of his hands is completely swathed while in the other he is holding a tong, at the end of which is a bluish black snake with prominent stripes. The deadly krait writhes and hisses as he holds it threateningly close to Sharma, just out of reach for the snake to strike him dead with its ten milligram cocktail of neurotoxin venom.

The President of Atman Group looks on with an unruffled gaze as his ex-PA cowers in fear—whimpering, tears streaming down his cheek.

'Now tell the boss who these people are, what they are after…' Bullet says, holding the tong with the krait threateningly above Sharma's head.

'Believe me, please, I don't have a clue. That email made no sense to me.'

'It was sent to you and some others asking for help. What sort of help? Evidently whoever sent it is known to you,' JRK said in a matter-of-fact voice while scrolling down the chief scientist's report.

'I have worked with you for twenty years, sir and never a word has slipped out from this mouth,' he looked at Bullet with fear-laced eyes. Bullet gnashed his teeth.

'We lost a genius scientist and no one still knows how. Then these emails to you asking to be prepared, asking for help— prepared for what? Then that dead girl. What is happening in this organisation? What kind of help are these people asking for? You cannot say you know nothing…' JRK fixed his gaze on Sharma and went on. Bullet cleared his throat, distracting him.

'And yes, look at this man,' he indicated towards Bullet, 'he went after a lead, thinking he had got to the bottom of all this mystery. And you see what has happened to him.' He raised his voice a notch or two, 'See what they've done to my most trusted bodyguard. Show him your burns,' he ordered calmly.

Bullet hesitated, his left hand being occupied with the snake tongs. He looked at his boss to be sure. Then he grabbed his shoulder bandage and gave it a sharp tug, revealing charred skin covered with a slimy white ointment and dripping yellowish pus. Sharma made a strange noise, his abdomen heaved and a jet of brownish liquid shot out of his mouth and sprayed on Bullet, drenching him with undigested remains of his last meal. The abruptness of this took Bullet unawares, and in the moment's confusion the tongs slipped from his hand and the krait slithered away and vanished under the boardroom table.

None of them dared move, fearing they would step on the snake in the semi-darkened boardroom. JRK felt a chill. A cold presence slowly slithering up his leg, up his knee, gliding over his Versace-wrapped crotch. Almost like a dream of a dawn faint as moonlight, close to a whisper, almost not there. Little alveoli stuffed with neurotoxins, a cocktail of magic drugs to change the world, this way or that. All the dreams of the world riding on him, or in those ten milligrams.

'*Behenchod*!' he hissed at the darkness.

OUROBOROS

She ran for her life. The flames were now licking the garage roof and racing towards the door. She climbed the fence at the back and then down the other side, there was no way she could safely enter the garage to get the car out.

A mushy waterlogged path, shoes squelching in the mud as she turned left, running as fast as she could. Behind her, the house was burning like a torch. The smoke and the sparks leaping at her till the deep night closed its arms around her.

She didn't know where to go. She had come out onto a narrow road flanked by office buildings and empty plots of land. Beyond the empty plots were the hills from which the hyaenas had come. She edged along the buildings, wary of pursuers. The street lights were out, sandpipers shrieked in the darkness high above the rooftops. She turned to look behind her to see if they were coming for her but it was all pitch dark. Sweat lined her face but the adrenaline kept her going. A dog barked and she stopped in her tracks. Was it barking at her?

Had it seen something? But then the dog barked again, and it was farther away.

What could she do now? Her mind buzzed with clashing thoughts, and blinking on and off, it went blank for a while. Who could she call for help? Who could help her in this forest of unknown dangers? She reached the main road. Here, the street lights were working. The sodium lamps threw vapoury beams of brooding orange at the rain-washed road which reflected the radiance, sending it away to the stars. The street was wide and empty. She could be easily spotted.

A ditch ran along her side of the road while the other side was blocked by the high wall of a factory. There was hardly anywhere she could go if they came after her now. She walked along the edge of the footpath faster now, as it had begun to rain again. If she could get an autorickshaw to take her to the train station, she would be safe. There was a stand for autorickshaws about a mile from the house but at this time of the night they would all be dead drunk.

The sultry-eyed women were still selling European holidays and hyaluronic acid in the middle of the night. The displays switched silently inside the glass and chrome light towers, and a model of indeterminate age came on with her botoxed grin. All along the street, in the rows of display boxes, she was grinning at the absurd downpour, ceaseless for a week.

Another mongrel barked. And then from behind, someone called out her name.

'Sujata.'

She froze in her tracks.

'We have been waiting for you sister,' the business-like voice was bereft of emotion, almost synthetic. Sujata huddled under a bus shed and turned to find herself looking straight into his eyes.

Tall and handsome as ever. Now in a brown leather jacket and charcoal black trousers. He had a cane in his hand and he bent forward slightly, transferring some of his weight to the stick. The leather wallets and belts were arranged on a polished wooden stand before him. The whirring of the display motor stopped as he spoke to her from within the light tower.

She was panting, a bit scared, and that made her angry, 'Yes, about time too, sir!' she said.

'They're after you.'

'Thanks for the information!' she said curtly. But still, she was thankful that he had appeared. But what should she do now?

'They tried to roast me with electricity,' she gasped, trying to check her voice, though on this midnight street there was not a soul; no pursuer in sight.

He nodded slowly as if he had just tallied grocery deliveries against orders. 'You have been protected by the Nine,' he said, then continued, 'your adversaries are dogged and ruthless. This is no common enemy.'

'Who exactly is this enemy that you talk of?'

'As you have been told, these are enemies of order, of the balance that keeps the world ticking, these are the reactionaries, inhabitants of the lower dominions but they have harnessed science-magic to trouble the earthly domain. They are worshippers of Mammon and Plutus, they are always trying to steal the Secret Books so that they can enter the mirrored chamber and become immortal while holding the higher and lower dominions in thrall. They want to see their pennants flying in all ten directions, their chariot wheels raising dust in the Four Quarters,' he finished in one breath.

'Erm, thanks for the lecture, but why are you here? To help me?' she asked.

'Later, Sujata. There is very little time to explain. They are after you so make haste! Maybe someday we will meet again,' he said, and looked deep into her marble black eyes, 'Do as I say. Run, even if you get drenched, towards that bridge over there. Cross it, and a little ahead there is a traffic island. Take the road to the left. Follow it till you reach the Circle of the Kings. Not very far. About a hundred metres from the island. There, just in front of you would be The Edifice. Once you are there, you will know what is to be done,' he said, and there was a faint whir of a motor.

'But, isn't that a shopping mall, what...?' she was about to protest. But before she could complete her sentence, the electric motor concealed inside the display box had come to life and Perfect Man had disappeared silently, and the sultry-eyed model selling holidays in France was back in business.

The Edifice was the biggest shopping mall of Bhaskarnagar. An ellipsoid structure of stone and glass with four sweeping wings, stretching their curved arms out in four directions. In drone photographs it looked like an alien spacecraft designed by a slightly mad architect. Sharply in contrast to the clean geometry of the Circle of Kings, the Edifice was a play of whimsical shapes, an amalgamation of ellipses, twisted cylinders, bent cones and curved lines, with slightly inebriated spheres piled one on top of the other—the dissonance of the forms purposefully growing as one went up to higher levels.

Sujata raced through the night rain and reached it in less than fifteen minutes.

A paved walkway went up from the road to the building. It cut through a well-manicured garden with monster-headed fountains, beds of exotic blooms and an eclectic collection of black stone statuary. There was a deer, Lord Ram in his forest exile, an archer shooting a fiery arrow, a crescent moon and star, a winged lion, the star of David, the Adoration of the Magi, an angel dancing on a grave, *apsaras* guarding the *kalpavriskha*, a cowboy on his steed, palanquin bearers, the Father of the Nation, a camel carrying tourists, the Buddha in the *bhumisparsha* mudra touching the earth and the ibis-headed Thoth, among many others. The statues had concealed lighting but tonight all of these had been switched off.

She strode down the path flanked by these silent shapes as the scent of night flowers made her dizzy. Then one of these statues sprung to life. The cowboy.

His steed started out on a trot and he signalled her to follow. The rain was coming in torrents now. She walked faster as the rider with the ten-gallon hat wove all the way around the giant building, stopping right in front of a shuttered iron door at the back. The horse stopped at the entrance and the cowboy dismounted. He pressed some buttons on a panel and, noiselessly, the steel shutters began to rise. Rolling up silently, the Edifice opened its door just enough to let her in. Then, as quietly as it had opened, the heavy shutters rolled down and the bolts snapped in place.

It was pitch dark inside. She switched on her flashlight and began to walk. In a few seconds all the lights came on, washing the interiors in a flood of radiance. She was standing at the centre of the atrium. Light washed the walls, reflected off glass, shone on giant banner advertisements dangling from the ceiling seven-storeys-high. Such a variety was advertised. From colloidal platinum incorporated serums to diamond studded headsets—it was all there. Just as she tried to focus on the confusing green on white signage, the giant banner advertisements like flags, the screaming three-storey high posters, the discount notices of the anchor store, the mannequins in the upscale apparel shops, the price lists of the gelato kiosks, the movie posters of the multiplex, the video game consoles at the games arcade—they all began to whisper. Soft, soothing, coaxing whispers, breathy at first, but soon getting louder, shrill and loud, and louder still till a roaring cacophony of voices charged at her from all sides—a tower of Babel working on speed:

Buy two get one free; The Ouroboros; Last Five Days-Super Diapers; Don't Use the Elevator; Major Discount Sale-Rush, Rush, Rush; Caution Wet Floor; Women Adore Platinum; Black is the Colour for Saturday; Work Hard Party Harder; Visit Switzerland; Party-Party-Party; Red Cottage; Wash Rooms This Way; Super Theme Parties; Unforgettable Dining Experience; Dr Subba's Slim Pills; G's Gelato; The Power of Knowledge; Chocolates for Every Occasion; Nine Unknown Men; Theme Party Tonite; Best Deals on the Planet; Unleash the Beast, Dance till you Drop; Offices, Restaurants, Bars…Bara Burger, Footlongs at Half Price …Half a Kilo of Sugar FREE! On every purchase… Shop More Live More…Fire Exit…

But then above that din in her head, a booming voice

came over the public address system of the deserted shopping mall, 'Come up to level seven', echoing in its metal and glass emptiness.

She headed for the escalator, which hummed to life soon as she stepped on.

As she approached level seven, a faint music brushed her ears. She couldn't make out where it was coming from. In a few moments it was more distinct. A low humming, like a chant, to the accompaniment of a brass gong and the rhythmic beating of a drum. She stepped off the escalator. A 'This Way' sign began to blink and she followed that direction. All the way down a long curving corridor with unoccupied shop fronts—empty and one-eyed, a curio shop, a lonely bookstore, boarded retail space and, right at the end, a huge ornate doorway.

The arched double-door of The Ouroboros was carved with the motif of the left-hand swastika repeated over and over again, enclosed in a border featuring the *Das-mahavidya*s— the ten Wisdom Goddesses and the five *dhyani*-Buddhas. The edges of the teak doors were clad in beaten copper plates inscribed with a script which Sujata could not recognise. At the entrance stood a man in the maroon robes of a monk. He had a terracotta urn in his hand.

'There will be a small cover charge,' the monk said.

Sujata looked at his face, put some money in the urn and

stepped into the dreamy darkness of The Ouroboros.

Lilting music wove through the shadows. Above it a chant, in a language faintly familiar. Drumbeats in the semi-darkness punctuated by the clang of brass. She walked down a passage that curved slowly leftwards till she entered a largish chamber. The drumbeats were louder here.

As her eyes adjusted to the faint light, she could see their silhouettes against the phosphorescent glow of the walls. It was a fairly large circular hall with a well-stocked bar on the end opposite to her. Nearer to her were low tables ringed around a dance floor. The tables all occupied. The phosphorus glow of the walls cycled between dark red to amber, blue and black.

The tables had been arranged in four concentric circles. The innermost circle closest to the dance floor had nine tables, the next had thirteen, then eighteen, and the outer circle had twenty-five tables. Each table had a seat in the shape of a large dice.

Nine men, who looked somewhere around their mid-forties, sat in the innermost ring. They were variously attired—one in silk shirt and dark trousers, another in a maroon robe like the monk at the gate, the next wore purple; if one was in a starched *veshti* and shirt, his neighbour wore a spotless white *kurta* and *churidar*, and at least one of them sported a turban or some similar headgear. Each of them had a garland of marigolds around their neck, and one man had very long graying hair.

The men sat with their hands on their laps, still, unmoving. And indeed, just as she had heard, their bodies didn't seem to touch the dice-shaped seats.

Sujata was getting goose bumps as she stared at them in awe. She had read about them in the books, heard stories about them later. How they could fold the dimensions and transform matter from one form to another. It didn't take a moment for her to realise the rare privilege she had been granted this night without an end. Sujata was standing at the court of the Nine Unknown Men!

DRY RUN

'So here we are comrade,' Lohit Joardar makes an expansive gesture as they step into the sitting area of his modest apartment. The place looks like it had been caught in a storm with piles of law books, clothes and personal effects strewn everywhere, and is in such disarray that it takes them close to an hour to find the extra futon which Kapoor was supposed to sleep on.

He sleeps like a dead man in the stranger's home while Lohit drives off in his Renault automatic and doesn't return till very late in the night. His host tiptoes in to find him awake, and so they chat a little over coffee, which kills the remaining fatigue from the bus ride. Then Lohit rolls a joint and lights up, and the papery smell of weed hangs in the air of the little apartment all through the night.

The host is quite affable, and Kapoor begins to confide in him soon. Though he was not sure whether they had really met before, the warmth and friendliness of Lohit Joardar and his offer of an accommodation persuades him to drop his guard.

Trust. A part of his mind begins to trust this ex-sailor who walked with a crutch. Also, lawyers can be very resourceful he had reasoned, perhaps he can help him with what he was planning. It was a risky decision no doubt but, right then, Lohit was his best bet.

Next morning after breakfast he was telling him a bit, and some more later that night. Lohit listened carefully as Kapoor narrated all that had happened: when he had first realised that an impostor has taken over his place while he was on an unplanned trip to Anantanagar, the house with old grandfather clocks, the night at the Imperial hotel, the hellish train journey, and about his continuing problems with the 'Nazi chocolate-maker'. How he lost his money and took the wrong train arriving in Bhaskarnagar instead of Aukatabad. He told him also about Sujata on the train and Choco Raja, and that he wanted her as the face of the chocolate campaign. He didn't reveal his weakness for her but told him why he couldn't trust her completely. Then about the floods, getting involved with the relief effort, and finally how he had run away from the middle of a street play for the affected. The journey on camelback and the bone-breaking bus ride.

Lohit listened, a twinkle in his eye, and got very interested when he began to reveal his plans. 'I have decided to strike back and unseat the fake Jayant Roy Kapoor who has taken my place, propped up by that Nazi enterprise,' he said.

'So how do you go about it?' Lohit asks when he returns late that evening. He apologises for being late, the smog has been getting worse over the days, slowing down traffic all over the city. Kapoor, who had been studying a map of the area around the Atman group head office, tells him about the failed attempt to contact some of his trusted men.

'The mailbox I created for this remains empty, except for marketing emails of Titanic impotence pills and Chinese dick enlargement kits.'

'Titanic, eh? But coming to the point, I think this strategy won't work, comrade. Don't try to contact anyone,' Lohit says, adding, 'You don't know who you can trust anymore.'

Is Lohit trying to dissuade him? Perhaps he had made a mistake by confiding in him too much.

His host seems to read his thoughts and he suddenly bursts out laughing. 'Come on man, you have to trust me!'

Kapoor raises an eyebrow but keeps quiet.

'Now, look here, you may not remember this but you and I go back far. Back in our town, the old bar with moths on the walls, you had once stood up for me when I was in a tight spot. How can I forget that? And besides, I may have my own reasons. Let's say I am a Nazi hunter. You just told me about that unscrupulous German competitor propping up the fake businessman,' Lohit says before retiring to his tiny room with a sagging spring bed and books of law lining the walls.

'What bar?' Kapoor raises his voice, 'I just met you the other day!'

But there is no response from the other side of the door.

Lohit is stuck in traffic again and returns late the next day. There is kebab and parathas in the fridge and they heat it up, but the meat is stringy and the bread has almost turned to rubber. Still, they are hungry and the food is polished off in no time.

They sit and talk amidst the disorderliness of the room as the city outside falls asleep. Lohit rolls another joint, and in between deep drags, says, 'Doesn't this man have a famous cat?'

'Of course. My cat, Prana,' Kapoor looks offended, 'What do you mean by this man. Prana is my pet. He's the darling of TV channels and mascot of my business empire. He's on our logo too, now what about him?'

Lohit caresses his chin and his eyes change colour, 'Oh! Nothing, just that it reminded me of Commander. You know, I still dream about him…and in there the parrot tells me stories of the sea, of shipwrecks and fierce storms. But he never says where he has gone, why he has been hiding from me. People who have never had pets would never know what difference they make to our lives.' His eyes glistened with tears and his voice was hoarse with sadness.

'Definitely, I agree, which is why I can't wait any longer. God only knows what that impostor has been up to, how he has been treating my pets and how fast he is wrecking the company. I have been thinking what would be the best way to unmask him. You said you had an idea?'

'Did I say that? Well, I could have suggested the legal route but now that he is already well entrenched, it would be difficult to make quick headway. Instead...' the gleam was back in his eyes, and his big face glowed under the light of the stand lamp.

'What?' Kapoor asks.

'We could track his movements and try an abduction. If we get him, we can press him hard to confess on camera.'

'What about bodyguards, security?' Kapoor wasn't too sure.

In fact, I should have warned him right then but he hardly acknowledges my presence anymore. We rarely talk and he has been too busy with his plans. Meanwhile, Lohit goes on insisting that his idea is foolproof.

'It might sound risky and difficult but because of the work I do, I have contacts in all walks of society. We have to gather information about his daily routine, that's crucial. But the main operation has to be handled by us. As for the getaway and shelters, all that can be arranged,' Lohit says.

Kapoor eyed him incredulously but I knew already he would get convinced. I always know these things about Kapoor, though I fail to change his mind. I can see him being drawn into this great danger but I have given up. He is not my lookout. We are independent. I will warn him, but that's the most I will do.

'We are tracking his movements, comrade,' Lohit was bursting with excitement the next day. 'We are doing it very discreetly, nothing can go wrong.'

With no other idea occurring to him, Kapoor nodded before returning to his maps of the city. Studying maps of the commercial centre where Atman's head office is located, making sketches of the office building, drawing plans and layouts and marking out streets of the area all this keeps him occupied. In the evening, he take swigs from a century old bottle of Jamaican that Lohit keeps locked in a safe, diluting the remains with tap water.

Soon they receive solid information from a contact. Sharp at 7:00 in the morning, the impostor comes for a walk in a park near the Gate of the Emperors, and leaves around 8:00. There are not many people around at that time.

It is time to get in on the act. It is decided that Lohit will be dropping Kapoor off close to the area and he would do a few recces, checking out everything before they finalise their plan.

They share leftover sandwiches and set out early the next day. A little while ago, Lohit had asked him not to smoke because strong smells can alert pets that accompany morning walkers. Kapoor didn't like that advice; he looks grim and is silent throughout the journey.

The city is swimming in a layer of smog, and the dust of the desert storms earlier that week had begun to gather in the air. The cars that are out on the roads this early have switched on their fog lamps.

Lohit drops him below an overpass and drives off. Kapoor looks relieved and lights a cigarette. He walks aimlessly through parks and gardens, admiring the flowers, watching the morning walkers who, despite the smog, have come out in hordes. He lingers in the shadows of the great jacarandas with their crown of purple blooms, takes a stroll through the lush lawns, and then along the pools of water near the gate with bobbing tourist boats painted red as blood.

He saunters up the low hill and gazes at the imposing structure of the gate with rising exhilaration: He is back in his city. Aukatabad. The centre of his business empire. A wave of confidence washes over him. The sun peeps above the jamuns and jacarandas. Kapoor rubs his hands, and his face brightens up. Very soon, he will be back at the helm of the huge ship that is Atman Group—an empire that nurtures and feeds thousands. Warmed by invigorating thoughts, he jogs all the way down and walks into an enclosed garden which Lohit's contact had marked out on the map. Seasonal flowers and giant trees everywhere. A couple of morning walkers here. He breathes in the air, looks around, and there he is!

Alone on the edge of a lily-pond with a marble fountain gushing in the middle. A fine spray falls on him as he skirts the pond and comes even closer to Kapoor. His neck is thick as a bull's and he walks with a swagger, planting each foot with determination.

Kapoor watches and the anger rises—annihilating rage coiling inside him, looking for release. In the shadow of a tree, he notices the armed bodyguard, buck-toothed with cut marks on his face. His head reels. He bites his lips hard as he watches the impostor come around, closer. The metallic taste of warm blood in his mouth. He bites his lips harder, canines puncturing soft tissue. Kapoor tries hard to stop himself from charging at him right then.

THE GREATEST SECRET

Sujata had stopped in her tracks. The inner circle of nine men was silent. They had their eyes closed and seemed to be listening to music. As she wondered what she should do next, a man in a colourful patchwork dress got up from the outer ring and came up to her. He was the blind baul Arup Das. Arup introduced himself and led her towards the centre.

The guests at the outermost circle of tables were the most animated. She found them all there. Fellow travellers on her journey. A post office clerk from the city who had helped her once before; Ishika, the dream-reader; Dutta and Kalam, the famous phrenologist duo; Khandelwal, a chiromancer hiding behind his thick glasses; the grey-haired tantric who claimed to have conquered sleep; Lady Rosebud, the tarot reader-in-residence at the Hotel Royal; the tasseomancer Anuradha, taller than the men; the satanist John Chillman, smoking a cigar; and Taru, the municipal Councillor and rhabdomancer, who could tell where treasures were buried and was currently being consulted by the metro railway project of Aukatabad.

Arup baul and Sujata cut through this group and reached the next ring of eighteen who sat quietly. They swayed to the music and chanting, which continued as she walked towards the centre of the hall. She noticed a few men in this group smoking long wooden pipes. They adjusted their eyeglasses as she passed. In this mixed group, she recognised the familiar faces of artists, scientists and authors from the last century. One of them looked like a famous Swiss psychiatrist, but she could not be sure in that light. Nor could the phosphorus glow of the chamber help her decide whether the man she had just passed was the scientist Jagadish Chandra Bose, one of the pioneers of radio transmission. Ahead of them now was a motley group of thirteen men and women from different parts of the world. One wore a wreath on his head, a few had donned cloth caps, another with long hair had tied it in a knot at the back; at least one carried a cutlass. Among them, Sujata recognised the figure of Roger Bacon, suave in a flowing tunic. He was gesticulating at a sharp-faced gentleman with prominent cheekbones, two seats to his left, pointing out something in a disintegrating volume of *The Mirror of Alchemy*. This person smiled, and in a second, Sujata recognised him—the greatest of Roman poets, and one of the early Masters of the hidden path.

She had now leveled up with the innermost circle of the Nine. The baul stopped here and pointed out the way to the centre. A shiny barstool that looked like a sea anemone was waiting. She stepped ahead with trepidation.

Sujata took her seat slowly. All eyes were on her, except for those that were closed in meditation. She looked around and now noticed another faint restless group beyond the outermost circle of twenty-five. They were airy and shapeless, most of them. Some were just a puff of smoke, while others were half formed, a limb or two sticking out of a gaseous blob, there were others whose shapes were topological problems, hard to describe. These shimmery presences were ranged along the walls of The Ouroboros.

'Good that you have come, I hope it wasn't too difficult getting here?' one of the nine men spoke. He had a shock of white hair, and was wearing a dark silk shirt which imparted an air of aristocracy to his person.

'No, sir,' Sujata said, her voice almost a whisper. She was tense, her heart was still going fast but she kept it to herself.

'Relax, sister,' the man said, adding, 'Meanwhile, let's sort out some urgent matters.'

Someone brought her a glass of a greenish drink which emitted light. Hope it's not radioactive, she told herself before taking a sip. It had the burn of alcohol and she immediately felt better.

Another of the nine addressed her. 'The seriousness of the issue can't be underestimated. As you know we are banking upon you,' saying this, he rose. He was the one with long graying hair, and he stood at more than six feet tall. His lips curled into a momentary smile. 'Sit comfortably, sister,' he said, 'we need to discuss this threadbare.'

Sujata sat erect, her large eyes in an unwavering gaze. The tall man continued to stand and speak, moving slightly, shifting his weight from one foot to the other, 'Look at this hall here. You are the centre now, right in the middle of it all.'

The music had still been playing faintly, but now it fell silent. The clang of brass also stopped and a hush descended upon the gathering. The hall reverberated with his booming voice. And though it was not even as big as a cinema theatre, it seemed she was hearing him in a huge auditorium. It was the richness and depth of that voice. 'You stand both at the beginning and the end of everything. Remember, it's a privilege to be where you are right now. As you look out, you see the past. We all arrived here before you, if you want me to put it that way,' he cleared his voice.

Sujata swept her gaze once more over the assembly. It was hard to put the Nine in any time period but she had been told they appeared on the scene about two thousand years ago, and with rigorous training under a Tibetan teacher, have mastered the energy wheels—making them completely deathless. The circle behind them was definitely populated by men of antiquity. She could tell from the way they were dressed, their hairstyles and everything. And the group after that was closer to the present. Finally, the outermost group was populated by men and women from these times. She realised she was really peeping into time through these figures—from the past to the present—while the future lay concealed, curled tightly into itself like a great serpent, somewhere, perhaps within these very walls of The Ouroboros. A feather of excitement stirred inside her.

She knew that each of the Nine had a particular responsibility which they had been bearing for millennia, a subject of human endeavour and achievement which they guarded from misuse. Just as classified military technology is not made available to civilians, the powerful society of the Nine have been guarding advanced developments in different fields from falling in the wrong hands. She tried to fix the identity of the one who was talking with her, and wondered what the specialisation under his watch was. But then, he spoke again, 'Serious misfortunes stare us in the face. Cunning people want to play God. They plan to sell *Moksha* from chocolate boxes. It's dangerous, and a huge threat. They also desire to steal the Secret Books. You know we cannot let this happen.'

What did she know? Sujata wondered, 'I know a little, sir, but much still escapes me,' she said haltingly.

'We will come to that but this is just to remind you about our responsibilities, about the powers the nine of us keep in our custody lest they become weapons in the hands of irresponsible people—lest they threaten Creation itself. Let me give you an example or two. Defence scientists have built ballistic missiles that can rain fire across great distances because some of the material from one of the Nine Books were leaked by mischief-makers. But we can never agree with the uses you have put these to. You build rockets to kill, weapons to vapourise cities, to obliterate and annihilate a great work. Same with unnecessary gene manipulation, same when you modify dangerous viruses!' his voice rose, but he soon regained composure, 'This is why our great emperor, the Beloved of the Gods, asked us to be careful. But as they say, we are human beings after all. There had been many instances when material from the Books was put to wrong use, and the results are for all to see. Today, you have the precautionary principle; technologies not well understood, which can possibly cause boundless harm and catastrophe are better not employed, they are better kept guarded, and that's exactly what we do,' he looked around his own circle, and the others nodded. Next, he made a hand gesture summoning someone from the back.

A balding man in a white cassock, red velvet cap and a dagger-like beard came shuffling. His dress was dirty, and there were stumps in place of his hands. He came and stood silently at the centre of the gathering.

'Meet Gerbert of Aurillac.'

Sujata rose to offer her seat. The other man declined, and his face remained stern and unsmiling. She had seen him when she entered but didn't recognise him then… Sujata stood still.

'Gerbert is a man of sharp intellect. As you know he went on to become Pope Sylvester II. He had read some of the Books and he had been gifted the secrets of building the talking head *automaton* by one of us here. But then…' at this, the Pope mumbled something which didn't convey anything to Sujata, 'yet he misjudged by sharing the secrets.'

The pope showed no emotions on his face but looked at Sujata in the eye. Heavy-lidded with sadness, crow's-feet all around. 'My bones will rumble each time they pass, every time they pass…' the pope said, and went on repeating the same words. A man in a dark cape came up and helped him back to his seat.

The hall was quiet for a few minutes. Her interlocutor had vanished; his seat remained empty. She was beginning to feel hungry and tired. It had been a long and stressful night. She took another sip of the glowing drink. She felt like digging into her knapsack for the chocolate, but controlled the urge. Chocolate would have helped her concentrate. How can they be so mean as to not offer her anything to eat when food had been served to many of them? Surely they knew what she had been through tonight. At least the Nine should know, they were supposed to know almost everything.

She felt uncomfortable, brushed by the gazes of the audience. The tall man returned from his loo break, and was speaking again, 'Now tell us how it has been going. We know they have tried to harm you. Of course, they couldn't. But explain to us why you have been unable till now to make Chanchal Mitra do what we want. Weren't you trained by the master Caligari in the dark arts? Why is this man, Chanchal Mitra, still not strong enough to work for us?'

'Maybe he will, soon,' Sujata blurted out without thinking, 'the flooding of the desert upset everything.'

'Inanities may be avoided, sister!' the voice thundered, 'May all present here be told what progress has been achieved.'

She told them briefly what she knew about Chanchal's condition. 'I cannot always predict how he would react to a suggestion. But I had been with him all this time. To prepare him for it, so one could gently suggest, coax the stream to follow the right course,' she completed in a worry-mixed voice.

A hum was heard among the circles. The airy shapes at the back kept very quiet. 'How then has the stream been flowing, oh sister? I heard that it now flows right through your heart…' there was a quiver of mockery. Someone whistled from the second ring. A momentary mirth rose from the gathering.

Her heart began beating fast. She was seized by a strong sense of disorientation. She had been fighting a battle against herself, never expecting this would be so difficult. Sujata suddenly realised that very moment under the phosphorous glow of the nightclub—woven together with all the dimensions folded upon each other, full of characters from the present and the past—that she had been fighting a losing battle against the formidable forces of love. Uncertain of her words, she blurted out, 'I have lost him, he fled!'

'Holy Cows of Ahimsa! How could you do that? This is sheer disobedience. Where is Caligari? Come up to the stage!' he thundered.

A hideous-looking man with wild eyes and unruly hair, who seemed to have emerged from the catacombs, shuffled through the crowd and stopped right in front of the first row. He wore the ragged clothes of a mendicant, and his skin was pale as wax. He scrutinized her with his fiery eyes, and although he had been her teacher, she flinched from his look.

'Didn't you instruct her how to induce the holy slumber in a person so that the subject would obey orders?' the voice was now steel cold, and the mystic-doctor who went by the name Caligari grew even more pale, so much so that the phosphorus glow of the hall filtered through his skin and he looked like a cadaver soaked in a jar of formalin.

'I swear by all the angels that I did,' and he glowered at Sujata, the look singeing the skin of her face.

'I am sorry. I lost concentration. I will…I will do it. I will find him,' she said.

'May no mistakes be made this time, otherwise the shit will hit the fan,' the tall man said forebodingly, then continued with a frown, 'pardon my expression, but that's what they say nowadays, isn't it?' Many of them nodded. Then his voice was more business-like, 'Jayant Roy Kapoor is a dangerous man. He wants to play God. We know he desires to become a Master of the Higher and Lower dominions. We suspect his sights are also on the Secret Books, which we have been updating and guarding for ages.

'There are others with his ambitions; there had been others before and there will be more to come, but he has gone too far. We got hold of the lab notes of his chief scientist Vincent, who died under unfortunate circumstances. We know exactly what he is after, and we have to sabotage him… at any cost.

'Remember, he is clever and ruthless. I don't want to scare you but we know he has a collection of shrunken heads of those who fell out with him. We need you to stop him for good. All of us assembled here are behind you, but we need the help of a brave woman. True, we are using cruel methods this time but this is the way the stars predict. I am certain you will be able to return Chanchal Mitra to his former self once the job is done, we will see to that. But we have to use him now, we need the courage of holy slumber. We need Chanchal Mitra to stop Jayant Roy Kapoor in his tracks.

'If Felicity—the drug he is trying to design—is successful, an endless night will befall us. We don't know right now how far he has progressed. From the dead scientist's lab notes, it seems he was getting close. Luckily, he is gone...but they have hired a new one and they are using AI deep-learning algorithms and other borderline technology which can speed up their work while giving rise to new and unpredictable risks. In any case, if his potion works, it will usher in the end of all order, for everyone will be free, there will be pandemonium, an endless rebellion will start that no power would be able to control, governments will fall and finally there would be cataclysm. JRK, and his circle of accomplices, will rule over the chaos—until he, too, will be sucked into it. No, we have learned our lessons when the secrets were leaked, and we have learned them well. We can't let him continue with his insane project.'

Sujata crossed her legs and held the glass between her palms. A few things were getting clearer. This is how Zeeta comes in the picture, she had been prying into this secret project of the businessman. Zeeta was on this side, and she is dead. Now she was being reminded of her duty to drive Chanchal crazier and crazier, so that he goes and finishes off Jayant Roy Kapoor. She was beginning to have doubts...was she up to the task? And if she failed, what will happen to her? To divert her mind, she said, 'Can I be told a bit more about Felicity, and the effects of this substance? How will it help JRK?'

'Yes, of course, we will explain. Some of us here already know,' and he looked around the gathering. 'This evil man is trying to sell salvation as chocolate. Salvation wrapped in golden foil at fifty rupees a slab. You understand how dangerous it will be when these chocolate bars—spiked with Felicity— reach every store shelve? When innocent men and women try this new chocolate and begin to enjoy their ecstasy? And come back again and again for a little more of the fix, to prolong their trip? He will have the whole country in thrall. And it will spread like wildfire, nation after nation will get hooked to his magic; he will hold humanity in stupor. And these stupefied multitudes will pray, obey, respect and love him like they pray, obey, respect and love their gods and their gadgets, their superiors, their laws, their loved ones. It's a potion for anarchy, anarchy of a dangerous and unforeseen kind, anarchy before which nothing, nothing at all is sacred.

'But this wicked business tycoon thinks that the opposite will happen. That charged by these ecstasies people will work even harder, and with joy. There is no guarantee for that and, in fact, we believe it will just be the opposite. People work to fuel their desires, desire helps us defy death. All the riches that people accumulate—Chippendale settees and Swiss watches, duplex apartments and fancy cars—are really to hide the finality of death from their view, and desire helps them get there. But if your desires pale into insignificance before the great chemical induced joy, why work at all?'

Sujata nodded. But isn't there such a thing as selfless service, or maybe that doesn't apply here. She was trying to make sense of what she heard. Was this the real plan behind Choco Raja that she had heard him talk about? Was this megalomaniac planning to get the whole nation hooked on drugged chocolate? But she had to ask a question, 'Why do you think the authorities won't be able to stop him when things begin to fall apart?'

'We are trying to find out more about the experiments. If he manages to do it right, then the amounts will be too small to detect with any known methods and I tell you he will not stop with chocolate. Very soon he will sneak it into other foodstuff. These transnational companies are immensely powerful... they can turn the world upside down in a day, which is why we always have our people on their boards. With this one we haven't been successful.

'Now talking about Felicity, we believe it will be synthesised using a very sophisticated process which cannot be easily replicated. It will be almost impossible to reverse-engineer it. And coming back to my point, I believe this mind-altering substance will put humanity in godforsaken trouble. Felicity will not only provide undistilled bliss, it will also affect reason. People will stop working, labourers will run away from factories, human beings will stop loving and finally they will all starve to death. For what is the necessity of troubled and uncertain ecstasies if Felicity gives a perfect trip each and every time? A trip better than sex, a forever ticket to a wonderland where work seems meaningless?

'But then, for a moment, let's assume his thinking about this is right. If in a state of chemical bliss people begin to work like machines, around the clock…imagine the whole blessed population working like maniacs with no need for holidays and little rest, and using the same dirty technologies and mountains of mined minerals. What will it do to Mother Earth? They have already screwed up the climate and we haven't been able to figure out how to save them from themselves. Just add the sauce of Felicity in this soup, imagine four billion working like mad, tirelessly, with little need for leisure or rest. The world will burn out like a box of matches. JRK is a madman and he needs to be stopped.'

Everyone was listening raptly. The servers who had brought food to the tables had left. Although people's plates were piled with *naan*s and *bharta*s, rice and *lal maas*, no one made an attempt to dig in.

'Now, some of you have asked whether this new substance will lead you on to a real Nirvana,' the tall man said, then continued, 'No, chemicals can never do that. Chemicals don't deliver *Moksha*, but they can create good approximations of the state of selflessness that is achieved by mystics. And it will work, because the blind man doesn't know which pigeon flies higher.' Arup, the baul, who was blind in one eye, stirred in his seat when he heard what the speaker had just said. He made a face.

'The ancients said "the All is mind" and, in fact, it is,' the speaker continued, 'But not really the mind, but the brain cells and the nerve endings that give rise to mental energies and vibrations. This is the secret right here inside us. It's all these little invisible receptors on those cells. They are the centres of greed and the lower *moksha*s. These are the seats of the Spirit, and the wheels of all the materialist systems of the world—capitalism, socialism, mercantilism, and what have you. Marx never went deep enough so he bunged it all up, pouring a shitload of authoritarianism and glazed-eye dictators on the planet. Meanwhile, capitalists loved the chemical soups that flood the nerve endings—where material civilisations are created and destroyed, where crime is committed and resisted—and they hoped to use these to their advantage, but the soups are too strong for capitalists too. They themselves couldn't resist the fire of greed begat by these powerful substances, and so we have wars, and climate change and doomsday machines. Gautama, of course, devised a way out, to dry up the most dangerous of these chemicals, to plug the maws of the receptors that drive us mad with desire. But who is listening? And this man, JRK, he is aiming for these same receptors with a truckload of nukes. He and his men are trying to shake up the right cocktail and deliver a close to brilliant *moksha*. But it will be a grim spectacle. The fallout will be devastating.

'Also, with Felicity sneaking into the food chain through chocolates and other stuff, people will begin to avoid the real teachers, the masters and the adepts, the true knowers of the Way. You understand what I mean, sister?'

She had to force a 'yes' out of her mouth. But neither the authority of the speaker, nor the weight of the arguments could touch her heart. She secretly cried for Chanchal. She began to hate herself for getting drawn into this business. This hate grew in her mind and tightened her face muscles. What would he be doing now, alone and vulnerable, with his strange ailment, she thought. How could she do this to someone who had been kind to her, who had tried to save her on the train from that knife-wielding junkie? And even before that when she was secretly at work. Is it right to sacrifice a kind soul for greater good, which itself could be dubious? Her invisible tears almost choked her, and she felt she might faint from the effort to maintain her composure.

She wanted to flee, extricate herself from the coils of The Ouroboros, run away from the past, and turn her back to a secret world that had once seemed enchanting.

'I hope you have no more doubts, sister?' the tallest of the nine men was asking her. She shook her head; she wanted to leave. All of them were watching her. She looked around the hall and hooked her fingers around the belts of her knapsack. 'I will do my best,' she said.

'Go back and take up the work where you left it,' the tall one said, and raised his hand in a gesture of protection. She stepped off the bar stool and was about to leave when he spoke again, 'But you have lost him, you said. Precious time! There can be no progress without him.' He considered something and said, 'Let me find out where he might have gone.'

With this, he fell quiet. His gaze turned inward and he began to mumble in a very low voice. Minutes passed, everyone was silent. He pulled out a small stone tablet from a bag and began to trace signs on its face with his index finger. His gaze was still turned inward as he drew these signs—his fingers shivering slightly as they slid along the face of the stone. Then he took a good look at it and began to speak. 'Chanchal Mitra is closer to his destination. He has reached Aukatabad. He had crossed the flooded desert. Our sister has let him slip away. But now she will be more careful. She has committed negligence but this is not the time to accuse her. The ship of the desert has been his friend. He has travelled. He has travelled on an omnibus. He is exhausted, but a stranger has appeared. He pretends to be a friend and they seem to know each other. Is he one of ours? We don't know yet but shall soon find out.'

HOLY SMOG

I'm terribly scared today, and hiding in the darkest corner of the house. What are they dragging me into? Will the Mitra name finally go down in ignominy because of these characters? That Kapoor refuses to hear anything I try to say, and now this one-legged outlaw, lamenting always about his lost parrot, is giving him ideas. Where are we headed? That woman who had sheltered us in Bhaskarnagar has also arrived. I heard the knock on the door …

A hesitant knock, just once. There's no bell at the door... Kapoor peeps through the kitchen window to check. Sujata is wearing a sienna-coloured beret at a rakish angle, down which the dark waterfall of her hair dangles like secrets yet to be revealed. Looking anxious, restless with her hands and trying to check for a name plate, but this guy Lohit hadn't put up any.

Kapoor lets her in. Though they had fought bitterly, he did miss her the few days since he had arrived. Still, he is wary. They had rowed badly about that climate book he found at the guest house. He couldn't trust her any more. And now she has suddenly appeared outside Lohit's Aukatabad apartment.

'Good heavens! How did you find me?' Kapoor asks, offering her a glass of water.

'I made some enquiries,' she says.

'Bollocks! No one knows I'm here,' and he goes back into the kitchen to fix his lunch, which is nothing but reheated kebabs from last night and basmati fried in ghee.

A little while earlier, he had returned from another recce of the Gate of the Emperors; and this day too, he had spotted his target. In fact, he noted that the bodyguard didn't accompany him right into the garden but hung back near the gate. Another armed guard waited outside the park where his car was parked, keeping a watch on the road. Perhaps they considered the garden, smack at the centre of the town, to be safe. This is good for their plan but somehow they have to trick the second guard.

He returns to the room with two plates.

'You think no one knows you're here…?' she asks, and there is a breathy absence in her tone which leaves much unsaid.

Could it be his host? He wonders. Do they know each other? That's highly improbable. He doesn't answer but looks straight into her eyes. In the webbed darkness of Lohit's apartment, they look even more unfathomable. Nothing to be found there. He will have to dig it out soon but right now he is immersed in planning for the big day. This cannot wait any longer.

'This bloody flat is like a dungeon, should I switch on the lights?' he asks.

'If you wish,' she says.

He offers her some fried rice with kebab, but she says she's not hungry and opens a packet of cashew instead.

Afterwards they take a walk through the little forest behind the house. The paths lined with kareel shrubs and thirsty eucalyptus trees are deserted, and they go deep into the wilderness.

'We have to leave this city,' she begins by saying.

'What do you mean we? You go wherever you want to. This is my city and I am going to unmask that fake before doing anything else,' Kapoor says, and begins to disclose their plan to abduct the fake and extract a confession that he is an impostor.

She turns pale and looks genuinely alarmed.

'Never, you're not going to do anything of that sort,' she says firmly, stopping in her tracks...

'For the last time!' He says rudely, 'Will you stop meddling in my affairs or do I take a drastic measure? I repeat, you can go anywhere you like. Once this cloud clears and that fake is exposed, you are welcome to be the face of my advertising campaign. But I won't insist.'

She falls quiet and they walk back part of the way to the hotel where she has booked a room.

'So you're leaving today?' he asks her when she prepares to go.

She gives him a strange look, 'You are making a deadly mistake,' she says suddenly, covers her face and walks away.

He stares in her direction for a while, then takes a bus to a market in another part of town. He buys ropes, gags, medicines, dry fruits and loads of energy bars before returning to Lohit's dungeon.

Lohit seems to be enjoying the preparations. He is even financing the costs, I don't see what interest he's got in helping that Kapoor. But I've kind of given it up to fate. At least he's the one who talks to me while Kapoor has been ignoring me altogether. The other day he was asking me about the bar on the Avenue of Egos back in Anantanagar. The one where the moths used to cover the walls. So we chatted about the characters we'd met there, those who are still around and those who have left for good. But he couldn't help me get back to Anantanagar; 'not yet', he said.

Meanwhile, he is dropping Kapoor off every morning for his scouting visits. At night they have long discussions, and this evening while they are planning finer details on a hand-drawn map, Sujata arrives again.

Once more, she tries to dissuade them from the attempt to kidnap the impostor. 'How can I convince you that this will be a big mistake? We will be in serious trouble,' she swings around to face Lohit, looking for support. But the old sailor just returns a smile, his eyes twinkling with mirth.

I hope I could help Sujata in convincing them. But I am very weak now and Kapoor won't listen to me. I cannot raise my voice and because there is little to do, I sleep most of these days.

Sujata stops trying to convince Kapoor about the dangers when she realises Lohit is also part of the plan. At their first meeting, she had thought the sailor-turned-lawyer was just trying to keep Kapoor in good humour without being serious. But now, she gives up.

Kapoor doesn't understand why Sujata was trying to stop them. To save her own skin? If she was working for the fake JRK, she can help the other side set a trap. Is that possible? Is it all part of some greater subterfuge? He doesn't know, and now they are too deep with the planning. Kapoor does two more recces of the garden where their target comes for his morning constitutional. Lohit drops him at a different spot each day, drives around to check possible exits, and the risks and advantages of each route before going off to work while Kapoor uses public transport to return.

Their target appears around the same time every day and takes a brisk walk in that garden before stepping out through the west gate, where a car picks him up. Sometimes he buys fruits from a vendor on his way out. There are many lonely paths inside the sprawling garden, flanking pools of water with just a handful of early birds, and Kapoor feels if they can time it correctly the whole operation will be a cinch.

They decide on a Friday morning, when the number of morning walkers is expected to be the lowest.

As luck would have it, Lohit develops a terrible stomach ache the previous night. It must have been the over-spiced kebabs reheated day after day, and his body had completely disagreed. He twists and turns in his bed, and unable to bear the discomfort, he sits up, takes his crutch and walks around in his swinging gait. He groans and howls while swinging around from room to room, cursing the butcher who sold him the kebabs. Intermittently he breaks into tears, lamenting the loss of his pet parrot, Commander. Kapoor tries in vain to console him, handing him Carmozyme mixture but to no avail.

Everything had been planned for the next morning. If they cannot do it on Friday, it will be another week's wait. Even Sujata had finally relented and agreed to meet them at a pre-determined spot soon as they were through with the job. But Lohit Joardar's digestive system had revolted.

The alarm clock rings. It is still dark outside. Kapoor checks with Lohit. The old salt is up and looking better. Kapoor suggests they postpone it for a week.

'No problem mate,' he slapped his tummy hard, 'these old guts are as quiet as a mouse now, let's go to battle. Winter is around the corner and he might just stop coming for his walks, or he might start arriving late when there will be too many people around,' he says, assuring him that he felt fit as a fiddle, and so they set out as planned.

I have no recourse but to accompany them. By now I am resigned to whatever fate has in store for me. I promise myself that if I return to Anantanagar in one piece, I will have a score to settle with this crutch carrying bandit who appeared like a ghost ship in the roiling seas of Aukatabad.

Morning tastes like a scrapyard. Morning smells like a farm fire. The yellow-grey walls of smog had grown darker. For days and weeks the dust of the desert, swept by freak and untimely storms, had thickened the haze and now the city was suddenly engulfed in coarse dust. It holds the streets in a stranglehold, blurring the borderland between night and day. The trees stand in whispery attention, dust-caked like dead soldiers. Lohit is behind the wheel of a beaten grey sedan with automatic transmission, Kapoor sitting quietly beside him. The hired car zips through the steel grey dawn, windows rolled up but the smell of burnt leaves overwhelms the cabin.

They drive east and pick up another person near the abandoned railway quarters. His name is Dhiraj. He has a square face with a snub nose and bloodshot eyes, and he hands a small pistol with a wooden grip to Lohit. Lohit takes a look at it and frowns before sticking it into his belt.

'Where the hell did you get this Soviet relic from? I asked for a bloody Glock!'

'Very dependable, sir,' Dhiraj says and takes the wheel.

They head along the perimeter road, turning sharply back into the city from the area of the old fort. From here, it is a southward drive but the smog is now so thick that they make slow progress and have to switch on the headlamps. A patrol car overtakes them near Citizen's Place, sirens blaring, rushing in the direction of the Gate of Emperors. Dhiraj slows down and steers the sedan into a different route which would take them to the westward flank of the garden. They get off the car on a road parallel to the one skirting the garden, and Lohit and Kapoor head for two different gates. Dhiraj remains at the wheel.

The path from the northern gate branches in three directions. One going along the line of trees on the far side, another passing close to them and the middle path shooting straight, bisecting a pool of water before snaking its way deeper into the garden. They keep a watch from a sunken flower bed edged with shrubs, which gives them a good cover.

The smog hangs thick among the trees, and they have to strain their eyes lest they miss him. A couple of joggers appear through the gate and continue along the far path, which vanishes after some distance beyond the line of trees. Lohit leans against a keekar tree, tapping the ground with his crutch, marking time. The birds are quiet today. And then they see him.

He comes walking briskly along the path closest to them. Just a few feet from where they are waiting, hidden. Shod in trainers, tracksuit and a baseball cap, which hides his face. He looks fit. Like every day, he is carrying a cane picnic basket for fruits. Behind him like an elf, and without any warning, appears the cat, Prana. His tail trembling in the air. The mascot of Atman group.

Lohit sees the cat, and a look comes over him. What kind of look it is, it's hard to describe. But his eyes sparkle like a child's and then throwing all plans to the wind, he lunges towards the impostor—before he has even levelled up to where they were lying in wait for him. Lohit bolts ahead on his crutch like a streak of lightning, stabbing through the smoky haze. The smog is like a black wall, grey with the desert dust. The smog is like the bitterness of the world congealed around the Gate of Emperors.

Shots ring out. Warning fire followed by the determined rat-a-tat of a machine pistol.

Kapoor freezes. They were supposed to check for the bodyguard. The smog made it next to impossible. He sees a figure approaching him stealthily. He would be a sitting duck if he spots him. It's the buck-toothed bodyguard. The muzzle flash of a gun.

The hiss of a bullet, inches above his head.

Kapoor is rolling on the ground, lucky not to be hit.

Cries of help ring out as bullets fly in all directions. Sprays of hot metal. Kapoor sits up in a crouch, holding his breath. Where is Lohit? A shot from their side, or what looks like their side anyway. More automatic fire. Kapoor runs for cover when he catches a glimpse of their target again. Cutting through the shrubbery, going for the nearest exit. Right then Lohit appears from his left, dashing towards him. But this man is fast.

Both of them close in on him. Lohit is about to grab him, he's pointing the gun at him. With a swift and powerful move he slams the picnic basket into Lohit's face. It hits him square on his chin. The gun jerks off his hand.

The imposter jumps across another line of shrubbery. 'Help!' he shouts, sprinting across the grass. More sprays of machine pistol fire from the lakeside trees. They are coming from behind.

Cries of the injured. Many morning walkers have been hit by the reckless firing. Lohit stands stunned by the blow, swaying on his good leg. Kapoor drags him behind the guard wall of a public loo. The air now smells like a scrapyard on fire.

Lohit covers his face with one hand as a trickle of blood runs down his chin. There is a loud splash. The picnic basket, after hitting him, had disgorged a load of Kashmiri apples. One of the bodyguards had skidded on these and landed straight in the water.

Lohit notices Prana, stiff on his legs, hissing aggressively. In a flash he scoops him off and then turning, digs his crutch in the ground and goes swinging ahead like a gymnast. Who can catch him? A stray bullet whizzes past them.

But the imposter has vanished and there's a sudden lull in firing. It's too dangerous to look for him now. They have to escape. They run for an opening in the railing that Kapoor had marked on the map. Rails removed by junkies to sell as scrap that paid for their daily fix. It isn't easy in the smog, but they find it somehow. Quickly, they slip through, the moans of the wounded behind them. The siren of a fast approaching patrol car comes from the street.

The cat seems stunned into silence. Dhiraj drives the getaway car, calm and unblinking. Like he's on his office commute. The smog gives them good cover from the traffic cameras. Driving south for some distance, he finally swings the sedan into the *pahadi* where the old forested hills meet the city.

An autorickshaw hidden in the clumps of keekar trees. Dhiraj steers the car through the gaps in the trees and leaves it some way off the road. They now shift to the auto.

They cross the river and drive west through industrial suburbs, and onto open farmland. The sun is hot on their heads when they reach a small building a little off the road. It's a cross between a vehicle repair garage and a modest residence. Lohit has the keys.

There is enough food for three people in the fridge. They eat hungrily, leaving some for JRK's cat Prana, who sits twitching his tail, observing them.

The garage at the front of the house is closed, and there seems to be no one around. Through the day, Lohit watches the street through a slit in the curtains, and then returns to his seat to check the news. The news looks bad. Three people have been grievously injured and one is fighting for his life.

The whole city has been alerted about the gunfight and the kidnap attempt, and the channels are getting descriptions from morning walkers who may have seen them. Luckily, these descriptions are all dramatic. One of them said they were three well-built Pathans with Kalashnikovs, driving a Japanese SUV.

'Holy smog! God give us more pollution!' Lohit cackles, turning off the TV. Kapoor gives him a hard look.

But the disappearance of Prana, the mascot of the Atman business empire, casts a pall of gloom over Aukatabad and beyond; and by the end of that day the entire nation is looking out for three gun-toting men in a Japanese car and a grey smoke cat.

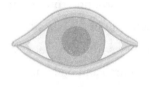

TELOS

FINAL ESCAPE

Now look what they have done! How many died? I am in a mind to give them away. Call the police. How the Mitra name will be sullied when all this comes to light! Wish I could quietly finish the two off and return to Anantanagar. Strangle this intolerable Lohit Joardar and Kapoor, who have been leading me into all sorts of dangerous misadventures. But I am weak, I can hardly move my limbs now while that one, that insufferable Kapoor does whatever he pleases. So I will try to rest, for now I will try to keep quiet…

'The city is too hot for us,' Lohit says, adding, 'We will have to follow the original plan. At least we have snatched his favourite pet.' There seems to be a hint of satisfaction in his voice while Kapoor is drowning in despair. It's a huge setback for him after such meticulous planning. He curses himself for getting Lohit involved in this business. It was he who had bungled it at the last moment.

'Why didn't you wait till he had levelled up with us before making a move? You exposed yourself and gave them time to react! Wasn't this what we had agreed?' he demanded of

Lohit, who was checking bags with dry fruits, energy bars and provisions for the road.

'The damned smog! You saw how thick it was in the morning. Packed with deadly particulate and the dust of the desert from where you came. It followed you. It's strange how the wind knows better than we do. How it plays with our well-laid plans. Besides, I told you both my eyes are bad. I reckoned it will be too late if I didn't make a move right then. Who knew that maniac bodyguard would be so close, emerging from those grey curtains like a malevolent spirit?' Lohit says as he bites into an energy bar.

'You have bad eyes! Wish I'd known that,' Kapoor says, with rising anger, 'Bloody smog, darned pollution and the evil wind. It screwed up everything!' And then he rushes off to the bathroom and bangs the door shut.

'Late stage cataract in the left…I think I told you,' Lohit mumbles to himself. He places a thumb below each eye, and with the index finger on his eyelids he tries to open the eye wide while rolling his eyeballs to look around the small room. Then he turns his attention to feeding the cat.

An hour after sunset, Lohit and Kapoor get into the autorickshaw again. Dhiraj drives them through the darkness along back roads till close to midnight they arrive at an abandoned filling station whose roof had caved in. Sujata is waiting for them there. She is anxious, and she doesn't utter a single word when she sees them. It is completely dark now, except for the fiery glow of Aukatabad lighting up the western sky. Crickets are chirping angrily in the fields and a torrid wind is coming in gusts from the north-westerly direction. Dhiraj switches on a small torch and leads them along a dirt road through the wheat fields. About a kilometre onwards stands a farmhouse with smelly cowsheds, a barn and stables. There seems to be no one around.

The ponies are bridled and ready. Lohit exchanges a few whispered words with Dhiraj before he leaves, and they mount the ponies and set out on a slow trot. Soon, they are riding faster down the dusty road that goes east. A boat moon travels with them through the night. Prana is sleeping in a basket on Lohit's pony. The old salt is keen to keep the cat with him during the journey and no one objects. Perhaps the loss of his pet parrot is fulfilled by the cat. Sometimes the dust clouds of passing trucks paint the moon red. Often the moon vanishes behind clouds, and the darkness of the endless road is complete. Like they are on the verge of the known universe and passing into the emptiness before the beginning. *Darkness wrapped in darkness.* Only the clip-clop of horse hooves anchors them to the ever-flowing present, shaken now with a roll of thunder.

They knew it wouldn't be an easy journey. But staying back in Aukatabad was not an option anymore. After they bungled the kidnapping and came away with Prana, the police had been put on high alert. They heard the news of raids and roadblocks even as they were leaving the city; and now, on the road, they can feel the cops breathing down their necks. They will be coming for them.

Sujata has fears of her own. How will her masters react when they find out she has neglected her duty? Will they let her go? Besides, the journey won't be easy for him. She worries how it will affect his mind.

The first night on the road, he is assaulted by panic attacks. He screams and curses, and they have to rein in the ponies and stop.

'I have benzo pills that might help,' Lohit tells Sujata.

'Not yet…we have just started,' she says.

'We will be attracting attention if he doesn't calm down.'

'Let me speak with him,' she gets off the horse, walks up to him and assures him everything will be okay. But it's not easy; and to add to their troubles, it begins to rain, further slowing their progress.

It's getting risky, though they are being very careful. Lohit seems to have made good arrangements in advance, which no doubt helps. They travel by night, and during the day, they shelter in safehouses which are situated away from settlements, and usually some way off the road. At the first of these, which is just a poultry feed store with two beds at the back, Sujata rolls up her hair into a grey turban, and puts on the kurta pyajamas of a villager. It is safer to be dressed like a man on these roads.

Next morning she sees the caked blood on his hands. He is asleep in a foetal posture, his face buried under a dirty pillow; there are splotches of dry blood on his shirt. He had tried to bite off his fingers. It's the same injured hand, the burnt skin still to heal completely. Lohit says he had tried to stop him but not quite successfully. He needs a doctor who could address everything. Sujata will have to find a doctor, but how. It was impossible to get one while they were on the run.

Things were getting completely out of hand. Did she harm him by doing what she had done? But she has stepped back and here she is, caring as much as she can. She hated the old seaman for fuelling his delusions and getting them in this mess. Worries line her face, casting shadows on her beautiful eyes, and she looks gaunt under the wraps of her turban.

Lohit suggests the pills again. But the benzodiazepine doesn't help much as he begins to feel drowsy, slowing down their progress. Also, his problems surface more frequently after taking that drug.

Lohit brews tea in an old kettle after cleaning the cobwebs inside. The tea is refreshing, and they are about to set out when he bursts into the room. It's the evening of their second day on the road. He stops midway, darting a look between Lohit and Sujata. His eyes are terror-stricken.

'What's the matter mate, everything okay?' Lohit asks in his most genial voice.

'Spirits! I am being visited by ghosts. Why are we holed up here with that insufferable Kapoor? I have to return to Anantanagar. What's happening to Mitra House with me away for so long? The maid must have left, she would take care if she was there. And my dog, is he dead already?' the soft unimposing voice of Chanchal doesn't surprise them.

Sujata unconsciously covers her mouth when he mentions the maid but nobody notices it. He looks downcast, weak. He scratches his head and looks empty-eyed at the medical gauze swathed around his palm. The toll on his mind and the strain of living two lives have begun to tell on his body. Something has to be done soon. Despite harbouring mistrust about Lohit, she looks at him for some kind of assurance but he seems distant.

Without any warning, an impetuous voice thunders at them, 'What the hell are we doing losing time?' The switch to the guttural voice is so sudden that they spring from their chairs. And right before their eyes, he changes. His face looks broader, more folds appear below his chin, his eyes begin to glint with a cold fire and he is stronger, taller and intimidating.

'We are trying mate, it will take time,' Lohit says firmly. Prana sits at his feet and he caresses his light silvery ruff as the cat watches them with his green opalescent eyes.

He continues in the booming voice, 'Every day lost makes that imposter stronger, his horses dance in my garden, trampling the flowerbeds. We have to challenge him now and shoot him down if he resists. A bullet between his eyes...Tell me, how much. How much money do we need for the job, to stop him...to annihilate that wanker?'

'Let things calm down a bit,' Lohit cuts in with an even tone, 'The law keepers are still too worked up about Prana's disappearance. We have served him a big blow right, the mascot of his business empire snatched right from under his nose—we have torn out his heart. The rest will follow. But this is not the time.'

He grunts an agreement and holds his head in his hands. 'OK, whatever you have to do, do it quickly! What are we doing pissing in this cowshed for the whole day? Let's get out of here!' he screams.

Sujata had tried to talk about him with Lohit earlier, when she had met him at the apartment. But Lohit only gave her a strange look and changed the subject. He was more keen to know about JRK's cat, and then he and Kapoor had been deep in their plans for the abduction. Now in the forced contiguity of the journey, it crosses Sujata's mind. Why has this old salt always seemed more interested in the cat than the mental stability of someone he claims to know from before, or the predicament they were in. Who is he? Is he really a friend or could he be one of *them*? Though Sujata didn't trust this giant of a person with that penetrating gaze, which burns through the shells of your darkest secrets, who was as swift on his crutch as an athlete on his feet, the common danger of the road slowly changed her mind.

The sun has set and they have to start soon. Chanchal sleeps like a dead man while Prana keeps watch. 'He is tired playing two roles,' Lohit says. He is massaging the ponies as they feed along a grassy patch. The ponies seem to enjoy it as his strong hands move against their backs, 'I think I know where he will be better. And it will be a good place to lie low till things calm down,' Lohit adds.

Sujata peers into his jackal eyes, trying to read his thoughts, trying to gauge his confidence. What else can she do under the circumstances, which were getting desperate anyway. She had finally agreed to his suggestion to head in the north-easterly direction, towards the mountains. But there still remained hundreds of miles between them and the great mountain ranges of the north.

They set off again with the stars coming out over the northern sky. Sujata rides next to Chanchal while Lohit leads. Somewhere, far into that darkness, were the high ranges, the melting glaciers and the mountain passes through which secret teachings have flown for centuries. Was that wicked businessman really planning to play God, like many before him? What if he succeeds and Felicity reaches the masses?

The world around them was quiet, too quiet, thinks Sujata as questions criss-cross her mind.

They ride for another hour, part of it across the swampy bed of a lake, and around midnight, see a big sky full of stars. They are nearing a river. A road bridge over swift flowing waters, and then down the embankment, a few more miles to a one-storey house deep in the woods. No lights shining through the windows. There seems to be no one here. Lohit asks them to wait behind the trees and whistles thrice, startling an owl hidden among the branches.

In a little while they hear a soft creak…the sound of a door being opened. Lohit's pony steps ahead, a few paces. 'Oh it's you, come inside,' someone says in a low voice. A torch is switched on for a brief moment, showing them the way through the door.

Their host has a square face with a thick, full moustache and he speaks in a low, whispery voice. They lead the ponies to a shed at the back of the house.

Two plain rooms, one doubling as kitchen. Folding beds, a work table, basic cooking arrangements and books of medicine. That's about it. Their host is a physician. His name is Indranil but Lohit just addresses him as 'doctor'. They get introduced while he goes about making arrangements for them to put up for the night. A meal of tarka and roti with a piece of fish as bonus. 'I arrived this week, otherwise I could have made better arrangements,' the doctor says apologetically.

'Not at all, this is king's fare,' Lohit says.

Chanchal is calmer this night. He listens to them, nurses his injured hand, offers a comment here and there.

Doctor Indranil tells them about his work in a hospital at Anantanagar. Every year he takes time off to visit far-flung districts of the country, offering free treatment and medicine to people who didn't have access to modern allopathy. He will be camping here for some weeks before travelling further north, where he will run a clinic for a few weeks more, before returning to his city.

How did he travel? 'Oh, there are people who come to collect me,' he says, but doesn't say who these people are. He is a raconteur with a vast store of experience, and his conversations keeps them up till late.

When Chanchal retires for the night, Sujata tells their host about his delusions and how the cat happens to be with them. She can tell from his reaction that he has already been informed about their arrival, and that he is someone she has to trust. 'You are travelling with the right person,' the doctor says about Lohit, who by then had produced a fat bottle of rum and was pouring large measures in three glasses.

'We are heading for the mountains, the *pahadi* winds will do him good. Let's drink to his health,' Lohit says, raising his glass.

'Just be careful so that he doesn't hurt himself, keep talking with him as much as you can,' the doctor says, 'and be very alert. This part of the country is unsafe and you seem to have made enemies. I'm told, the police have been tipped that you could be hiding in these parts. They have instructions to stop and search strangers. If I were you, I'd have waited for a few days before continuing. This place is safe.'

But Lohit thinks they should get going. 'I know that but there will be friends along the way. We will be careful; I guess we fit in well. Don't we look like farm labourers from the north?' He laughs and his eyebrows make a crooked dance.

Three rounds of drinks with Sujata's inexhaustible stock of salted cashews. After which she retires for the night. Sleep eludes her, chased as she is by her own demons.

Till late in the night she can hear them talking—the mysterious doctor Indranil who has appeared like an angel in this forest of the night and the old salt who calls himself Comrade LJ. Clinking glasses and talking of old times. This is when she learns how Lohit lost his leg when their ship had been taken by pirates near the Horn of Africa. He had put up resistance and was shot. She wondered about this man. How did he know all these people, all these safe houses? Just because he is a lawyer? But her eyelids were getting heavy and sleep carried her off to safer places, far from the darkness of the road.

Everyone wakes up late. The doctor is busy soon, setting up his temporary clinic at the back of the house. Lohit vanishes in the forest and returns around midday with a bagful of red berries. They rustle up a quick meal and wait for it to get dark.

Chanchal is quiet today. He asks their host how far it is to Anantanagar. When Lohit tells him that they are headed for the hills first, he doesn't protest but nods sadly.

They are on their way just after the sun sets and the river turns blue in the twilight. The ponies, rested and fed, go on a canter and soon they are among wheat fields, huts in the distance with flickering lights. The country smells of cow dung cake fires seeping through the scent of freshly cut hay. When the ponies get thirsty, they stop at a well and a village girl draws water for them, pouring it into a hollow in the earth.

There is still some light in the western sky; perhaps there's a city in that direction. A shepherd comes from the other side with his large flock of bleating sheep and goats. They let them pass. A tractor appears far away, almost hidden in a cloud of dust. The cloud grows bigger as they ride towards it, and finally the smoke-belching, rumbling machine appears, moving slowly and moodily as if it was still deciding where it should go. Their eyes meet the driver's. A blank stare, no greetings exchanged. The lumbering machine passes them, engulfed by another great dust cloud.

They are avoiding the highway as far as they can, using longer detours but this is slowing them down. Sujata knows her disguise isn't great. Will Jayant Roy Kapoor's personal security come after them before the police does? She remembers the two men trying to roast her alive in that guest house. She doesn't discuss this possibility with her co-travellers but hopes the journey will end soon and they arrive at Thunder Mountain, where Lohit says there will be arrangements made for their stay. And Chanchal could be treated there. When things go quieter, they can slip back to Anantanagar.

A little later, and by then it's completely dark, they see a light on the road—a swinging yellow flame. Sujata and Chanchal pull back their ponies while Lohit rides ahead. A tall and sinewy man wearing a large turban is waving and signalling at them to stop. Lohit brings his pony to a halt a few feet from him.

The flickering light illuminates the stranger's face as they watch from a distance. He has unusually dark eyes and an unwavering magnetic gaze. He seems to be clenching his jaws as he stands ramrod erect, waiting for Lohit to alight.

Sujata is certain this is a policeman in mufti. So the game is over. She watches Chanchal's expressions but he doesn't seem to care. He has alighted from the pony and is looking at the horizon. Sujata knows a police jeep will appear any moment to pick them up and they will have to spend the night in some dreadful lock-up of a town *thana*, and next day they will be sent to a district court where they will be charged—and later would be sent to jail for life, if not worse. After all, they were responsible for the death of innocents. She can feel fingers of ice brushing her spine and holds her breath.

Lohit is having an animated conversation with the stranger and it looks like an argument. Should she step back and disappear into the night? No way! But then the stranger with the light cracks up, his teeth glisten in the lamplight and Lohit, balancing on his good foot, swings his crutch—something she had seen him do when amused.

He turns back and signals at them to lead the ponies, and they all begin to walk. The tall stranger with Lohit, Sujata and Chanchal a little way behind. The cat is asleep in a saddle bag, his head barely visible.

As the road turns, a lake appears in the distance, big trees forming a ring near its bank. The stranger with the lantern and Lohit walk down the embankment. They follow. On a large meadow between the trees are parked wagons and carts. A number of rough blanket tents have been put up, and Sujata can hear the animated voices of children within. The bleating of a large flock of goats kept nearby punctuates these voices. Women in colourful costumes with strong bodies, some wearing silver anklets and tinkling bangles of glass, watch them from the folds of their tents. There are really no words Sujata can think of to describe her relief after this long and arduous trek. She thanks Lohit for as he had assured her the night before, they have been welcomed by the Barefoot Tribe.

BAREFOOT TRIBE

Prana is an immediate hit with their new hosts, who are a large group of herders travelling east. The small children play with him and the women feed him goat milk. He had been quiet and gloomy all this while, only acknowledging the presence of his human subjects from time to time. Otherwise, he would be napping. But among the children of the herders, he changes completely. He plays with the little ones, chasing and being chased by them, hiding behind trees and purring in affection.

This group of pastoralists, locally known as the Barefoot Tribe, had been travelling this route for generations, long before railway tracks connected Anantanagar to Aukatabad. They are warm and friendly with the visitors to their camp. They put them up in a tent and give them a hearty meal of smoking hot rotis and vegetables.

During the day, the women join the menfolk in grazing their goats and sheep, and a blacksmith in the group turns out snake rings. The rings are serpents eating their tails. Sujata buys a few and asks him where he got this design from. 'From the road,' he says.

The man who invited them is the leader of the group. He is busy through the day, but in the evenings he chats with Lohit by the lakeside. He talks about how they have to go further each year for the greener grass as the land dries up. 'We take little from this land and try to return what it gives us. So did our forefathers and all those who walk this country with the animals. But the settlers in villages and cities never tire of drawing out the last drop of earth's riches,' the leader says.

Lohit sighs but his mind is elsewhere. He worries that he might be bringing trouble to this blameless group of herders from the western lands.

The leader makes hot tea with goat milk and they sit for long, sipping the thick brew, talking and listening to the herders' story of the road. Lohit listens as he sings a song about man breaking his bonds with the earth, which is like falling out of love that one considered eternal.

Sujata feels relieved as she stretches on the soft grass and looks up at the sky. The sun has set but there are patches of wet orange near the horizon. Marmalade skies. It could be raining in the north. A woman prepares a meal on wood fire; Sujata watches her from a distance. The scent of rotis stir up her appetite. She opens another pack of cashew and watches her cook as evening spreads thickly over the world.

She wishes to stay longer, few more days. Her mind turns to Chanchal. Will he want to stay back, she wonders.

The herders had all returned to camp with their flocks and they were mostly in the tents behind her, near the water. To her right, at some distance, is the road but tonight there are no signs or sounds of its presence. Has the highway been closed for some reason? She feels an odd tingle at the back of her neck but in the moment that it takes her to swing around, the attacker descends upon her like a thousand storms.

Before she can yell out for help, a spade-like hand covers her mouth, another grabs her throat. His wild eyes glow in the night, close to her face as she sinks her teeth in his flesh. His huge translucent body presses her down as she knees him hard in the groin. An unearthly sound comes from deep in his throat. For a moment the pressure on her throat eases. There's blood in her mouth.

'I'll lock you up for eternity, witch!' He swings his arms and slaps her so hard that it sounds like a thunderclap. A dog barks. Then another. He presses down on her throat again and she begins to choke. She tries to shake him off but he is too big for her. The overpowering stench from his monk's habit hits her. She begins to gasp for breath as his fingers close in on her windpipe.

He has pinned down her arms with his feet. She tries desperately to free herself. If she could only join her hands in the protective posture…but will it work against him? She gathers all her energies in her solar plexus and unleashes it at one go. Swinging him off violently, but he is on his feet in the blink of an eye.

His waxen face looks harder than the time she had seen him last. A sharp whistling sound and she sees a large net falling heavily over her. She crosses her hands but before she can form the protective mudra, she hears the low barks close by... Dogs!

Angry snarls and growls follow. The herders' dogs appear in a flash and Caligari freezes. His eyes go wide with fear as they bare their fangs at him ready to bite. With a whipping motion he pulls away the net and sprints towards the highway, fast as the wind. The dogs give chase, barking and racing but he was too fast for them. He crosses the dark fields in leaps and vanishes, leaving the overpowering stench of rotten flesh and tombs hanging around Sujata.

The growls and barks have brought the herders out from their tents. What can she tell them? Perhaps it is best to hang back a little and stay where she is. But what if he returns? Shivers go down her spine. She keeps lying in the dark, watching the tents and the men who have stepped out. They look around the meadow with torches to see if some beast of prey had attacked their herds. She massages her throat, still aching from that iron grip. She is in one piece, luckily no bruises. She closes her eyes, takes a deep breath and sits up with a start. What if that pale-faced man attacked Chanchal? Where is Chanchal?

Lohit had been sitting with the leader of the group by the water's edge, but she doesn't find them there. Perhaps they have gone to investigate the dogs, but they should have passed this way. Should she return to the tents and take someone along to look for Chanchal?

Small cooking fires are glowing near the tents where food is being prepared. The herders gather just a bit of firewood through the places they pass, never denuding an area. As she nears the cooking pits she sees small children playing among the parked carts. Their tent is empty. There seems to be no one about. She decides to go up to the lake again. She will go alone. She isn't scared of attackers, but Caligari is no ordinary assailant. She hopes the dogs will keep him away. She takes a turn away from the camp and towards the lake shimmering in the starlight.

Sujata begins to skirt the lake. A goat bleats in the distance, a night heron calls out. A shadow near the water. Someone sitting on the bank a little distance away.

It's him. Chanchal. Alone by the water. She walks closer and stands a little distance away from him.

His face is glowing, wiped of the darkness that clouds it most of the time. It's as if the sky is reflected there. He hasn't seen her; should she distract him now? But it is not right to keep watching him like this when he is not aware of her presence. She can sit down beside him. She goes down to the bank. He sees her and smiles.

They sit quietly. Ripples break on the lake, softening up the starlight. They watch without words. The campfires are on the other side—bright and exuberant. Someone there begins to play a stringed instrument. The plaintive air floats over the waters as an elderly man sings out about the passing of seasons. Then another sings,

> *A roti if you don't turn, will burn.*
> *Horse tied to a place will lose its pace,*
> *A leaf stuck to the soil will rot,*
> *Knowledge that does not travel will shrivel*
> *…So we stay moving with our herds*

Chanchal hums the tune. Sujata feels relieved and says a silent thanks to the singer.

The herders would be moving camp in two days. They are also headed east. This group will be walking mostly on foot with their herds, along their centuries-old routes while some of the women and children will get lifts in the carts drawn by two tractors. Four hundred miles. Lohit knew this beforehand.

Sujata feels assured. With these nomadic people, it is unlikely for them to get spotted. They rest for these last two days, dipping into the slow, peaceful life.

There is a time early in the morning when local farmers pass by the camp on their way to the fields. Some would stop to get their fortune told by a wrinkled lady in a bright red and blue skirt who is always bedecked in colourful stone jewellery, and has tattoos covering her hands. She has raincloud eyes—Sujata adores this woman. Sitting beside her in the evening, listening to her speak to the herders, Sujata feels she can bring her world together again.

Chanchal watches the old lady read palms. He looks fine. He asks Sujata if she will come for a walk. They climb up the embankment and on to the other side of the road, then through the fields and towards a stand of trees to the north. He tells her about his time back in Anantanagar; when he was working for the newspaper. She knows all of this but he tells her nonetheless... About how his father died, the clock Visigoth, and all that happened that night. He looks a little agitated as he speaks.

'Try not to remember what happened. It's been a long time,' Sujata says.

He then tells her about Idris and the promoter's men, how the diamond souk had raised its head beside Mitra House, and the countrywide adulation of the business tycoon, the stories, the reports, the interviews…and as he mentions him, he begins to transform. His face gets drained of colour, 'He is a big man, big and powerful…' he repeats again and again.

They turn back and cross the road, and are walking towards the camp. The day is almost dead. Clouds have gathered across a bleak mid-summer sky and the light is slipping away. 'I feel unwell,' he says, and as they near the tents, he switches.

'I have always been wary of you! In fact, both of you. You are kidnappers, you are working for those Nazis who installed that man in Aukatabad! Why am I here? *What* exactly are we doing here with these bloody shepherds? I want a clear answer!' he glowers.

She makes a secret sign seeking the help of the stars. 'Soon it will be night, and tomorrow we shall resume our journey,' she tries to placate him.

'Where to exactly—to that dying city of the east?'

She keeps quiet, leading him with her eyes.

Wood smoke rises from the camp, hovering undecidedly over the lake. It blots out the trees, spreading its tentacles like some mythical beast, till the camp is also shrouded by this smoke of cooking fires, through which the hushed voices of herders beckon like dim stars. Her eyes are smarting.

He suddenly stops in his path, turns and gives her a hard look. Shaking his head violently, he says, 'Okay, this is the last time I am doing what you say."

'Night is coming,' she says, 'let's find our friend.'

'I think he is over there by that tree, he is always with their leader.'

She is relieved at the hint of softness in his voice.

The Barefoot Tribe is preparing to break camp. They have been putting their meagre possessions together. That night everyone except the cattle guards sleeps early.

They fold their tents and set out early next morning. Before they part ways, the leader shares one last smoke with Lohit. 'There will be heavy rains in the mountains where you are headed. I can smell it in the air,' he tells him.

'As long as it doesn't leave us stranded, we should be okay,' Lohit says, his bright eyes gleaming.

'Listen to the hills before you step on her. We have been doing this for centuries but now…now we can't hear her clearly like before. We have to try hard, the mountains…the land, they are speaking in strange tongues,' he says. Lohit nods as the tall herder speaks before leaving.

The three of them and Prana travel with the carts for small children and women. The herders, with their leader, set out with their flocks. The tractor-drawn carts move slowly, the ponies keeping pace with them. A few young men from the group drive the tractors and ride the ponies part of the way.

The ponies glide by, sometimes falling back. A man in the first cart cracks jokes which are relayed to the horseriders. There is laughter, and then there are long hours when no one speaks. The road travels with them, it becomes their home again, it cradles them, it puts them to sleep, the wheat fields wrap their soft green and golden blankets around them, the smoke of woodfires circle and dance above their heads, the cat keeps an alert watch as the creaking procession journeys through time—beyond histories and limits—tunnelling through ideas, revolutions, desires and memories etched heavily across the face of a tortured earth.

They stop at night close to a town. Food is simple but their tired bodies enjoy the meals. But Chanchal isn't doing well. He is getting terrible headaches and has been yelling at Sujata. Lohit tries to calm him down in vain.

Sujata is at her wits' end. She had hoped the countryside was curing his fears, and in fact, his episodes of delusion were becoming rarer; but now, he was falling apart again. She discusses with Lohit what they should do. He believes things will get better when they reach the mountains, but that is too distant to lay her worries to rest.

On the third day they arrive at the outskirts of a cantonment town with chimney stacks and a river choked with refuse. The Barefoot Tribe will take a different route from here. The ponies go with them. After wishing each other luck on the road, the three of them go looking for an address. With some trouble and after raising the suspicion of a shopkeeper at the bazaar, they find the house of an elderly chemistry professor known to Lohit. He sees Chanchal and exchanges a knowing look with them. 'Let me know if you need anything at night. All other arrangements have been made,' he assures them and drives off on a scooter. They don't see him again.

That night Chanchal tries to run away but Lohit's foresight saves the day. Lohit, who had cannily decided to sleep next to the door, stops him. But they have to keep a vigil for the rest of the night.

Even the most difficult times come to an end, and so this night slips by too, and the morning looks different. Slightly cloudy skies but there's a pleasant breeze blowing. Chanchal has removed his bandage, his hand has healed a lot. And most of all, the morning brings a welcome surprise: an ambulance with a trusted driver is waiting at the door to pick them up. It's early and perhaps no one notices the three of them and the cat slip into the vehicle, which will ferry them to their final destination—Thunder Mountain.

Sujata marvels at the resourcefulness of Lohit. Comrade LJ, that's how he wants people to address him. How does he manage to do all this? Is he working for *them*? Those she had last met at The Ouroboros after the intruders tried to burn her alive? Those from the invisible world, who have been shadowing her ever since she learned to think for herself. The instructions drilled into her head, the nine men, the maimed pope and that satanic Caligari who had followed them this far. Is he lurking around somewhere near, ready to pounce on her and punish her for insubordination?

The scenes are fresh in her mind, their words still ringing in her ears. But something has changed. She is not the same person anymore. She is ready to take on ghosts, imaginary or real, for him. This soft-hearted man flung into the middle of shadow games not of his choosing. She will see Chanchal out of this mess.

'How do you know this chemist who hosted us?' she asks Lohit as the ambulance bounces along a bad stretch of road. 'Old comrade, he used to be a bomb-maker,' Lohit says, rubbing the cat's chin.

The ambulance is the perfect cover. And it is much faster than tractors and ponies. They begin to gain time. Back to speed and cold-blooded internal combustion. It burns, burns, burns and the road slips by. Cities and towns approached, negotiated, left behind. Big and small rivers crossed, forests sped through and forgotten. A tyre changed, and freedom really has no end.

The country gets greener and people speak in new tongues. A soft lilting language, almost like music. They have made it to the East. But then the skies close in and they drive into the rains.

Heavier than they can imagine. It slows them down and it takes them a day to reach the gates of the mountains. The rivers are boisterous and overflowing, the skies are being torn apart by forests of lightning. The great snow-capped peaks from where these rivers emerge have vanished behind walls of water tumbling down from the skies. After an hour's rest, they will seek a passage into that dominion.

THUNDER MOUNTAIN

The ambulance slows down as it begins climbing the rainswept road after driving through the dense green terai. The mercury begins to drop quickly, and soon it's teeth-chattering cold. From time to time, Sujata looks out through the rear window, worrying about pursuers. She has this uncanny feeling that their enemies—and now they have many—haven't given up yet.

The road is flanked by a deep gorge, which is now a smoky vortex of rain and mist. Down there somewhere is the road to the end of the world. Looking down, a cold fear brushes her cheeks and she tries to hold the cat for comfort but Prana easily slips away. The groans and whines of the engine is upsetting the cat. All along this journey he hasn't bothered them much, travelling quietly and keeping to himself. He napped happily; and whenever they were sitting down, he parked in a spot near Lohit, who indulged him with fish bits or scratched him gently between his ears, and the cat purred with pleasure. Now, he looks nervous.

A steep wall of rock rises to their right as they climb higher. Sometimes there are openings in the rock wall and a gushing waterfall would be washing that side of the mountain. As they ascend, they are drawn into a kingdom of mist. Prayer flags in many colours dripping wet from the incessant rains, and hill women in bright dresses sitting in momo shacks, waiting.

They rise higher among the clouds. At many points landslides have carried away parts of the road, and the driver has to be very careful negotiating these stretches where the vehicle hangs by its teeth at the edge of the gorge, as it advances inch by inch.

Little hamlets shrouded by rain appear as they drive cautiously on the road to Thunder Mountain. It seems the small wooden houses have been standing like that forever, standing outside time—waiting for some traveller, who will appear centuries later with the secret of reading the maps of clouds.

Wooden houses, rolling tea gardens, children in red and blue school uniforms, and colourful raincoats. Great pine forests, home to orioles, and emerald doves, now washed by grey sheets of water.

Here and there, the hillside is completely denuded by reckless logging; and down those slopes, the water rushes down in torrents, eating away the mountain beneath.

Boulders block the way and they have to turn back and take a more precarious route, higher and higher, up a razor's edge.

Lohit sips rum from a flask. The toll of the road has deepened the furrows and creases on his face, but despite the grime and dust a hard-jawed determination shines through. He is trying to have a conversation with Chanchal.

Chanchal looks composed but he is not here. Kapoor has surfaced again sometime back. But still, something is different. This is a quieter man, though his attitude and body language is not his own. He sits with his feet spread wide, and he has been speaking in that deep, gravelly voice. Still, he is ready to listen to what Lohit has to say.

But who can tell what lurks underneath the apparent calmness. There is a waxing and waning of his moods, and he could erupt without warning. He would swear, scream and shout, and then get tired because of these outbursts. 'Foul weather. Otherwise it would be great to go for a walk. No one will recognise us, and there's hardly a soul where we are heading,' Lohit says.

'We should build a golf course down there,' Chanchal says, peering down at the valley.

Lohit steals a gaze at Sujata and continues, 'Sure mate, when the time is right. But let's look forward to our stay here. It will be pretty when the rain has stopped.'

Sujata nods noncommittally. 'I think we should be careful,' she says. The incident at the herder's camp is still fresh in her mind. She always worries that some harm will come to them. From which side? Will it be the police arresting Chanchal and Lohit, or will it be JRK's men bumping them off. It could also be *them*.

Lohit notes her words and falls silent. The cat watches him from the jump seat but becomes disinterested after a while. The vehicle passes another small hamlet.

Majestic pines, stately oaks and rows of dreamy Japanese cypresses behind the little wooden houses on both sides of the road. Momo shacks, steaming hot tea. A group of lamas walking slowly in their maroon robes. She peers at their tender faces; they seem to smile back. A little ahead, only a slither of road remains, part of it having slid into the gorge. They move cautiously. The man at the wheel, who never speaks, stops the vehicle and asks them to walk that stretch. 'Too risky,' he says.

The rest of the distance is covered in an hour, and they climb up a side road to a small red-tiled house complete with a garden, a few kilometers from the edge of a little hill town. 'Captain Samanta', the weathered name plate says, but a fat lock is hanging at the door.

Lohit gathers a small slab of concrete and flings it against the lock with all his might. A few times. The lock breaks and falls to the floor, the doors creak open. They look at each other, and then at Lohit.

'Never mind, Captain Samanta wouldn't care, and he won't be coming here anytime soon. Maybe never,' he says, and lays back on an easy chair near the door, putting up his good foot on a carved wooden table with dragon heads. The cat leaps on his lap and goes to sleep. Sujata eyes him warily.

The house has four rooms and Lohit picks the one closest to the main door on the ground floor while the two of them take two upper floor rooms. They have electricity, but water supply is erratic and unpredictable.

The night is very cold, and so they light the fire in the evening and sit around it talking. There is tinned fish in the store and noodles, enough for a couple of days. They have noodles topped with smoked mackerel and fried eggs before turning in for the night. Next morning the rain stops, but heavy mist engulfs Thunder Mountain. They stay indoors. Chanchal paces the corridors and chats with Lohit, but later descends into a black mood and locks himself up in his room.

The headache has returned; and when in pain, he is becoming abusive. Sujata is not confident about giving him the benzo pills anymore. She tries to hold his hand but is rudely brushed away, and she worries he will hurt himself again. Late in the night when the woodfire has died and the sitting room is dark, she finds him alone there, mumbling to himself. It seems to be gibberish at first, but then she hears him talking in the darkness about the enormous losses he has suffered because of that fake business tycoon in Aukatabad.

Meanwhile, Sujata gets some names from Lohit and tries to contact people in Anantanagar for a doctor; someone who can advise on Chanchal's condition. That evening a young boy comes wandering up hill, thinking the house to be empty. He stands in the courtyard and plays the harmonica to the wind. It's a folksy tune she can't recognise, which nevertheless weaves a note of joy through the house. Prana, equally gloomy these days, stirs up and Lohit hides behind the window to watch and hear him play. Sujata tiptoes up behind him, and finds the old salt has his gun in his hand while he listens to the boy sing.

She steps back softly, knowing it is not over yet and at night, she double locks the main door. But in spite of all precautions, one evening Chanchal slips out of the house without telling them.

Sujata had been sleeping. Chanchal had had a severe panic attack the night before, which kept all three of them awake. At last, he had fallen asleep in the morning and when in the afternoon he felt better, he put on a coat and walked out. Lohit, who was supposed to be downstairs, was nowhere to be seen, nor was the cat.

Darkness comes unannounced to the mountains. Like a mythical bird of the night, it flies in and perches on the hills. When it approaches, its giant wings beat the light away, sweeping time away with it, and all of the visible world.

It gets dark as he takes the road that climbs higher from the house—a series of steps, through a rusty iron gate of an abandoned chalet, a garden overgrown with weed and up still, a narrow path, lined by primroses, twisting and turning between tall conifers and massive boulders. He climbs, his feet slip a few times but he doesn't fall; and at last, he reaches a path high up in the mountain from where he can see the lights of the hill town gleam far below. This path goes up another hillside to a high stony ridge, where the twilight still lingered.

Darkness had engulfed the mountains by then, and the path by which he had arrived has disappeared somewhere among the spindly trees and giant boulders. But he is oblivious of all this. He inhales the fresh mountain air and sweeps his gaze over the valley below, lit up by the glow of a large hydropower station. Power—that magic word, casting its spell over the world. He stands watching, hands on his waist, his feet wide apart.

He is so engrossed he doesn't hear the patter of hooves. Like phantoms, two thuggish men riding mules creep up the path from the other side of the high ridge. Clip-clop, clip-clop, the sound of hooves ring out clear now. Stealthily, they approach the top on the backs of the sure-footed beasts. The first man is large, almost a giant, while the one behind him is shorter, stockier. They are both wielding clubs and have guns in their belts. They are almost near the top, a few feet from where he stands.

A few rocks roll down the side of the hill and Chanchal steps back. There is a moment of absolute silence—nothing moves. Then a low rumble, like the growl of a ferocious beast deep inside a cave, followed by an earth-shaking noise tearing the mountains apart, reverberating through the valleys. The hill moves, and Chanchal is thrown to the ground. A few feet from him the mountain opens its jaws wide. A giant dust cloud rushes towards him, engulfs him and charges ahead. The jaws open wider and wider. The mules whinny and buck, throwing the riders off. One of them grabs a rocky outcrop and goes on screaming wildly at the face of death. With a thunderous rumble that shakes the heavens accompanied by the roar of a thousand monsters, half the ridge with the other rider collapses into the valley below, on the villages of innocents, smashing the lights of the hydropower power station till all the lights of the valley go out.

Everything happens in a matter of seconds. The sound of rocks raining down fills the world.

As the dust around him begins to settle, in the gauzy starlight he sees the figure of a tall man emerging from where the mountain had opened up. His forehead is furrowed with a hundred lines, and his powerful jaw is shaded by grey stubble.

He seems to have walked out of the grave of the hill. Like a rock he stands there, silhouetted by the starlight; his eyes, faintly aglow, are fixed on Chanchal.

Chanchal sits up. Stiff and petrified, not sure what's going to happen next.

'Who?' he asks.

'I come from another world,' replies the confident voice, and he walks up to Chanchal. 'I hope you are not hurt. It's late and we should get going. Sister will be very worried.'

Chanchal looks dazed. He gets up slowly and brushes the dust off his clothes.

'Okay Pontius,' the man claps, signaling to the giant crab that crawls up the side of the ridge, 'you don't have to rip off the flesh of that screaming thug down there'. He flicks on an electric lantern, 'Let's get going.'

TALKING HEADS

It was a night, warm as this one. He had just returned from Switzerland. His father, a high-ranking minister of the ruling party, had sent him to a Swiss college for a degree in hospitality management. Back home, vacationing in Goa, he had been toying with the idea of a pharmaceutical manufacturing license when he had met her. The warm and salty sea air blowing through the windows of the Calangute villa had been suffused with the scent of marijuana, and a tattooed man with a cheerful face and rotten teeth was going around yelling '*Boom Shankar*', offering his *chillum* to everyone. They had driven out into that night, rich with possibilities, with the rotten-teeth man in the backseat, and then thrown him out somewhere on the road to Anjuna.

Tonight, the briny sea breeze has been replaced by blasts of desert air. But he hadn't retired to his suite. The fragrance of wild roses sneaks into this private balcony framed by a *jharokha*, where he sits in her company, watching meteor showers against a diamond-studded sky. He has decided to sell this palace hotel at the edge of the desert to a Swiss hotelier. Increasing water scarcities in the area and the loss of local support staff—migrating elsewhere—compounded with other setbacks, pushed him towards this decision. He wanted to spend one last night here with his beloved.

She faces him. The cord from the stone canopy of the *jharokha* hangs right at his eye-level. Her eyes still closed; her face, calm as ever. The fairy lights on the crenellated ramparts filter through the gaps, casting a river of shadows across his face.

'Now that my world is unraveling, will you forgive me?' There is no response but he thinks he can hear a faint sigh.

'It makes no sense apologising for what can't be undone, but I still say sorry for what I did to you in a fit of rage,' he breathes heavily, and his shark eyes lose their wicked light. Then an afterthought, 'Bullet could have ignored my order, stupid low-life!'

'Bastard!' the word comes floating at him, a whisper on the wind, singeing his ears. He swallows but quickly composes himself, and says, 'Bullet is dead. Crushed by a landslide and I am literally at the end of my tether. At least allow me to atone for my sin.'

'Rot in hell, Jayant Roy Kapoor!' says the shadows of the night, and he sees those lips move. A cold fear grips him but it is laced with excitement. His breath comes in short gasps.

'Okay, I'm already there and I am not scared. But you cannot blame me for everything. The chocolate business was your plan, and whatever came along with it. Felicity, this insane desire to control minds, to play God—it was you, you who planted all that in my head!' he blurts out.

A jet of spit hits his face as he tries in vain to twist himself out of its way, almost falling from the chair. There is a rumble of thunder. She has opened her eyes. Cold limpid fires of another world.

He tries to get up but his legs have frozen into stone. For minutes he sits staring at her, his heart thumping away madly. Owls screech in the distance. A few minutes later, he moves to cover his face with his hands. She's still watching him, hate dripping from those eyes.

Slowly, he raises his head and looks into her eyes. Calm, as he watches her with a steady gaze. 'Felicity was an ill-conceived plan. Now I know. It is always dangerous to play God but I never had an inkling of the sinister forces I was pitting against. The secret enemy has been relentless and I still don't know who they are. No, it's not Ghaswala. Things don't add up. It cannot be my competitors working against me. This is an insidious, far more powerful adversary. Perhaps they are unknowable. Perhaps you could explain, Clara?'

Swarthy cloud masses from the west are obscuring the heavens, burying the stars, and the little verandah is now pitch dark. There is another clap of thunder and the ramparts of the old fort tremble as the booming sound reverberates through its halls, passages and lover's alleys.

Jayant Roy Kapoor shivers and grabs the vodka glass on the ornate table. He raises the glass and knocks back the drink. 'They poisoned my best scientist. I could see that someone was not happy with Felicity; but not one to chicken out so easily, I went ahead with increased determination. We got this brilliant Israeli professor working for us. And he picked up the trail left by Vincent pretty quickly, but then…but then he succumbed to bubonic plague. Just think about it, bubonic fucking plague! And no antibiotics worked. The doctors were flabbergasted. It all began with my chocolate factory. Twice, the production line was contaminated by salmonella. Luckily, we stopped the distribution in time. Then those strange messages to my staff, asking them to stand by for orders. What orders? Who are these people? Why did they try to kidnap me in that park while killing and injuring so many? They took away Prana, they just snatched away my beating heart. That was the last straw. Without him, I am finished. Destroyed! Do you understand?' he screams. 'Nothing makes sense anymore. I have decided to shelve Felicity,' he pauses to look up and see if his words were having any impact.

The wind has grown stronger and it rattles the doors of the hotel suite. The curtains behind him are flying with abandon, and lightning flashes glitter on the white gold of his Sky Moon Tourbillon. It's midnight. A bolt comes at him, tearing the sky apart. A terrible explosion and a palm tree goes up in flames. A ferocious wind rises, spraying mountains of dust into the hotel.

The flash of lightning has blinded him; and dazed, he stands up, pushing the chair back. The *aandhi* is raging now like it never has in a hundred years. Great clouds of dust are washing away the world from his vision. The sky has vanished, and the fairy lights on the ramparts have gone out. Though it's a warm night, he suddenly feels a cold chill. He begins to shiver. Teeth chattering and with trembling hands, he goes to the door leading into his suite and with one yank, tears off the lace curtains.

More lightning strikes his hotel. Where has the staff gone? Have they deserted him in fear of their lives? The roar of the wind that seemed to emerge from the depths of the desert blots out every other sound of this world. He goes closer to the edge of the *jharokha*, and with the dust and wind beating him blind, he searches for Clara till he holds her between his hands, between his cupped fingers, and says, 'I have abandoned Felicity. I am tired, I want to give it all up but will they leave me in peace?'His voice is breaking with despair as the buffeting winds slap his face with the dust of the night... And it is, as he realises; it is she hitting him with her stone cold hands, hitting him mercilessly till his head reels from the blows. Her icy hands on his throat now, and he blinks his eyes open for a moment and sees her...the flesh of her face fallen off and the bony remains of empty desires staring back at him, at his face, at his glassy eyes from which the breath of life has been wrenched away a moment earlier.

PONTIUS AND
HIS MASTER

The untimely passing of Jayant Roy Kapoor was big news all across the land, and in places far beyond. It hogged the airwaves and social channels for days, with commentators arguing about what exactly killed him. Whether it was frustration, personal issues, or even a secret enemy. The storm or the possibility of a lightning strike switching off his heart wasn't once mentioned. Bad weather doesn't kill big men. Weather is largely manageable. Despite the fact that the powerful Nazi war machine was stopped by an early and particularly harsh Russian winter, notwithstanding the evidence that empires grow strong or weak as the weather changes, ignoring the manifest truth that everything from deadly smog to unnatural rain and lightning strikes can change the course of lives, there is solace in the fiction that we are in charge. So the other stories of what really could have happened and how all this came to be were whispered and quickly forgotten.

In the quiet corner of Thunder Mountain, Kapoor's passing creates small ripples and is soon forgotten. People hardly remember the gunfight at the park and the failed kidnap attempt of the now dead business tycoon. Most do not. Which is good for the three of them sheltering, after breaking into Captain Samanta's house.

The arrival of the military doctor, Gupta, is a moment of hope for Sujata because he is a psychiatrist. Chanchal doesn't seem to remember this detail but he didn't fail to recognise him on that mountain top after the doctor helped him to his feet. But this ray of hope is clouded by the disappearance of their fellow traveller, the bright-eyed Comrade LJ. In fact, he is not seen again from the same evening that Major Gupta, the healer of minds, arrives. When they trudged back home through the darkness, and knocked at the front door, he was already gone.

Sujata had been sleeping, so she didn't know when he had left. They waited for him till midnight, thinking he had gone to meet someone and would come back, but he didn't. Nor did the cat. Prana, the mascot of the Atman business empire, had disappeared with the old salt. Later, they found a note on a window but it didn't explain why he was leaving suddenly...but he did say that he was taking the cat because he had developed a bond with him.

Sujata only wished that he could have told them before he left; and though psychiatrist Gupta's arrival was reassuring, she couldn't help but feel a little disappointed he had gone without a word. At the back of her mind she had always harboured doubts about Comrade LJ, and had been especially upset when he joined the kidnap attempt but he had been a friend on the road.

After dealing with the attackers, Gupta had led them back to the house by the light of his electric lantern. He seemed to know the way and didn't miss a single turn. They had sat around the fire till late in the night, discussing where Comrade LJ might have gone, but Sujata soon realised she knew very little about this man. Major Gupta left the house around midnight, whereto…they didn't ask, but the town was quite a few kilometers away, and there was no traffic on the road below after evening. But he was back the next day.

'Down at the taxi stand in town, they have seen a man on a crutch leaving with a cat,' Gupta told them next morning.

Sujata looked scared. What if they link us with the kidnapping?

Major Gupta seemed to read her thoughts and said, 'I found out discreetly. For some years, I have been living in the hills, so people know me. Being a doctor helps.' She poured more tea for him and Chanchal, who was in a grim mood that day.

'Otherwise I wouldn't have found you out. They told me,' he said, but who these people were was never revealed.

That he was a friend of Chanchal's father was good enough for Sujata, and that he was a psychiatrist was even better. She had tried contacting people but they hadn't been able to find any doctor she could trust. With the death of Jayant Roy Kapoor, things should calm down but she knows, for her, this is not over yet. And Chanchal's treatment was just beginning.

The fact that Gupta had known Chanchal's military engineer father helped. He knew that his mother had died young and the boy had been lonely. He asked Sujata questions about the recent past, noting details, pausing to think between the conversation.

He gave her instructions, and asked her to be with Chanchal as much as she could. 'You can help me pull him out of this. I need your help,' he told her. 'But if you follow my advice and help me, I promise he will improve a lot. The rest,' he paused, bunched up his eyebrows, and looking straight into her eyes, said very quietly, 'is beyond my powers. You can understand that.' She flinched from that penetrating look, lowered her eyes, and nodded mechanically.

The landslide had severely damaged the hydropower station, and for days, there was no electricity in the area around Thunder Mountain. The young hill, tortured by tunnel digging for the hydropower project—and ceaseless rains in the previous weeks—had given up, and in a final show of disapproval, had made a death dive at the power plant. It was much like a kamikaze raid.

It is difficult to live in the house now without lights or running water; but the doctor thinks the isolation and the mountain winds will help. It doesn't look like the owner of the house will be coming anytime soon and if he does, she will have to handle it, now that Lohit Joardar had disappeared without a trace.

Gupta begins his work. Once a week he comes over to meet Chanchal, and the sessions continue for hours. He tells Chanchal how to create a safety plan, and put it to work whenever he feels things are getting out of hand. 'You have to be strong. I am with you,' he would say repeatedly.

Sujata is always with Chanchal. They go for walks up the path to the ridge where the two men came for him, or down into the valley to buy fresh vegetables and oranges. The cat having disappeared, they find the crab Pontius to be a nice creature to know, so Sujata always insists that Gupta bring him along. But this is not always a good idea. Once the doctor got down with his patient, Pontius would roam free and one day, finding the front door open, he had ventured out. He went all the way up the path towards the ridge and got lost till a kind-hearted lama returned him to the house. Sujata doesn't ask him how he found them.

Chanchal remains calm through the first few weeks of therapy, but then he switches. First he becomes irritable and loud, later he begins to order everyone about in that throaty voice which is not his own. 'Why are you holding me here?

That impostor is dead. Good riddance but what is happening to my business? Who called you, Mr Therapist? Get lost!' He tries to rush out of the room and when Gupta asks him to stop, he grabs the main door and bangs his head against it—once, twice, three times. Crac… crack…soft bone hitting heavy teakwood. Sujata comes running to stop him but he has hurt himself already.

In the next session, the doctor gives Chanchal practical hints to explain he has been imagining much of it. 'We are friends and I understand you are upset. But it's not all that bad. We will find a way out of your trouble,' he says in his mild suggestive tone that isn't easy to ignore. But Chanchal is hardly listening. He holds his head and grumbles. He is still in pain but over the days and weeks, the doctor's suggestions seem to be taking a hold on his mind.

Major Gupta explains his illness, that it is manageable, and that he would be all right. Chanchal watches him with tired eyes. 'We all play many roles in our lives. And it's not unnatural to get a bit more attached to one role or the other,' Gupta says. 'When I was in the Army and watched the young *jawans*, the glow on their faces, the simple-minded determination to lay down their lives for the nation—the tales of valour—I, too, began to think I was more a soldier than a therapist. I dreamed of driving one of those big Russian tanks, of receiving medals for bravery. But then my training intervened. I was back at my job every day at the Army hospital. And I knew those were dreams and dreams only, and not to be indulged in much.'

They sit in the huge living room of the Captain who never comes to claim his house. Chanchal takes the easy chair; Gupta settles down on one of the rosewood armchairs. The doctor explains, 'Chanchal, there is a part of you which thinks itself to be someone else. This someone has been fed on dreams which float about in the air around us, ready to snare the unsuspecting innocent. We begin to live these dreams and then the dreams get bigger than us. This is something that can happen to any of us. Sometimes it's our past that makes us more vulnerable, more credulous to the seductions of the present. An unfortunate incident, some trauma, it can be anything. And then we seek refuge. We get divided into two or more to resolve the past and engage with the illusions of the present. A present of many spells being cast, to entice and control us. We create new personalities within ourselves to try and cope with those memories, the small failures of our lives, we take refuge in the personalities of heroes or apostles. Between them, these new personalities or identities can share traumatic incidents, aspirations and memories as they have different tolerance levels—and sometimes, completely different approaches to life. But over time, this division becomes taxing on the individual. It begins to affect that person. There is no good alternative to wholeness, we have to face our present and our past being one.'

On good days, Chanchal listens intently. Early in his illness, he had discovered the other man, Kapoor, who was around him somewhere, distant but always there. This understanding helps his recovery. But it is still slow progress, a step at a time, climbing up the sheer rockface of normalcy from the precipice he had fallen into.

He slips and falls back many times. Each time, Kapoor resurfaces and has arguments with the doctor. Kapoor tries to injure himself when Chanchal has disappeared.

Gupta reminds him of the safety plan. 'Make a contract with yourself not to hurt anyone—inside or outside,' he says repeatedly and persuasively. The plan doesn't always work and once, when it gets really bad, he has to be put on medication.

Winter arrives in the hills, and in the early days, heavy rains lash the mountains. The runoff water from the ridge high above the house sluices down in a stream, bringing with it dead leaves that look like human hands, and a tumult of rocks that have broken off from bigger chunks which hang precariously from the hillside. The rain brings with it more landslides. The young hills tortured by untimely rains, plagued by tunnelling for power, stripped of the trees where birds and beasts found a home, stricken by dreams of civilisation, sheds its burden on the earth. A long stretch of road disappears near the town square.

The people of the little town, their mouths gaping open in surprise, look at each other and shake their heads in disbelief. They retire to their homes, grim-faced under their baseball caps. The lamas in their maroon robes float about in the empty town square, and the mountain wind can be heard whistling down the streets.

Sometimes Chanchal goes for walks and as advised by Gupta, always carries a sketch pad. He has been improving, and the doctor believes he can negotiate with his surroundings better. He has also been advised to write, and has begun to keep a notebook. Beautifully decorated with images from the Jataka tales on the cover, that notebook soon fills up—and a thicker one appears. And then another, continuing with the same motif of the past lives of the Buddha on their covers.

Summer brings trekkers with their heavy equipment to the mountain. They crowd the town square and walk up and down the snaking hills roads with tents and rucksacks, their eyes alight with determination and something more. Doctor Gupta has now reached that stage of treatment where he can summon and talk with the two different personalities of Chanchal. Sometimes he addresses them together. 'Both of you listen,' he says, 'this is important. The two of you have to try and talk more with each other, have meaningful conversation. That would make our work easier.' There are also occasions when he needs to use hypnosis to bring out the more adamant Kapoor and give him specific advice like 'you have to stop hurting yourself by all means and concentrate on your pictures. Some of these are so good. I am interested in this drawing you made of this monk on horseback. Can we talk about this now?', and he enters into a deeper discussion.

At one level of the therapy, a heavenly figure emerges in Chanchal's mind. He is tall and he wears a spotless white dress of unstitched cloth, and there is a golden aura around him. His hair is blazing white and he has a permanent smile on his face. Around his neck is a garland of tuberoses, and he holds a crystal ball in his hand. The appearance of this figure who Chanchal calls 'The Smiling Father' makes it much easier for the doctor to work with Chanchal's traumas.

They are soon discussing, in session after session, the death of his father in the clock chamber, Chanchal's loneliness as a child and, finally, the more recent past. His days as a journalist at *The Trumpet*, the changing city, Idris—the man with the missing ear and the allure of the changing times. But these memories are less and less stressful, the baggage of torment, craving, dissatisfaction and oppression they carry is lighter as the weeks pass. The Smiling Father is always at their side, even when they begin discussing the madding rise of Jayant Roy Kapoor.

THE WORLD AT EVENING

There is little left to say. Except for what happened at the very end. It took the doctor more than three years of work with Chanchal Mitra. Thirty-two months into the therapy, they reached a stage where the two personality states within him could discuss memories with each other. As they continued to talk about the past and how it had affected them, the painful past gradually lost its bite and became a matter of frank discussion. Interestingly, the stronger and aggressive Kapoor helped in coping with what was particularly traumatic for the weaker Chanchal. And as these sessions continued, the two distinct identities discussed and coped with the brazen and troubling past, and went about negotiating present time with the help of the doctor; time, which is a river of images, sounds and words…which, like sea shells or broken mirrors, gather on the shores of the mind; they learned, slowly, to live together—an ordinary balanced level-headed individual; they slowly climbed the difficult road to fusion, they learned to be a harmonious whole, one and singular.

When Jayant Roy Kapoor completely disappeared and the old Chanchal was back and stable, Doctor Gupta invited them for tea to his house—an ancient bungalow hanging precariously on the other side of the ridge where the two men had tried to attack Chanchal. It was a clear and bright day, and the white peaks were leaning at them through the windows. Everyone looked cheerful.

The tea exuded a fruity aroma. Taking a small sip, he looked at Sujata and then Chanchal, and said, 'My work with you is over.' Lost in thought for a moment, then he continued, 'This is a work that the two of us have created with extraordinary effort, and we should be ever-dedicated and ever-alert so that no harm comes to it. Living as one is difficult but it's the only way we are allowed to live here,' he beamed, and the furrows on his forehead danced in agreement. 'If you need help again I will be there, but I have to leave soon. There is a lot waiting for me in another world,' he grinned, a mischievous twinkle in his eyes.

They chose a weekend for the journey to Anantanagar. Chanchal and Sujata took a car for the overnight trip along the north-south route, which connected the mountains to the city.

Anantanagar. City without end. The house on Four Horse Street was just the way he had left it—the giant clocks, the potted cactus plants and the piles of business magazines were all there. The storeroom with his father's old electrical gadgets and tools had signs of a fire that had damaged the old radio sets. He will have to clean up the mess. But Champakali was not there anymore, and his dog Mastan had also disappeared. No one could say where he might have gone. He only hoped Mastan had found a good home.

'We need a dog in the house,' Sujata said, and he agreed.

The street outside had transformed further. More cars, more heat and definitely more people. The neighbourhood had turned touristy, and many of the residences had morphed into restaurants or heritage hotels. Fashion houses had opened shop and on the southern end, a glitzy shopping mall had sprung up next to an old hotel.

The house where the priest lived had been repainted and clad in chrome and glass, it drew an endless stream of shimmery-eyed young women in red skirts, white tops and fishnet stockings, who hung out at the bus shed, turning it into a magnet for male shop assistants. The priest had sold his house to an air-hostess academy, a business which flourished in every city and town as dreams took wings. The spell had been cast wide.

Sujata had taken up a job giving spoken English classes at the air-hostess academy while Chanchal had been writing almost regularly. The handmade notebooks with the Jatakas on their covers were kept in a neat stack on the green secretariat table. The room looked cleaner.

Sometimes, he painted. He had dusted the old easel and started painting people. Faces, portraits, groups. When he was not writing or painting, he would go for walks all the way to the river. Sujata would accompany him often.

Right at the end of the cobbled stretch of Four Horse Street, they would sometimes sit down on the green wooden benches to watch the world go by. They would talk about the difficult time that seemed to have passed. They would discuss winter flowers for the garden or plan to visit an exhibition. He looked content. Rarely did anyone bother them.

Just across from these benches was an upscale bar which sold overpriced cocktails and played songs of protests from a time long gone. They would sit and watch the stream of middle-aged patrons arriving, then leaving slightly tipsy; and one day, Chanchal spotted him. His old business partner Idris was stepping out from the bar.

Idris saw them and waved. He walked up and hugged Chanchal; grinning, he held out a hand to Sujata.

'Idris. Have we met before?'

'I guess not,' she shook his hand stiffly.

'Oh, where have you been all this while, sir?' he asked Chanchal.

'Health problems, I had been away. Now I'm getting better,' Chanchal said.

'And you, madam, hope all is well with you?'

Sujata nodded stony-faced, but right then a blast of music came through the doorway of the bar and the conversation faltered for a moment.

'You had left me in deep water,' Idris complained to Chanchal, 'but I have managed. We are doing new things.'

'I am sorry Idris. It was not my intention,' Chanchal said.

Sujata wished to go to the bookshop. Chanchal remained for some more time with Idris. He asked him about Champakali but Idris said he had no idea what happened to her; that he will let him know if he finds out. It looked like he was keeping something from him, but Chanchal didn't press him any further.

That night, Sujata was restless in bed. She fidgeted, she tied and untied her hair. She sat alone by the window, staring into the night, warily watching the shadows that moved. Loiterers and drunks—some lying face down on the benches, their legs splayed, as if hurled down from a great height.

Weeks went by. The branches of the pomegranate tree near the gate and the evening breeze which sometimes blew in from the river, played a game with the lights of the Diamante. In that play of shadows, they sat and talked and went far. Too far to notice the scent of white flowers that had begun to carpet the driveway.

They would be talking about their long trek across the plains—following rivers, along country roads, through villages and farmland, and about the people. Strangers that had given them shelter, those that had passed them by and the dangers of the road. Secret pursuers breathing down their necks, unexpected friends, their sunburnt faces, those bold moustaches, the tattooed fortune-teller with raincloud eyes, the village girl drawing water for their horses. And about the wide open country—green, brown and gold—miles upon miles under the sun. They remembered what they learned from the road. How, from the breeze in the evening, they could say they were nearing a river.

The memories of the breeze carry them back to this garden. Here, the river breeze has died. Their shadows are blue against the light-washed wall of Mitra House, the roar of automobiles in the distance, the smell of combustion pervades the world.

When the evenings began to arrive early, they stopped sitting out in the garden. Chanchal had started to work for another media house. He would be busy poring over his notebooks when he returned while Sujata's hours at the air-hostess academy had increased.

The academy had piled on extra work. She was later than usual that night. She walked up to the next block where their favourite pizza shop would be open at that hour. But it was not. She turned the corner near the Viennese style tearoom. It, too, had downed its shutters for the day, and she could see a single white-uniformed waiter through the French window. He was folding the tablecloth, arranging the bone china and keeping the chairs upside down over the tables. The other staff had left.

The gift shop next door had also closed. She peeped at the displays as she rounded a corner. A glass swan went up and down, dipping its beak in a bowl—the dream of perpetual motion. Limitless energy, limitless power. She stopped to watch it, but it didn't cease. It went on diligently, back and forth, on and on.

As it was a chilly January night, all shops had downed their shutters. She left the swan to herself, and was passing the lighted displays of a fashion store when she noticed him and gulped in recognition He looked a little older; there were lines on his face she hadn't noticed before, and he was wearing a ten-gallón hat. The cane was gone.

Sujata drew in her breath. He had seen her too. But he was not smiling. He grabbed the brim of his hat and then he took it off, and in one swift motion stretched out his hand from the glass box and flung it at her. It came whirling around in circles, gathering the night around it, landing square and perfect on her head.

Her head spun. Dizziness enfolded her like a lost friend. She was on a roller-coaster, rushing at great speed. It went faster still and the world came crashing in from all sides. Crowds charged at her, waving placards; grey blocks of concrete swayed and toppled all around, raising clouds of dust; an ocean erupted and came down upon her in torrents of plastic and bleached coral; forest fires lit up the miles.

Stars changed places in the sky.

The stars whizzed by, slicing through the darkness, their hot breath licking her skin. She found herself under the wings of a giant bird with shiny talons. The bird screeched and whistled. Loud and clear—the shrill piping call, rising high above a city, asleep, for it was the middle of the night and below that endless darkness, like an ocean of candlelight, flickered street lamps, shop signs, neon-lit boards, lighted clock towers and monuments, railway signals and lamps high up on bridges, offering their prayers to the darkness. The bird piped and whistled as it flew, clutching her tight. And as the lights came closer and the tower blocks looked bigger, and the roads like glowing centipedes crawled through the darkness, coming from nowhere with nowhere to go, she heard their voices—clear, crisp and calm, 'Welcome back, sister.'

The people of the city woke up the next day to find that Perfect Man had found a lover. A woman with a waterfall of hair and eyes dark like murder. A knapsack across her shoulder. She wore a ten-gallón hat. The Couple, as they came to be known, stared back from billboards and light towers, and from pages of magazines and websites. The new advertisements ramped up the sales of the accessories brand. Every young man and woman in the city now sported a broad-brimmed hat and slung on leather knapsacks. Women grew their hair long, painted their lips crimson with cochineal and switched to black denim boot-cuts. College campuses and nightclubs bristled with copycats of Perfect Man and his lover. Everyone was happy for they felt he had been alone for too long.

The airhostess academy where Sujata used to give English lessons was not amused when she disappeared without a notice. They lodged a police complaint and because she had taken a loan, they engaged a private eye. But Chanchal was of little help to the balding private eye who came to question him, and there seemed to be no one else in the city she had known. Yet the detective tried. The company that owned the leather accessories brand was cagey, and didn't return calls. Nor did *Le Neuf*, the little-known agency that had created the Perfect Man campaign. In fact, it turned out pretty soon that their telephone numbers were false, and a search for the names of the directors couldn't go much further either.

ACKNOWLEDGEMENTS

I owe a debt of gratitude to my climate activist colleagues, academics, editors, journalists and fellow writers who have, through their enthusiasm, example, and by creating opportunities, allowed me to engage with planetary crises through my fiction, non-fiction and activism. Here, I must mention Liz Jensen, Sam Beckbessinger, Ben Grant, Arunava Sinha, Anu Kumar, Chandril Bhattacharya, Prasun Chaudhuri, Medha Dutta-Yadav, Tarun Goswami, Krishnan Unni P., A.J. Thomas, Jeffrey Barber, Mary Woodbury, Bodhisattva Chattopadhyay, Sami Ahmad Khan, Anuradha Kumar, Zafar Anjum, Lopa Ghosh, Pradeep Mehta, Christoph Rupprecht, Sarena Ulibarri, Steven McGreevy and Sally O'Reilly, among several others. I would also like to thank *Eclectica* magazine and its editor, Tom Dooley, for publishing an early chapter from this book.

My editor Vibha Chakravarty Kumar worked on the manuscript with care and diligence, for which I am very grateful. Her suggestions, insights and ideas have definitely enriched these pages. I must also thank Nirmal Kanti Bhattacharjee, Editorial Director at Niyogi Books, for championing this book.

Amitav Ghosh, through his fiction, non-fiction and occasional messages, has always been an inspiration in my journey. I am, likewise, deeply indebted to authors Ramkumar Mukhopadhyay and Anita Agnihotri for holding my hand along the way, and to poet and academic Sanjukta Dasgupta for believing in my work.

The interface between mental illness, spirit possession and the effect of entheogenic drugs on our minds are subjects that have often intrigued me. For this, I am indebted to the writings of Aldous Huxley and Sudhir Kakkar, among others. However, this book wouldn't have been possible without the insights of a student of Kakkar, psychiatrist Anurag Mishra. Dr Mishra, who is the Chief of the Psychonanalytical Unit at Fortis Healthcare and Founder of Psychoanalyis India, helped me dig deep into the nuances of certain types of mental illnesses that inform the plot of this novel. Besides hours of long discussions, face-to-face meetings and email exchanges, he also helped me secure a Livonics fellowship, which helped me research and write this book.

The character of Caligari in this story is inspired from Dr Caligari of the well-known work of German Expressionist cinema *The Cabinet of Dr. Caligari*. Also, the

Spellcasters

pastoralist's song that appears in the Barefoot Tribe chapter is quoted from Sushma Iyengar's article in *Pastoral Times*, 2 December 2016.

For centuries, Indian kings are known to have maintained talented courtiers from different disciplines for advice and enlightenment, the most famous of which would be the *Navaratna*, or the Nine Gems, of emperor Akbar. While bearing some resemblance in name, the Nine Unknown Men of this book are from a period much before Akbar's. Extremely successful in erasing their presence from the pages of history, the secretive Nine first made an appearance almost a century ago in the fiction of Talbot Mundy. Later on, they found a place in the cult classic *Le Matin de Magiciens* (The Morning of the Magicians) by Louis Pauwels and Jacques Bergier. Although many of their secrets remain protected to this day, a few contemporary writers have noted their presence in their works. I do hope, with some trepidation, that the secretive Nine wouldn't mind my giving away a few more of their secrets.

Finally, I must thank my partner Anuradha for her enthusiasm about this book, and as always, for being my first reader.